THE DARK SIDE OF THE ROAD

BAEN BOOKS
by SIMON R. GREEN

ISHMAEL JONES MYSTERIES
The Dark Side of the Road
Haunted by the Past (forthcoming)

Jekyll & Hyde Inc.

THE DARK SIDE OF THE ROAD

SIMON R. GREEN

THE DARK SIDE OF THE ROAD

A Baen Book

Baen Publishing Enterprises
P.O. Box 1403
Riverdale, NY 10471
www.baen.com

ISBN: 978-1-9821-9221-1

Cover art by Kurt Miller

First Baen printing, September 2022

Distributed by Simon & Schuster
1230 Avenue of the Americas
New York, NY 10020

Library of Congress Cataloging-in-Publication Data

Names: Green, Simon R., 1955-, author.
Title: The dark side of the road / by Simon R. Green.
Description: Riverdale, NY : Baen Books, [2022] | Series: Ishmael Jones
    mysteries
Identifiers: LCCN 2022021259 | ISBN 9781982192211 (trade paperback) |
ISBN 9781625798770 (ebook)
Subjects: LCGFT: Detective and mystery fiction. | Novels.
Classification: LCC PR6107.R44 D37 2022 | DDC 823/.92--dc23
LC record available at https://lccn.loc.gov/2022021259

Printed in the United States of America

10 9 8 7 6 5 4 3 2 1

THE DARK SIDE OF THE ROAD

✜ ONE ✜
INTO THE TEETH
OF THE STORM

CALL ME ISHMAEL. Ishmael Jones.

I got the phone call in the early hours of the morning. I was in the main bar of some hotel in London. Don't ask me its name; they all blend into each other after a while. I have no home of my own. Never have. Too risky. I just move from hotel to hotel, using this name or that. Makes it that much harder for people to find me. But the Colonel always knows where I am. That was part of the deal we struck, all those years ago.

It wasn't much of a bar, but then, it wasn't much of a hotel. Not a salubrious, or even a cheerful place. The lighting was too bright, the fittings and furnishings more functional than comfortable. And the background music was such an offence to the ear that I ended up having to bribe the barman to shut it down. I sat on a stool at the bar, so I wouldn't have to keep getting up to order more drinks. It was that bleary-eyed time in the early hours when the night life just gives it all up as a bad idea and admits defeat. I was the only customer left in the bar. Everyone else had gone home, or gone to bed, or both. The bartender was standing around with his arms folded, looking worn out and resentful. Wishing I would leave, so he could shut the bar down and turn in. But I wasn't going anywhere. I didn't feel tired, or sleepy. I wouldn't for several days. I keep strange hours because I lead a strange life.

I looked at myself in the mirror behind the bar. My reflection met my gaze with a cold, mistrustful stare. A very familiar face because it hadn't changed in so very long. Not the one I would have chosen, but good enough. I was tall, slim, dark-haired and handsome enough if you weren't too choosy. A long rangy figure who appeared to be in his mid twenties. Dressed well, but anonymously. The kind of stuff you can buy anywhere, so you can fit in anywhere. An easy smile, a casual look, and dark eyes that gave away absolutely nothing. Someone who had learned to walk through the world without making ripples because he couldn't afford to be noticed. Who lived under the radar because he couldn't afford to be found out. A man who drove on the dark side of the road. I toasted my reflection with my almost empty glass. I thought I looked pretty good, for someone whose appearance hasn't changed a bit since 1963.

And that was when my mobile phone rang. Or, rather, shuddered in my pocket. I always keep it on vibrate. Because a sudden ringtone can make people look at you, and remember you. I took my time hauling the phone out. I knew who it was, who it had to be. The Colonel's the only man who has my number, these days. I work for the Colonel and the Organization he says he represents. Whatever that might be. Some day, I hope to find out exactly who and what I'm working for. It would be nice to know. But as long as the Colonel continues to protect me from all the people who want to find me, and as long as he keeps pointing me in the direction of really bad people who need taking down, and as long as he keeps paying me really good money to do it . . . I'm happy to go along.

I put the phone to my ear. "What do you want, Colonel?"

"And merry seasonal greetings to you, dear boy," said the Colonel. "How would you like to come and join me for Christmas, in the grand old country house of Belcourt Manor? Deep in the heart of rural Cornwall, far away from all the hustle and bustle of the big bad city. Good food and good booze, and who knows? Maybe even silly hats and party games till dawn. Only several hours' hard driving from where you are now, if you start straight away. I need you with me at the Manor, as fast as you can get here. The situation is . . . somewhat urgent."

"What's the mission?" I said.

"Oh, not a mission at all, as such, old bean," said the Colonel. "More like, a personal favour to me. Tell you all about it when you get here. Never know who's listening in, these days. It used to be just us, but then the Government insisted on getting involved. I don't like how it feels down here, at the Manor. Could be wrong, of course. I could just be jumping at shadows. In which case, we'll all have a jolly old time eating too much, drinking too much, and dozing off in front of the television. The usual deeply religious Christian celebration."

"But you don't think you're wrong, do you?" I said.

"Of course not, dear boy. Or I wouldn't be calling you. Will you come?"

Of course I said yes. I couldn't turn him down, not after everything the Colonel had done for me. He gave me the address in Cornwall, and enough general directions so I could be sure of getting there even if my satnav threw a wobbly, and then he hung up. Before I could ask him any questions. Like what it was at the Manor that had spooked him so badly. Or what it was he wanted me to do for him. I put my phone away and nodded to the quietly seething bartender to fill my glass again. One more large drink, and then off into the night, and the dark, one more time. To do things in the shadows that the everyday people don't need to know about. Because someone's got to slay the dragons, even if the armour isn't as shining as it used to be. And because if you have to hide in the shadows, it helps if you thin out the predators that want to hide in there with you.

I drove my rented car a lot faster than was safe, pressing on into the winter storm with cold determination. The wind howled like a demon on the loose, and everywhere I looked heavy falling snow was burying the open countryside under gleaming white shrouds. The road ahead was almost completely blocked, but I just aimed my car like a bullet and put the hammer down. Everything forward, and trust in the Lord. I hunched over the steering wheel, peering through the windshield at the deadly white world outside.

The wipers were doing everything they could, but the wind was blasting so hard now that it was practically snowing sideways. I'd been driving for hours without a break, and what had started out as a pleasant snowfall when I was leaving London had quickly degenerated into the kind of vicious blizzard that ends up in the history books. More and more, I was driving by guesswork and instinct.

My satnav kept telling me I wasn't far from my destination, but I wasn't sure I believed it. I was out in the middle of nowhere, hammering down a narrow country lane, surrounded by miles and miles of endless white. It felt like I was driving on the moon, surrounded by nothing but open space, and not a landmark anywhere. The car's tyres lurched and skidded over the undulating snow, sometimes digging in unexpectedly; and then the steering wheel would do its best to rear up and hit me in the face. Or deep snow ridges would throw the car back and forth so violently that it would end up bouncing off both sides of the road; and then I had to fight the wheel for control until I could force the car back in the right direction. So far, I was winning, through a combination of stubbornness and brute strength ... but it was starting to look like a race as to which would wear out first: my hands, or the steering column.

The calm-voiced announcer on the car radio (no doubt sitting safe and warm in some BBC regional studio) seemed to be taking great pleasure in informing me that I was caught right in the middle of the worst storm since modern records began. That most of the roads were snowed under, the trains weren't running, and the airports were all shut down ... And that no one should try and go anywhere unless their journey was absolutely necessary. *Stay at home, stay inside, where it's safe.* The announcer allowed himself a small chuckle. *We all like a little snow at Christmas, but this is overdoing it, just a bit. So stay warm, and have a very happy Christmas.* I turned the radio off. It was either that, or reach down the radio and rip his heart out.

With the radio off, the roar of the heater filled the car; it was doing its best to take the edge off the cold and mostly failing. The best you could say was that it was probably warmer inside the car than out. Any normal man would have known better than to be out in conditions like this, but I've never been a normal man.

I clung grimly on to the steering wheel and kept my foot down hard on the accelerator. Because I was determined to reach remote Belcourt Manor, even if I had to drive through hell itself to get there.

✛ ✛ ✛

My first meeting with the man who called himself the Colonel was almost fifteen years ago now. In one of the better bars, in one of the better hotels in London. Full of well-dressed people, looking very prosperous. Lots of friendly chatter, none of it aimed at me. I didn't want to talk to anyone, and they could tell. I was just hiding out in the middle of a crowd, trying to figure out how best to disappear from the bar and the hotel without paying my bill. I couldn't risk using any of my credit cards, with any of my current names, for fear of attracting attention. And I was going to need what cash I had on me.

I hadn't made up my mind where I was going yet, preferably some small and understanding country, with pleasant weather and no interest in extradition treaties, and a flexible attitude towards people who just wanted to be left alone. There used to be a lot of places like that, when I was starting out, but the world is a shrinking place, these days.

The Colonel appeared out of nowhere. Just sat down beside me at the bar and fixed me with a cheerful smile. I looked steadily back at him. There aren't many people who can sneak up on me. I'm really very hard to surprise.

He nodded briefly to me. "Hello, Ishmael," he said. "I'm the Colonel. I'm here to offer you a job, or perhaps, more properly, a position."

"Not many people know me by that name," I said. "And most of them are dead."

"I think that says more about you than anything else," said the Colonel.

I looked him over, taking my time. He was a big man, just hitting thirty. Broad shoulders, powerfully built, holding himself with easy confidence and a practised casualness. Sharp features, piercing cold blue eyes, a quick and mostly meaningless smile. An expensively tailored suit, though he wore it like a uniform. And perhaps, for him, it was. The closely cropped blond hair and severely trimmed moustache suggested a military background. Or, at least, ex-military. He looked like a man who'd had blood on his hands, in his time.

He ordered a single malt whiskey, with water in a separate glass, and the bartender jumped to obey. The Colonel had that kind of voice. He raised an eyebrow at my empty glass, so I seized the opportunity for a double brandy. Alcohol has no effect on me, but I've learned to enjoy the taste. The Colonel and I just sat and looked at each other until our drinks arrived, like two fighters in a ring checking each other out before the bell rings. The drinks arrived, and we toasted each other, and drank.

"So," I said. "You're not here to kill me?"

"No," said the Colonel. "Or you'd be dead by now."

"Then you can buy me as many drinks as you like," I said. "And as long as you keep on buying, I'll sit here and listen."

The Colonel dropped a generous bribe in front of the barman and gestured for him to disappear for a while. The bartender made the money vanish, and then made himself scarce. Several people trying to order a drink raised their voices in protest. The Colonel looked at them, and they went away too. And they hadn't even noticed the Colonel's concealed gun. I'd spotted it the moment he sat down. I wasn't worried. I have secrets of my own.

The Colonel looked me over, like a racehorse he was thinking of buying, or at the very least, placing a decent-sized bet on. "I have heard, my dear Ishmael, that you are no longer working for Black Heir."

"Not many people know me by that name," I said. "And even fewer have heard of that very secret organization. Heard, you say? From whom?"

"Word gets around," the Colonel said easily. "Especially in

our line of work. Secret agents gossip like teenage girls, just because they know they shouldn't."

"You do know what Black Heir does?" I said.

"The United Kingdom's very own department for alien affairs," said the Colonel. He sipped carefully at his drink, as though it might surprise him. "Real aliens, that is. Visitors from Beyond, and all that. They will keep coming here, even if no one on Earth knows why. Someone has to clean up the mess they leave behind and cover up the damage when things get out of hand. The general public is much better off not knowing who and what walks among them, unseen. I was given to understand that you had a really good track record at Black Heir. A real gift for tracking down those who had gone . . . off reservation. And for keeping a lid on things, with a deft and only occasionally violent hand. So I have to ask, why did you walk out on them, Ishmael?"

"I don't approve of their new direction," I said steadily. "Someone higher up the political food chain decided that the old ways, of containment and observation and handing out the occasional spanking, just wasn't good enough. So from now on, official policy is: kill the aliens. Friend and foe and everything in between. Then dissect their bodies and steal all their belongings. I told them this was a bad idea, and they told me to shut up and do as I was told. They should have known better."

"Too tender-hearted?" said the Colonel.

"I don't believe in making unnecessary enemies," I said.

"What a very sensible attitude!" said the Colonel. "Why can't we all just get along, eh?" He gave me a thoughtful look. "I have to tell you that the current directors of Black Heir are very unhappy with you. They really don't like it when one of their own goes walkabout. Especially given all the things you know, and all the things you've done."

"I know there are people looking for me, with bad intent," I said. "I'm safe enough here. Black Heir won't risk trying anything in plain sight. Because they know it would get messy. My leaving shouldn't have come as much of a surprise. I did make my feelings perfectly clear. I won't kill something just because it's different. Whatever name I use, and whoever I work for, there's always a line I won't cross."

"So I understand," said the Colonel. "You've worked for a great many subterranean organizations, down the years."

"You don't know that," I said. "You're just guessing."

"Perhaps. But these are educated, informed guesses. Come and work for me, Ishmael. I could use a man like you."

I smiled. "There are no men like me."

"Exactly!" said the Colonel. "That's why I want you."

"To do what?" I said bluntly.

"To search out secrets, investigate mysteries, and shine a light into dark places. And, now and again, punish the guilty that no one else can touch. *Pour encourager les autres.* I know, dear boy, sounds almost too good to be true, doesn't it?"

"Most things that sound too good to be true usually are too good to be true," I said, meeting his guileless gaze with one of my own. "What if you and I were to have a difference of opinion, at some point, over whether something really needed doing. Or whether someone really needed killing. What then, oh my Colonel?"

He shrugged easily. "On every occasion, I will see to it that you are provided with all the information you need to do the job. I will never ask you to do anything you're not happy with. I represent a large Organization, with a great many agents. I always make it a point to fit the right man to the right mission."

"But why me?" I said. "Why do you want me?"

"You have qualities I admire," said the Colonel. And that was that.

"I don't know you, Colonel," I said. "Which is odd because there aren't many in our line of work I haven't at least heard of. I have made it my business to know who's out there. So who are you really? Who pulls your strings? Who do you answer to?"

"I am the Colonel, and I represent the Organization. That is all you'll ever need to know. Safer that way, for all concerned."

I looked into my glass and was surprised to find it empty. "What makes you think you know anything about me, Colonel? The real me?"

"What does anyone really know about anyone else?" said the Colonel. "I have followed your career with great interest, for some time. From a safe distance."

"No one was ever supposed to know what I do," I said. "No matter who I was working for. That was always part of the deal."

"You've done very well at being invisible," the Colonel conceded. "Always been very good at moving unseen, in the darker places of the world. I like that. I can use that."

I gave him my best hard look. "What's the catch?"

To his credit, he didn't budge an inch. And I've made grown men wet themselves with my hard look. He just smiled calmly back at me.

"If you say yes, you belong to me and my Organization, until I say you can leave. Is that acceptable to you?"

"Of course," I said.

We both knew he knew I was lying, but we raised our drinks and toasted each other anyway. Because that's how deals are made, in our line of business. And so I worked for the Colonel, and whatever his Organization was, for almost fifteen years.

I did good work for him. On his order, I broke into places

that didn't officially exist, to steal information that powerful people didn't want to admit existed, and then I made it public for everyone to see. I travelled all over the world, passing through dozens of countries under dozens of names, from the biggest cities to towns so small that they didn't even show up on the maps. I investigated strange situations and impossible stories, and did things about them. Always moving under the radar, never making waves. I drove on the dark side of the road, in the darker places of the world, dealing with people and things that the world was better off without. Sometimes, I killed people. And sometimes I killed things that weren't even a little bit people.

And I never felt bad about it once.

I followed my satnav's directions through the blizzard, hoping it knew where it was going because I'd lost all sense of where I was. The machine spoke to me in cool impersonal tones, which I preferred to any of the current celebrity voices. I've never liked machines that pretend to have personalities. Technology should know its place. Actually, the thing hadn't talked to me in some time, because there weren't any side turnings. I hoped it was still working.

On the brief occasions when the wind did drop, presumably to work up more spite and malevolence to throw at me, all I could see ahead and around me was snow and more snow, stretching away into the grey distance. Not a living thing to be seen anywhere.

The last village I'd passed through, half an hour back, had been two rows of dark-stoned houses, crouched together for warmth and support. Dim lights glowed from curtained windows, while people hid from the killing force of the cold and the deadly violence of the storm. I could have stopped, if only to check my location and maybe grab some hot food and drink...but I couldn't shake off a terrible sense of urgency. The Colonel never asked for personal favours. He just didn't. So I drove on, into the snow and the wind and the storm, fighting the car as it did its best to slam me into snow banks, or send me spinning out of control as it skidded round a corner.

The satnav finally condescended to point out a non-signposted side road that I'd never have spotted without its advance warning. I hit the brakes, but they didn't want to know, so I just waited till the last moment and then hauled the steering wheel all the way round. I hung on grimly as the car threw itself into the side road. The wheel fought me savagely, and I fought it back, holding it firmly in position even as the steering column made ominous, unhappy noises. For long moments the car just slid sideways, none of the tyres able to gain any traction...and then suddenly they found gravel underneath the snow and dug in, and the car leapt forward.

The falling snow let off for just a moment, so I could see the narrow side road stretching away before me, bounded by two low drystone walls that had all but vanished under piled-up drifts. I drove on, bouncing and shaking over snow and hidden ice. I'd had the headlights on for some time, but they didn't help much. The windscreen wipers...were doing their best. I almost missed it when the road came to a sudden end. I could just make out a tall stone boundary wall up ahead of me, stretching away in both directions until it disappeared into the storm. And right in front of me, getting closer by the moment, a pair of massive black iron gates. Very firmly closed.

I hit the brakes and the clutch, slamming both feet down hard, and the car shook and shuddered as it slowed. The gates loomed up before me. I really hoped I was going to be able to stop in time. Marking my arrival at Belcourt Manor by crashing through their front gates would not make a good first impression. But the car skidded to a halt two or maybe even three feet short of the huge iron gates, and I kicked the car out of gear, hauled on the hand brake, and then just sat there for a while, breathing hard. I took my hands off the steering wheel and opened and closed them several times, till I got the knots out. I'd been clinging on to that wheel for so long that I almost didn't know what to do with my hands any more.

The old stone walls on either side of the gates were rough and bare and featureless. Surrounding the family estate, presumably. They looked like they could keep out most things. The gates had no decorations, no stylistic flourishes. Just brutal uprights and heavy cross bars. I probably wouldn't have crashed through them after all. Just totalled the car. Not that I cared. It was only a rental. I looked for a sign plate somewhere, to confirm this was Belcourt Manor, but there didn't seem to be one. Presumably you either knew where you were, or you had no reason being here. The satnav chose that moment to announce *You have reached your destination* in a very smug tone, so I shut it off. I studied the gates through the falling snow and could just make out a numbered keypad and an intercom grille, tucked neatly away in a niche in one of the stone gateposts. I sat and looked at the niche for a while.

The Colonel hadn't provided me with an entrance code for the keypad, presumably because he didn't trust an open phone. But I really didn't want to get out of my nice warm car. I sounded the horn several times, but even to me the sound seemed small and pathetic in the face of the raging wind. There was no response from beyond the gates. So I sighed heavily, pulled my coat around me, and pushed the car door open.

That took rather more strength than I expected. Ice had built up all across the outside of the car, sealing the door shut. And even after I got the thing open, through a winning combination of brute strength and bad temper, the roaring wind just slammed it shut again, hitting the door like a battering ram. Unfortunately for the wind, I was in no mood to be messed with, so I just put my shoulder to the door and forced it open again.

I clambered out of the car, one careful movement at a time because I didn't trust the snow and ice under my feet, and made myself stand upright in the storm. The cold cut at my bare face like a knife, and the freezing air seared my lungs as I breathed it in. The wind snatched the car door out of my hand, and slammed it shut again. I lowered my head, hunched my shoulders, and headed for the iron gates. One step at a time. My shoes sank deep into the piled-up snow, and it was hard work pulling them out again. The gusting wind hit me hard, slamming me this way and that with a bully's enthusiasm. I just kept moving. The cold and storm might have stopped anyone else, but it wasn't going to stop me.

I reached the niche in the gatepost, brushed away some of the blown-in snow, and then hit the call button and yelled into the intercom. I said my name loudly, several times, and added a few shouted *Hellos!* for good measure. There was a long pause, while snow accumulated on my head and shoulders, and then a far-off voice emerged from the grille. It sounded frankly astonished that there was anyone there.

"Hello?" it said. "Who is this?"

"Ishmael Jones!" I shouted back, fighting to be heard over the roar of the wind. "I'm expected!"

"Yes! Yes you are!" said the voice. "Of course you are! We just didn't expect anyone to . . . I'll open the gates!"

I refrained from saying a great many things and went back to the car. Getting the door open from the outside proved even more difficult, but I wasn't taking any nonsense from the car now I was so close to warmth and shelter. I put one foot up against the rear door, hauled the driver's door open and dived back inside. I had to clear the inside of the windscreen with my coat sleeve before I could see out again. I revved the engine a few times, and then edged the car forward as the gates swung slowly open. I urged the car on. The engine was making sounds I didn't like, and I wasn't sure how much longer the thing would last.

I'd barely got the car through the gates before they started swinging shut again. Someone at the Manor really wasn't keen on letting in unexpected visitors. I made a mental note to learn the correct numbers for the entrance keypad, first chance I got. I hate feeling trapped. Though the stone wall that surrounded the estate was barely ten feet high; I could jump that, if I had to.

I drove on, following the gently curving drive. An old-fashioned manor house loomed out of the falling snow ahead of me, along with several smaller outbuildings. I skidded to a halt before the main house. Belcourt Manor was a huge structure, squat and square, centuries old. Only four stories high, but with a dozen windows along every floor. All of them currently concealed behind closed wooden shutters. Glints of light showed through cracks in the ground floor shutters. No lights on anywhere else. No gargoyles on the roof, and no arched gables, just basic functional guttering with icicles hanging off, and a sloping slate roof.

A medieval tithe barn stood to one side of the main house, all rough stone walls and an arching roof, while a long terrace of Victorian cottages huddled together on the far side. No lights on there, either.

Something caught my eye, and I looked quickly up at the top floor of the Manor. Had there just been a flash of light up there, as though someone had opened a shutter to look down at me? Someone interested in my arrival? I thought so. I watched for a while, but all the shutters seemed securely closed.

I looked around for a garage, or at least somewhere sheltered I could park my car, out of the storm, but there didn't seem to be anything. Half a dozen large white objects set out before the Manor were quite clearly parked cars buried under quite a lot of snow. So I just manoeuvred my car carefully between the still white shapes and parked as close to the front door as I could get. And then I sat there a little longer, peering out at the falling snow. What was I doing here? This didn't feel like the kind of job the Colonel usually needed me for. Something about this whole set-up didn't feel right . . . There had been something in the Colonel's voice, something I wasn't used to hearing from him. If I hadn't known better, I would have said he was scared . . .

So the sooner I got inside, got the Colonel alone, and got some answers out of him, the better. I grabbed my battered suitcase from the passenger seat, forced the car door open again, and ventured out into the snow one last time. The wind had dropped away to nothing, not even murmuring; the falling snow just drifted down, casually, almost listlessly. It was like standing in the eye of the storm. I looked past the long row of cottages and could just make out acres of grounds, with cultivated flower beds, trees and hedges, and a whole bunch of sculpted topiary shapes already losing the details of their identity under piled up snow. It probably all looked very impressive, when the weather was behaving itself.

I trudged through the thick snow to the front door, my

shoes sinking in deep with every step, making loud crunching sounds. It was really very cold, but I'd faced worse, in my time. And then, when I finally stood before the front door, I discovered there was no bell button. Not even an old-fashioned pull-chain. Just a single great black iron knocker, in the shape of a snarling lion's head with a ring in its jaws. I took a firm hold of the ring and banged it hard. I don't feel the cold like most people, but this was a serious storm. Winter with attitude. Enough to affect even me, maybe, if I stayed out in it long enough. So I banged the knocker again, putting some power into it. The people inside had to have heard. They could probably hear it on the moon. The huge door swung suddenly open, and I barged on in without waiting for an invitation.

A blast of warmth embraced me like a favourite aunt, and I stopped dead in the hallway to let out a long, contented sigh. I dropped my suitcase on the heavily carpeted floor and stretched slowly, getting the kinks out. Clumps of snow fell off my coat, to melt and soak into the expensive carpet. Like I cared. The door slammed shut behind me, and a huge overbearing gentleman in a formal butler's outfit came forward to tower over me. He was exceedingly tall, with a muscular build, and he was also quite indisputably black, with a gleaming shaven head. He held himself sternly erect, the better to look down his nose at me. I let him look as I beat the rest of the snow from my clothes and stamped hard to shake the ice off my shoes. It felt good to be out of the storm and inside somewhere civilized. I shook myself hard, and just like that the cold was gone from my bones, and I was toasty warm and entirely comfortable. The butler watched me dripping snow all over everything, clearly considering whether he should just throw me back out. I smiled at him brightly, and he nodded briefly.

I could see he had a great many things he wanted to ask, so I let him wait. Never show weakness; they take advantage. Instead, I took my time looking around the long entrance hall of Belcourt Manor. It was huge, and determinedly old-fashioned, with no expense spared. The walls were covered with portraits of grim-faced people, presumably family ancestors, along with traditional country scenes in a variety of undemanding and unadventurous styles. The furniture was large and sturdy, undoubtedly antique, and all of it dusted and polished to within an inch of its life. The hall was also just a bit gloomy, despite everything modern electric lighting could do. Doors led off on both sides, the entire length of the hall—which stretched away into the distance before ending reluctantly in a great sweeping stairway, with stout wooden banisters. I must have seen a larger entrance hall somewhere, but I was damned if I could think where. I'd lived in hotel suites that were smaller. So of course I made a point of appearing entirely unimpressed, as though this was all business as usual, to me. I nodded back to the butler.

"I am Ishmael Jones," I said. "I'm expected."

"Of course you are, sir," said the butler, in a rich cultured voice. "I am Jeeves, butler to Walter Belcourt, master of Belcourt Manor."

"Of course you are," I said.

"The most recent weather reports would seem to indicate you are very lucky to have reached us at all," said Jeeves. "The storm is growing worse by the moment, covering all of Cornwall and Devon, and most of South-West England. It seems likely that in a few hours the blizzard will have sealed the manor house off completely from the rest of the world."

There was something in his voice, and his look, which suggested very politely that I was a damned fool for trying to drive through such extreme conditions in the first place.

"I'm stubborn," I said. "I don't take no for an answer."

"Indeed, sir," said Jeeves. "May I take your coat, sir?"

I peeled off my heavy coat. Melting snow had soaked through to the lining, even in the short time I'd been exposed to the storm. Water dripped from the bottom of the coat like a leaky tap. Jeeves took my coat from me and held it out at arm's length, between thumb and forefinger, as though he didn't want to catch anything from it. I gave him a hard look.

"Take good care of that coat, Jeeves. I have had it a long time, and I am very attached to it. That coat has travelled with me through many adventures, in many wild territories."

"I did get that impression, sir," said Jeeves. "I have rarely encountered an article of clothing that appeared so... hard done by."

"So treat it respectfully," I said. "Or I'll set fire to your shirt-front."

"Of course, sir," said Jeeves. "I shall find somewhere appropriate to hang it up. Somewhere it won't feel crushed by the proximity of other coats of a less boisterous nature." He then looked down his nose at my suitcase, which had also, it must be said, seen better days. Jeeves made no move to pick it up. "Do you wish me to fetch your other bags from your car, sir?"

"No," I said. "That's all there is. Travel light, travel fast."

"Indeed, sir. You must positively skip along. Not to worry, sir. I am sure we can supply you with everything you might need, during your stay here."

"Is Jeeves really your name?" I said, bluntly.

"No, sir," said the butler. "But for the money Mister Belcourt is paying me, if he wishes to call me Jeeves, I am perfectly happy to answer to that illustrious name. Though I feel I should point out that I do not mix cocktails or provide helpful advice to those who find themselves in a bit of a pickle, and neither do I untangle emotional difficulties. I just buttle."

"Have you always been a gentleman's gentleman?"

"No, sir. I have led a wide, interesting and most satisfying life."

"Only I couldn't help noticing the gun concealed in a holster at your back," I said. "And the knife in a sheath up your left sleeve. And the powder burns on your shirt cuff, indicating you fired a gun recently."

Jeeves looked at me for a moment. "You can see all that, sir?"

"I've been around too," I said.

"A butler's responsibilities are many, sir," said Jeeves. "If you'd like to wait here while I take care of your coat, I'll take you in to see Mister Belcourt. He was most insistent that he wished to speak with you, the moment you arrived."

"I'm more interested in speaking with the Colonel," I said. "He is why I'm here, after all."

"Ah," said Jeeves. "Mister James Belcourt."

I raised an eyebrow, despite myself. "James?"

"Yes, sir. Eldest child to Walter Belcourt."

"The Colonel . . . is James Belcourt," I said. "Well. I never knew. This is his family home?"

"Yes, sir. He arrived late yesterday evening."

"And where is he right now?"

"I really couldn't say, sir. I'm sure he's around, somewhere."

I was actually shocked to discover the Colonel's real name so casually. In all the years I'd worked for him, I'd only ever addressed him by his rank. He never once discussed his life outside our working relationship. And as long as he never asked me anything, I never asked him anything. Some things are all the more binding, for being left unsaid. And then I looked round sharply as a harsh commanding voice barked my name. The master of the house, and of the family, was striding down the hall towards me. I'd known he was there for a while, but it had seemed only polite to wait until he made his presence known.

"Thought it had to be you!" Walter Belcourt said cheerfully, in a loud and carrying voice. "Heard voices in the hall, thought: that must be our impetuous young guest. Ishmael Jones, how do you do!"

The old man stomped steadily down the hall, leaning heavily on a plain wooden walking stick. A good-looking woman edging reluctantly into her forties moved smoothly along at his side. Walter Belcourt looked to be well into his seventies, but he seemed sharp and hale enough, despite resembling nothing so much as a stooped and fiery-eyed vulture. Once a large man, he was now much reduced, all bone and gristle, with a face that had fallen in on itself. He was mostly bald, with a few tufts of flyaway white hair. His blue eyes were still sharp and knowing. His bristly white moustache reminded me irresistibly of the Colonel's. Walter wore a country squire's tweed suit, with tall woolly socks and heavy footwear, for long walks in the countryside. He finally slammed to a halt before me, took a moment to get his breath back, and then smiled briskly. He thrust out a hand and shook mine firmly. Just to make it clear who was the boss in Belcourt Manor.

"Any friend of James is always welcome at the Manor!" he said cheerfully. "Come far, did you?"

"I drove down from London," I said. "Made pretty good time, allowing for the weather."

"Good God, man," said Walter, honestly taken aback. He looked shocked and a little impressed. "You drove . . . all that way?"

"In this weather?" said the woman at his side. Walter ignored her.

"The Colonel seemed to think it important I get here as soon as possible," I said. "And I always do what the Colonel says."

Walter let loose a quick bark of laughter and nodded quickly. "The Colonel. Yes . . . James always did prefer to be addressed by his rank. Even if he won't tell me what it is he actually does. Won't even say which regiment he's a part of . . . Still! None of my business, I suppose. Security, and all that . . . Yes . . . Glad to have you here, Ishmael! Just a family Christmas gathering, nothing too formal. Just good food, good drink, and better company! Eh?"

"Such a pity James could never find the time to join us for Christmas before," said the woman at his side. "How many years has it been, dear?"

"Now, Mel," growled Walter. "You know how busy the boy is . . ." He fixed me with his fierce gaze again. "You work for my son . . . In the military?"

"I work for him," I said. "And I think that's all I'm allowed to say. You know how it is."

Walter grinned suddenly and actually winked at me roguishly. "Military intelligence, right? Couldn't tell me anything if you wanted to. I get it, I get it. Probably why James is still just a Colonel, after all these years . . . But then, he always knew what he wanted out of life. What mattered to him, and what didn't. Always went his own way, that boy!"

I nodded respectfully. It was hard to think of the Colonel as a boy, after all the years I'd known him.

"He hasn't been back to visit his old home in . . . I don't know how long," said Walter, frowning. His gaze softened, became suddenly doubtful, lost in the past. He looked at me vaguely, as though he'd forgotten why he was talking to me. "What . . . what was I saying?"

The woman at his side slipped an arm firmly through his. "You were just telling Mister Jones here how pleased you are that James has come home for Christmas, this year."

"Of course!" said Walter, his gaze immediately snapping back into focus. "Of course I was! Where is that boy? Arrived late last night, straight to bed, didn't even join us for breakfast . . . Where has he got to?"

"I'm sure he's around, somewhere," said the woman. She squeezed his arm, meaningfully.

"Ah! Yes! Allow me to present to you my wife Melanie!" said Walter. "Don't know what I'd do without her. This is Ishmael Jones, dear."

"I know, Walter," said Melanie. She bestowed a welcoming smile on me and gave me the tips of her fingers to shake.

Melanie was very blonde, very trim, utterly assured, and good-looking in a characterless way. Up close, I could see she was well into her forties, though she dressed younger. Fashionable enough, and entirely undeterred by expense. She also wore strings of pearls round her neck and diamond earrings so heavy that they brushed against her shoulders. I could see signs of surgical improvement, in her face and in her neck.

"I'm Walter's second wife," said Melanie. And given the difference in age between the two of them, the words *trophy wife* drifted across my mind. Melanie considered me thoughtfully, frowning just a little, as she realized my details didn't add up to any kind of man she was familiar with.

"Ishmael Jones . . ." she said finally. "What an unusual name."

"I like it," I said. "I chose it out of thousands. I didn't like the others. They were all too ordinary."

Melanie nodded vaguely, suspecting a joke had just gone over her head, but not ready to admit it.

Walter stepped quickly in. "We'd almost given up on you, Ishmael. What with the weather, and all. Beastly stuff. I mean, we all like a little snow at Christmas, for the festivities, but this is beyond a joke, eh? Eh?"

"Yes, dear," said Melanie.

"Still, James was certain you'd be here," said Walter. "Now, what are we all standing around in the hall for? Big fire in the drawing room, to warm a traveller's bones, and a hot toddy, to warm the inner man. That's what you need. Come along! Jeeves . . . Jeeves! Where is the fellow?"

"Here, sir," said the butler, hurrying down the hall to join us. I'd spotted him sneaking away with my coat and suitcase, while I was talking with Walter. Jeeves bowed briefly, to Walter. "I have placed Mister Jones' bag in the Rose Room, sir. I trust that is acceptable."

"Fine, fine," said Walter. "Just the one bag, Ishmael? Never mind. Jeeves can rustle up anything you need. He's in charge of everything practical round here. Aren't you, Jeeves?"

"Of course, sir."

"What is it exactly that you do, Mister Jones?" s Melanie.

"I work for the Colonel," I said.

"*Yes*," said Melanie, drawing out the word till it so more like *no*. "I got that. But what do you do fo exactly?"

"Whatever he asks me to," I said. I met her ch gaze steadily. "He asked me to join him here, so h

"But this isn't work," said Melanie, with the scoring a point. "This is Christmas. A time of c

"I'm always working," I said. "Wherever I a

"Don't press the young man, Mel," said Wal

there are things he can't talk about. Can I at least ask you, Ishmael, how long have you worked for my son?"

"Must be fifteen years now," I said.

"But you're not even thirty yet!" said Melanie. "Did the Colonel take you straight out of school?"

"I'm older than I look," I said. "But then, aren't we all, these days?"

Melanie's left hand went instinctively to her throat, where she'd had the most work done.

Walter plunged in, to fill the gap. "Must be more than fifteen years since James was last here for Christmas!" he said. "Good to have him back, of course, but . . . You probably know him better than I do these days, Ishmael . . ."

"The Colonel has always played his cards very close to his chest," I said carefully. "He only ever tells me what he thinks I need to know, when I need to know it. But I would be happy to sit down with you, at some point, and share my experiences of the Colonel with you."

"Yes," said Walter. "Yes, I'd like that."

"My daughter is here too," said Melanie. "Penelope. Lovely girl. Almost indecently intelligent. The two of you should get on well together. I'm sure you'll have lots in common."

"Really?" I said. "That would make a change."

"Penny! Yes!" Walter said cheerfully. "You'll like her, Ishmael, everyone does. Now come along, do; come through into the drawing room and meet the others."

He turned abruptly and strode off down the hall, his walking stick thudding loudly on the carpet, Melanie floating along at his side. Jeeves had already disappeared again, off about his business. I followed Walter and Melanie down the hallway, thinking: *Others?*

✦ TWO ✦
CONVERSATIONS AMONG
THE DAMNED

WALTER SLAMMED OPEN the drawing room door with a grand gesture and strode in with Melanie hanging on his arm. The gesture was somewhat spoiled by an uproar of raised voices blasting out of the room. Walter had walked in on an argument; an angry one, at that. The noise gradually died away as Walter and Melanie entered, and I hurried to catch up with them so I wouldn't miss out on the fun.

The few remaining voices cut off completely the moment I entered the extremely large room. I stopped just inside the door and looked interestedly around at all the flushed faces and startled looks. Everyone moved to stand a little closer together; it might be all against one and one against all in private, but they automatically closed forces in the face of an outsider. It was so quiet that I could hear the wind outside the shuttered windows. Walter drew himself up to his full height, slammed his walking stick on the floor, and glared about him.

"I've told you all before, no arguments at Christmas! This

is a time of peace and good will, and by God you'll all play nicely together or there will be no presents in stockings for anyone! You leave your problems behind when you come to my home for Christmas, is that clear?"

His voice cracked like a whip, and his gaze was cold and merciless as he glared round the room. There were a few reluctant nods among his guests and a lot of lowered gazes. I used the opportunity to take a look round the oversized room. You could have played five-a-side football in the space available while swinging a whole bunch of seriously annoyed cats. The room was dominated by a massive Christmas tree that took up one whole corner all by itself, its top bent over as it brushed against the patterned ceiling. Wide spreading branches were weighed down by any number of shiny balls and baubles, along with tattered lengths of tinsel and strings of old-fashioned flickering lights. Long-established family favourites, brought down from the attic for the occasion, I presumed. Someone had spent a lot of time dressing the tree, but it still looked like the Christmas fairy had thrown up on it. Cheerfully wrapped presents had been piled up around its base, all with carefully applied name tags. Someone liked their Christmas traditional and well organized.

The drawing room was overpoweringly large for the handful of people standing around in it, as though the room had originally been intended for much larger gatherings. Large bulky pieces of antique furniture stood awkwardly around, like guests hauled in to make up the numbers, and the truly ugly carpeting looked much used and even worn away in places. An open fire crackled loudly in a massive stone fireplace. I could feel the heat it was putting out all the way across the room. But then, this drawing room was almost large enough to generate its own weather conditions.

I half expected to see rain clouds forming around the heavy brass chandelier, which looked sufficiently precarious that I made a mental note never to stand underneath it.

Dozens of assorted Christmas cards hung from lines stretched across the wall above the fireplace, as though to say: *Look how many people we know!* A radio was playing traditional Christmas carols, sung by syrupy massed choirs without an ounce of real sentiment, but turned down to an unobtrusive volume so people could talk over them. There was even a sprig of mistletoe, hanging miserable and unwanted in a far corner, just to keep the Druids happy. All in all, it could have been a jolly enough gathering, if not for the heavy silence my arrival had plunged the room into.

"This," growled Walter, "is Ishmael Jones. A friend of James. So I expect you all to make him feel welcome!"

Everyone in the room reacted when they heard I knew the Colonel, everything from dropped jaws to narrowed eyes. But none of them said anything, even as they looked me over in their own interested ways. Whatever they'd just been arguing about was clearly forgotten now they were presented with the possibility of a new target.

I gave my fellow guests my full attention and smiled easily about me. Most of them managed some kind of smile in return.

Walter took me firmly by the arm and urged me forward. "Come over by the fire, Ishmael. Warm yourself up! You must be frozen, after driving so long through the damned snows to get here."

An attractive young woman in her mid-twenties immediately came to greet us, and Walter's habitual scowl disappeared in a moment as he beamed fondly on her.

"This is my daughter Penny, Ishmael. By my second wife Melanie, of course. Sometimes, I think Penny is the best thing this family has produced in a long time. Until the credit card bills arrive."

"Hello, Ishmael," said Penny. Her smile seemed genuine enough, as though she was actually pleased to see me. "A new face at Belcourt Manor! How delightfully unexpected. Are you my Christmas present? I can't wait to unwrap you..."

"Dear Penny," murmured Melanie. "Always so ready to say something inappropriate."

"Sorry, Mummy," said Penny. She didn't sound it.

She put out a hand for me to shake, and then raised an eyebrow as my hand closed around hers.

"How very warm your hand is, Ishmael! I'd never know you'd been out in the storm. Don't you feel the cold?"

"I'm very warm-hearted," I said solemnly. "Can I have my hand back?"

Penny let go of my hand, her scarlet mouth making a brief moue of mock disappointment. Melanie sighed quietly, while Walter chuckled. And only I saw Melanie's pale pink lips silently form the words: *Must you always be such a slut, dear?*

Penelope Belcourt had long dark hair, flashing dark eyes, a pretty face with a good bone structure, seriously dramatic make-up, and a smile that suggested there wasn't much she took seriously. As though the whole world was one big joke laid on for her entertainment. Just standing still, she burned with barely suppressed nervous energy. Like someone who had a lot to give and was just looking for the right person to give it to. She was dressed fashionably, but sensibly, for a weekend in the winter countryside. No jewellery, as though she didn't want anything about her that might distract you from looking at her.

"It is interesting that Daddy didn't see fit to inform any of us you'd be joining the party," Penny said smoothly.

"Well, given the weather..." said Walter.

"I didn't know I was coming here till I got the summons from the Colonel this morning," I said.

"And you always do what James says?" said Penny.

"Always," I said. "Except for when I don't."

"Penny, darling," murmured Melanie, "do get our new friend Ishmael a glass of our special hot toddy. Just the thing, to warm the inner man."

Penny shot Melanie a quick look, and then grinned briefly. She picked up a heavy china mug from a side table and presented it to me gravely, holding the mug carefully with both hands so as not to spill a drop. Heavy steam rose up from the mug's dark contents. There was something in Penny's gaze as I accepted the mug from her, so I sipped the stuff carefully before giving my opinion.

"Vile," I said. "Truly vile, with a creeping undertaste of Oh My God."

I handed the mug back to Penny, who laughed out loud, delighted. She put the mug back where she found it, beside several other untouched mugs.

"At last!" she said happily. "Someone who's actually prepared to speak his mind! How charming . . . You're quite right, of course, Ishmael, it is a truly awful family concoction that only appears at Christmas gatherings. I think for the rest of the year they use it as a horse purge."

"Really, Penny! It's an old established family recipe." Walter was trying to be annoyed with her, but couldn't quite manage it. "Just a bit of an acquired taste, that's all."

"Then why don't you ever drink it?" Penny said sweetly.

"Well," said Walter. "A toddy that good isn't something you want to overdo." And he smiled briefly at me, as though I'd passed some kind of test.

Penny nodded, thoughtfully. "You'll do, Ishmael," she said. "You have possibilities."

"Oh, I do," I said. "Really. More than you can imagine."

Walter took me by the arm again and led me away. None of us had said anything to the young man who'd been hovering sullenly at Penny's side all the while. No doubt we'd get around to him, in time.

"Now this, is Alexander Khan," said Walter, as we stopped before a slender, dapper Indian gentleman in his fifties. He wore a sharp business suit, complete with a snazzy waistcoat and shoes so brightly shined that you could see their maker's face in them. I said hi, and Khan bid me welcome in the clipped English tones of someone who'd learned the tongue as a second language. Sleek dark hair, dark skin, and a round face with deeply pouched eyes. He looked hard-used and overworked, and not at all interested in partaking of the Christmas spirit.

"My business partner," said Walter. "Helped me rebuild the company, many years ago, and make it what it is today. I'm semi-retired now, but I still take a healthy interest in what's going on."

"Not quite as retired as some of us would wish, alas," said Khan, looking at me rather than Walter. "If you will insist on still being a part of the decision-making process, Walter, you must shoulder your responsibilities. Important decisions will not wait, just because it is an official holiday."

"You don't approve of taking Christmas off?" I said.

Khan smiled frostily. "I am a Hindu, Mister Jones. I do not celebrate Christmas."

"That's Alex for you," said Walter, chuckling loudly in an only slightly forced way. "This man has a hell of a lot of the old-fashioned Protestant work ethic in him, for a Hindu. Always weighed down by responsibilities and worrying where we're going next. I keep telling him: slow down and learn to smell the coffee, or you'll be dead of a heart attack long before you reach retirement age."

Khan nodded absently. He was staring into my face and regarding me oddly. "Pardon me, Ishmael, but . . . It does seem to me you look remarkably like someone I used to work with, back in the eighties . . ."

Walter let out a sharp bark of laughter. "Well, it could hardly be the same man, could it, Alex? That was thirty years ago! Ishmael wouldn't even have been born, back then!"

"Perhaps you knew my father, Mister Khan," I said. "Which puts you one up on me, because I never met the man."

"Yes . . . Of course," said Khan. "That would have to be it, wouldn't it . . ." He gave me one last curious glance and then turned away, dismissing me so that he could give all his attention to Walter. "You and I need to talk, Walter. It is very important! You can't keep putting it off!"

"I think you'll find I can, Alex," Walter said cheerfully. "I will do whatever I damn well please, in my own home."

He moved away, and Khan immediately set off in pursuit, still trying to talk business while Walter talked loudly about anything but. I looked after Khan, remembering. He'd been perfectly correct, of course. I had known him in the eighties, back when we both worked for Black Heir. He left years before I did, one step ahead of being fired with extreme prejudice. He'd smuggled out a particular piece of alien technology, when he thought no one was looking, and used it to buy his way into one of the big communication companies. I hadn't known it was the Colonel's father's company.

Khan covered his tracks with all his usual thoroughness, but I knew what he was going to do before he did. I could see it in his face, hear it in the things he carefully didn't talk about. I could have stopped him, but I didn't see why I should. I was already starting to lose faith in Black Heir, and his more obvious actions helped draw attention away from my own less noticeable sidelines. It wasn't as though Khan had taken anything dangerous, or disturbing. Just some basic alien comm tech, sufficiently advanced to give any Earthly company a head start over its rivals. But not anything that might be... noticed. If it had been anything dangerous, or disturbing, I would have made it dis-appear, along with Khan. There is a line I will not cross.

Alexander Khan and I worked in the same department for several years, but I can't say I ever felt close to the man. We were colleagues, not friends. Khan had a lot of colleagues. And he was always a bit too ready to endorse terminating a stranded alien, instead of kicking its arse and sending it home. Still, it did seem I had made an impression on the man, that he could recognize me so quickly after thirty years.

While I was considering that, another of Walter's guests came forward to smile at me. A woman in her late sixties, grey-haired, with a wrinkled face that still held the remains of what had once been great beauty. She wore stylish but understated clothes that spoke quietly but persuasively of the virtues of another era. When people wore clothes to make them feel good about themselves, rather than just show off the latest labels. She wore a hell of a lot of jewellery, in all shapes and sizes, as though to say: *See? I was lovely, once. Men gave me all this, because I was so lovely.* She extended a slender veined hand for me to shake, and I did so carefully because she seemed fragile.

"Hello, Ishmael Jones," she said, in a warm and still quietly thrilling voice. "I'm Diana Belcourt. First wife to Walter. Welcome, to what used to be my home before Walter gave me up for the more obvious charms of Melanie. I do miss this place... Just one of the many things I had taken from me in the divorce. Because Walter controlled all our finances, he could afford better lawyers than me. I suppose I could have fought more, but in the end I just wanted out. Everything I gave up was worth it, to earn my freedom. It was hard work, being Mrs. Walter Belcourt. There's nothing like being married to a Great Man of Business to force you into the shadows."

I was saved from having to respond to any of that by Walter's return. He nodded easily to Diana.

"Still living in the past, my dear? You can't expect to move forward if you're always looking back over your shoulder."

"You've redecorated again, Walter," said Diana. "I don't like it."

"Mel does," said Walter.

"She never did have any taste," said Diana. "But then, that's why you married her. You know, you never used to give in to me that easily, when we were married."

"Well, one of us had to mellow over the years," said Walter. "And it wasn't going to be you, now, was it?"

"Are you sure the two of you aren't still married?" I said. "You talk like you are."

They both smiled. "We're all on good terms," said Walter. "None of us are the type to bear grudges."

"As long as the alimony cheques keep coming," Diana said sweetly. And then she paused and fixed me with a thoughtful look. "James is my son. I don't think I've ever met anyone before who worked for him. He's always kept himself to himself. I'm glad I've finally got to meet someone from that side of his life. He emails regularly, and phones when he can, as a good son should, but I haven't seen him for years. He does like to keep himself a mystery."

"Yes," I said. "I would have to agree with that."

Another woman came forward to join us, a remarkably

good-looking woman in her thirties. Walter and Diana both smiled on her, in their different ways.

"Allow me to present my good friend and companion, Sylvia Heron," said Diana. "She makes sure I'm where I'm supposed to be and doing what I'm supposed to be doing. Don't know what I'd do without her."

Sylvia gave me a wide smile, as though I was really only there to meet her. A warm, suggestive smile, backed up by a steady gaze, as though we were the only people present in the room. Having Sylvia bestow her full attention on you was like staring into a spotlight. She shook my hand heartily, and her fingertips brushed against mine as she released her grip. I felt a definite spark, just for a moment. Which wasn't something that happened to me very often. Sylvia was the kind of woman who could make a man feel like a man, and make him feel special, just by recognizing his existence. She looked me over, quite openly, and without saying anything made it very clear she liked what she saw.

Which was all very pleasant, but I couldn't escape a strong suspicion that she treated everyone that way.

"Stop it, Sylvia," said Diana, amused, but with just a hint of warning in her voice. "You can't have them all, or there won't be enough to go round."

"Sorry," said Sylvia, grinning. She didn't sound sorry. "My eyes always were bigger than my stomach."

"Well, don't eat the boy alive—at least, not until he's found his feet."

"Why waste time, that's what I say," Sylvia said artlessly.

She dressed glamorously in rich colours and clashing shades, and got away with it because her presence filled the room like a naked flame. Her face was just that little bit too long and horsey to be a classic beauty, but she could still take your breath away every time she turned her gaze on you.

With a face like that, and one hell of a body to back it up, Sylvia could get away with anything where men were concerned, and she knew it. She dressed a lot younger than her age, like Melanie; but unlike Melanie, Sylvia could carry it off.

So I just smiled back at her, making a point of being entirely unmoved by her spectacular presence. Because I'm not easy. I can't afford to be.

Sylvia blinked, just a little taken aback. "How lovely to have you with us, Ishmael," she said. "I only agreed to come to this draughty old heap to keep Diana company. I was expecting a dreary old-fashioned Christmas, but now it seems things are looking up. Always good to have new blood at an old gathering." She took a healthy drink from her champagne glass, made a moue when she realized she'd emptied it, and just stuck the glass out in mid air for someone to refill. Walter was quickly there, to do that little thing for her. Sylvia didn't even notice. She was busy looking at me, thoughtfully. "Diana's told me a lot about James. Your Colonel. I never expected to meet him here this weekend, or any of the mysterious people who work for him. Don't worry if you can't tell me any of your secrets; just make up some fascinating lies. That's what I always do."

"I'll do my best," I said.

There was general laughter from everyone listening, which was ... everyone. They'd all been drawn forward by Sylvia's performance, like moths to a flame. She might only be there as Diana's friend and companion, but she knew she was expected to be part of the entertainment, and she had no problem with that.

The group broke up as Diana led Sylvia away for a few private words, and general conversation resumed. Without being too blatant about it, I watched Sylvia work the room with ruthless efficiency, moving from person to person and group to group, charming and sparkling and flirting outrageously with everyone, while making it look effortless. The lady was a professional. I made a mental note to keep my distance from her, because I knew a predator when I saw one. I'd met Sylvia's kind before, at all sorts of gatherings. The professional friend and the perfect guest. The kind who's always ready to latch on to the right people, to be a friend and companion to those in need, so she could always be sure of being invited to the right places and the right parties . . . where she could attach herself to someone better. That was Sylvia. Always moving on, always moving up, until she finally allowed someone big enough to pursue and catch her, and persuade her to settle down—in sufficient luxury, of course.

Question was: what was Sylvia doing here at Belcourt Manor? She couldn't be after Walter, surely? Maybe she was just looking to make connections. Or maybe . . . she had her professional eye on something more solid. If I'd had any valuables, I'd have locked them up somewhere very secure while Sylvia was on the prowl.

I seemed to have made a complete circle of all the guests present, because I ended up back with Penny, who seemed happy enough to see me again. She might not be as glamorous as Sylvia, but she was a lot easier to be around. If only because she seemed to mean it when she smiled. The young man was still standing stubbornly at her side and made a point of stepping forward abruptly—ostensibly to introduce himself, but more noticeably to place himself between me and Penny.

"Roger Levine," he said shortly. "And I don't want you bothering Penny."

"Ah yes," I said. "The young man who's always at Penny's side, even when it's obvious she's forgotten you're there."

"What?" he said, bristling immediately.

"I'm afraid you rather walked into that one, Roger darling," said Penny. "You can't act like a brute and a bully and not expect to be called on it, eventually. Now behave yourself, and be nice to our new guest, or I swear I won't say a single word to you all weekend."

Roger started to say something, and then fell silent under the force of her glare. It was clear he wanted to stand up to her and equally clear he didn't know how. Self-confident and self-contained women were always going to be a mystery to a man like him. So he just shrugged quickly, turned back to me and thrust out his hand. I shook it carefully, and then let him have it back again. I did my best to look at him understandingly, and he nodded briefly, as if to say, *What can you do?* Thus love makes fools of us all. Love, or something like it.

Roger was in his early twenties, tall and gangling, in an expensively tailored suit that hung badly about him because he couldn't be bothered to stand up straight. Slouching and sulking were obviously full-time occupations for him, because he didn't understand why wealth and position couldn't get him the things he really wanted. Like Penny. It was also clear he was only here for the Christmas gathering under protest, to be with Penny. And even more clear that she didn't want him there. You only had to look at their body language. Roger did his best to project confidence, or at least arrogance, but was undermined by a weak smile and shifting eyes.

"So," I said. "What brings you here, Roger? You're not family . . ."

"I nearly was," said Roger, deliberately. "And I might still be."

"Oh, Roger!" Penny said sharply. "Don't go on. I told you,

it's over." She shot me a look that begged for understanding. "Roger and I were engaged to be married, but that is very definitely in the past. We're just good friends, now."

But all I had to do was look at the way Roger looked at Penny, to know that as far as he was concerned, it would never be over until he said it was over.

We chatted a while, about this and that. Penny filled the air with bon mots, while Roger mostly just grunted. It was actually a relief when Diana arrived, to take me aside for a quiet word. She studied my face for a long moment.

"I'm sorry, Ishmael, I know I'm staring, but . . . You remind me so much of someone I used to know. Back in Paris, in the late sixties."

"That would have had to be Ishmael's grandfather!" said Walter, passing by.

"It might have been," I said gently to Diana. "I believe he was in France, about that time."

And I moved away, ostensibly to get myself a glass of mulled wine. I really hadn't recognized Diana until we'd spoken. She'd changed so much, since she and I were lovers in Paris, in 1969.

I took a sip of the mulled wine, decided one sip was enough, and put the glass down again. There had to be something here worth drinking. I stood alone, doing my best to look lost in my own thoughts, and listened to what everyone else was saying. I can follow any number of conversations, even when several people are speaking at once. It's a good way to pick up on things you need to know, that other people don't want you to know.

Alex Khan still wanted to talk business with Walter, who didn't. Walter avoided Khan by attaching himself to every group as it formed. Talking cheerfully and loudly, he made sure he was never left alone with Khan. Fuming quietly, and sometimes not so quietly, Khan ended up talking with Roger, who'd been left alone because Penny wasn't talking to him just then and nobody else wanted to. The young man looked sullenly at the floor while Khan spoke to him, quietly but forcefully.

"I have been a good friend of your father for many years, Roger," said Khan. "And while he may be gone now, I know he would want you to do the right thing. You promised me you would invest a substantial sum of money in my company, and I am holding you to your word."

"That was when I was engaged to Penny," said Roger. He still couldn't bring himself to meet Khan's burning gaze, but his voice was firm enough. "The investment was to be my wedding present to her. Well, now the engagement is off, you and your company can whistle for the money."

"You can afford it," said Khan.

"That's not the point!" Roger raised his eyes from the carpet to glare at Khan, his cheeks flushed. "You want the money? Then make Penny like me again!"

"Be reasonable, Roger . . ."

"No!" said Roger, rather more loudly than Khan was comfortable with. "I'm tired of being reasonable. It doesn't get you anywhere. It just means you get taken advantage of and people walk all over you. I'm tired of doing what everyone else wants. Penny led me on and then dropped me, like I was nothing. As though what I wanted didn't matter. I don't like feeling like this. I want Penny back. I want things to be the way they were, when I was happy. So, you want the money, Khan? Then you know what you have to do to get it." He turned his back on Khan and walked away.

Khan seemed actually startled that Roger was capable of such strong-minded behaviour. He looked around for Walter and caught him in an unguarded moment, alone at the drinks cabinet. Khan hurried over to back Walter up against the cabinet, blocking his escape. Walter scowled at him, but short of shouldering Khan bodily aside, there wasn't any way out.

"I told you," Walter said stubbornly. "I won't discuss business over Christmas!"

"You have to!" said Khan. "The whole company is in danger of going under!"

"You're exaggerating."

"It is my company. I know what is going on."

"I think you'll find it's still my company, Alex," Walter said calmly. "Been in my family for generations..."

"It isn't your company, Walter, and hasn't been for some years now. We only keep you on as Chairman of the Board because your name still has some value in the City. But it is the Board who make all the decisions now, and they look to me to take the lead."

"And see where that's led them," said Walter, nastily.

"You aren't the only one who will lose everything, if the company collapses through underfunding," Khan said stubbornly. "It nearly went under before, remember? If I hadn't brought you that new communications technology... But the market has moved on and threatens to leave us behind. We need fresh investment to support our research labs, so we can come up with a new cash cow."

"I don't have that kind of money any more," said Walter. He looked quickly around, to make sure no one was listening, and lowered his voice till Khan had to lean forward to hear him. "I have the house and the land, and the money they bring in, and that's it! More than enough to see me out in comfort and leave a nice nest egg for Melanie and Penny, but that's all. I won't risk that, to prop up your dreams of what's best for the company!"

"You own things, Walter," said Khan, entirely unmoved. "Art, antiques, land. All worth a great deal of money. Sell something."

Walter smiled at him mirthlessly. "Are things really so bad, you think you can pressure me? All I have to do is wait, and the Board will recognize how worthless you've become. And then with any luck they'll have a rush of sense to the head and throw you out."

"I will remove you as Chairman of the Board, if I have to," Khan said flatly. "By force, if necessary."

Walter looked at him sharply. When he finally spoke, his voice was calm and controlled and icy cold. "You'd have to persuade every single member of the Board to vote together, to outnumber the shares I still command. And there's no way in hell you'll ever manage that. Too many of those people owe me."

"You are talking about the past, while I am talking about the future," said Khan. "You are talking sentiment, and I am talking business. It doesn't matter what you've done for those people in the past; they will vote to back me because it is in their best interests to do so. Money trumps friendship, or loyalty, or guilt."

Walter grinned at him unpleasantly. "If I do go down, I'll take every single one of you with me. I know where all the bodies are buried, because I helped bury most of them. You tell those treacherous little shits on my Board to behave or I will bury them. And what I will do to you, Alexander Khan . . . I would hate to see done to a dead dog." He scowled heavily. "Now see what you've done! Completely spoiled my holiday mood! Mel, where are you, girl . . . ?"

Melanie came quickly over to stand with him, and Khan gave up. He strode away, while Melanie fussed over Walter, making sure he had a fresh glass of champagne, and cheering him up again with happy inconsequential chatter. I couldn't help noticing that while Melanie was always ready to be instantly protective of her husband, she left Penny strictly alone. As though Melanie expected her daughter to be able to look after herself.

Meanwhile, Sylvia was still busy being the life and soul of the party. I watched her make a point of talking to everyone, individually and in groups; they were always glad to see her. Laughter followed her round the room, and there wasn't a man present who didn't look at her in a thoughtful sort of way, if only for a moment. And yet she didn't seem to want to talk with me any more. Perhaps because she could tell she'd be wasting her time. I think I puzzled her, a little. She was used to being able to con people, and you know what they say . . . one predator can always recognize another.

Roger finally got Penny all to himself by backing her into a corner and not letting her get past him.

"You can't keep avoiding me like this, Penny!"

"I think you'll find I can, darling. I'm actually getting pretty good at it."

"You said that if I agreed to come all the way down here, to this horrible old haunt in the back of beyond, and spend Christmas with you and your ghastly family, then you'd talk about us getting back together again!"

"I said nothing of the sort!" Penny said sharply. "You insisted on being invited down here, even though I told you it was a bad idea. I said that we would talk about this one last time, and we have. I don't want to be engaged to you any longer. How many times do I have to say it?"

Roger scowled at her, like a little boy being told something he didn't want to hear. "Why don't you want to be engaged to me? We had good times! We were happy together!"

"You were happy," said Penny, not unkindly. "I just went

along, I think, because it made Daddy happy. He so wanted to see his little girl safely married and off his hands. Someone else's responsibility. But in the end I decided that my being happy was more important than his being happy. You're not a bad sort, Roger, but you're not what I'm looking for. Sorry."

Roger stared at his shoes, because he couldn't face terribly understanding gaze. "I suppose you're about to say: *It's not you, it's me.*"

"No, I'm pretty sure it's you, Roger," Penny said firmly. "You're sweet enough, I suppose, when you're not thinking about yourself. And yes, I suppose we did have some good times together. But that's no basis for a marriage! You're not what I want, and you're very definitely not what I need. Just put it down to experience, Roger, and move on. I have."

"What is it you want?" Roger said desperately. "Whatever it is, I'll get it for you! I promise I will. Just . . . tell me what you want me to do."

"And that's your problem right there, Roger. I don't want someone who wants me to tell them what to do. Especially when I don't know what it is I want. Only that I'll know it when I see it. Or him."

She turned and looked right at me, and caught me studying her. Roger looked at both of us, and seemed more tired and hurt than angry.

I carefully looked away. I didn't want to get involved with these people. I was here for the Colonel . . . and there was still no sign of him.

I turned away, for something to distract myself with, and saw Diana standing alone for a moment, looking thoughtfully at Sylvia as she charmed and sparkled her way round the room. Perhaps Diana wasn't sure that bringing her new friend and companion with her had been such a good idea, after all, because there had been a time when Diana herself would have been the one sparkling and charming and catching everyone's eye. I remembered her doing it, in the days of her beauty. And perhaps Diana was realizing there was only one real prize in this gathering for Sylvia to go after, and that was Walter. Diana might be divorced from the man, but that didn't necessarily mean she wanted to see him thrown to the sharks. But even as I thought that, Sylvia turned away from Walter and went back to talk with Diana. And within moments the two of them were chatting and laughing together, happy as two teenage chums. Sometimes, I really don't understand people.

Melanie and Khan were standing close together, with their backs to the fire, talking quietly, as though they'd just happened to end up in the same place. But there was something in the way they stood together, in the way they held themselves, that caught my eye. I listened carefully.

"Have you talked any sense into him yet?" said Melanie.

"I'm trying," said Khan. "It's not easy. Your husband can be very stubborn."

"I know," said Melanie. "Trust me, Alex, I know. Do whatever you have to. I am not losing Belcourt Manor, and all that goes with it, just because Walter won't see sense. It's well past time he retired fully and left the company in more proficient hands. Your hands."

"Will I see you later?" said Khan, still staring carefully straight ahead of him.

"We'll see," said Melanie. "We're going to have to be very careful, Alex. We can't risk—"

"No," said Khan. "We can't. So we will just have to be careful."

They moved off, in different directions, to talk with other people.

Sylvia made a beeline for Roger, who'd been left standing

on his own again. I nodded to myself. People like Roger would always be easy prey to people like Sylvia. He didn't want to talk to her, because he didn't want to talk to anyone but Penny, but Sylvia fluttered before him, hanging on his every word and laughing happily at anything that might have been humorous. And Roger started smiling, and even laughing, in return. He seemed a lot more likeable when he lightened up. Every now and again, Roger would shoot a glance at Penny, just to see if she was noticing him being happy without her, but on the few occasions when she did notice, she actually seemed happy for him. Which wasn't what he wanted at all.

Jeeves the butler entered the drawing room, moving so quietly and smoothly that he hardly seemed to be there at all, bearing a fresh set of drinks on a silver platter. He moved around the room in a most professional way, his dark face calm and impassive, offering drinks to the guests. No one seemed particularly interested, but Jeeves didn't leave.

"Coffee and hot chocolate are also available," he announced his deep rich voice, breaking effortlessly through the general chatter. "I can always send down to the kitchens..."

"Ah! Yes," said Walter. "Are you sure dinner will be on time, Jeeves? I mean, given that Cook is down there on her own..." He looked around him apologetically. "No staff, you see. Couldn't get any of them to come in over Christmas, no matter how big a bonus I offered. We're lucky to have Mrs. Bridges. First class cook. Jeeves found her for me. Didn't you, Jeeves?"

"Indeed, sir," said Jeeves. "Cook has assured me dinner will be served exactly on time, sir. With the approved Christmas menu. The lady is a treasure."

"She'd better be," growled Walter. "She's costing me enough..."

"Now, Walter, I'm sure she's worth every penny we're paying her," Melanie said firmly. "Everybody else wanted to be with their family over the holiday season." She stopped and fixed me with a speculative gaze. "Won't your family be missing you at Christmas, Ishmael?"

"I have no family," I said. "They're all gone. There's just me, now."

Penny stepped forward, immediately touched. "Oh, that's so sad! Well, for this Christmas, you must regard us as your family! Isn't that right, Daddy?"

"What? Oh, yes! Of course! Glad to have you with us, young man," said Walter. "Any friend of James..."

I decided I'd been a polite and patient guest long enough. "Where is the Colonel? I haven't seen him."

I still couldn't bring myself to call him James—not after he'd been the Colonel to me for so many years.

"Yes..." said Penny. "Where is my dear stepbrother, who I've been so looking forward to meeting at long last?"

She looked at the others, and they all looked blankly back at her. And then they all looked at each other, before offering different ideas as to where the Colonel might be. In the Library, in the Study, in the Billiards Room... Even resting upstairs, in his own room. Eventually Jeeves cleared his throat meaningfully, and everyone fell silent to look at him.

"If I might take the liberty... Thank you. I have made my rounds of the entire house, checking that all the shutters are properly closed and securely locked. I have been in and out of every room, on every floor, and I haven't seen Mister James anywhere."

There was a long, awkward pause as everyone looked at everyone else. In the sudden hush, we could all hear the wind howling and rattling the heavy shutters outside the drawing room windows. It was a cold, ugly, threatening sound. One by one, everyone turned to look at the shuttered windows, thinking about the conditions outside Belcourt Manor, and they all shuddered, just a little. There was a general feeling of *he couldn't be outside, not in that . . .*

"He'll turn up!" Walter said briskly. "I mean, come on! He won't want to miss dinner. We're having his favourite dessert. He won't want to miss out on his first dinner at home, not after so many years away." He looked around, almost pleadingly. "His job keeps him out of the country a lot of the time. Isn't that right, Ishmael?"

"Something like that," I said. "Have none of you seen the Colonel today?"

No one had anything to say. I was liking the situation less and less.

"He's got to be around here somewhere!" said Walter. "He wouldn't just leave. It's a big house, Jeeves! You must have missed him. Look again."

"Of course, sir," said the butler. He didn't sound convinced.

Walter looked slowly round the huge drawing room, as though suddenly aware of how the size of the room dwarfed the small number of people present.

"There used to be so many of us," he said slowly. "There's something about Christmas, out of all the holidays, that makes you aware of how many people you've lost. Mum and Dad, of course. Gone almost twenty years now, but there isn't a day goes by that I don't think about them. And my brothers, Paul and Eamon. Both of them so much younger than me . . . I never thought I'd have to go to their funerals. All the aunts and uncles, the cousins, the wives and husbands and children . . . I stopped going to the funerals. I couldn't stand it. And now . . . This is all that's left of us. No one ever tells you that the hardest part of growing old is to go on living, when everyone else just goes . . ."

Melanie and Diana closed in on him from both sides, holding his hands and patting him on the shoulder. They murmured comforting words to him, but he didn't want to be comforted.

"Where's James?" he said loudly, close to tears. "I want my son!"

"I'm sure he'll turn up for dinner," said Penny, just a bit desperately. Not knowing what to say or do for the best. "He can't have gone anywhere—not in this weather."

Walter glared at her. "I always thought James would be the one to provide me with grandchildren and continue the family line. But now, I don't see that happening. So it's down to you, Penny girl. Stop being so damned fussy and do your duty to the family!"

"Yes, Daddy," said Penny. Not because she meant it, but because she didn't want the old man more upset than he already was.

"Could James have gone outside?" said Sylvia. "Maybe for a walk, in the grounds, before dinner?"

"In this weather?" I said. "Have any of you seen how bad it's getting out there?"

"Well, no," said Melanie. "The shutters are closed."

"I will search every room in the house," said Jeeves.

"James will turn up," said Walter, nodding vigorously. His eyes had gone vague again. And then he looked at me sharply. "Perhaps you'd like to freshen up, young man. Change your clothes, before dinner?"

"Of course," I said. "I'll see you all later. Lead the way, Jeeves."

I followed the butler out of the drawing room. There were some things I needed to ask him, in private.

✦ THREE ✦
MEMORIES ARE MADE OF THIS

I FOLLOWED JEEVES up the wide curving stairway to the next floor. It was a steep climb, and Jeeves kindly slowed his pace to allow me to keep up. It was all very well for him to go bounding up the steps like a gazelle on steroids—he hadn't been fighting a car through a blizzard for hours on end. Even I have limits. I took a good look around me as I slogged up the stairs, pretending I was interested in my surroundings to excuse my slow pace. More old-fashioned carpeting, so thick and deep that my feet barely made a sound. Heavy wooden banisters, the top worn smooth by generations of hands sliding up and down them. And yet more portraits, of more sullen-faced ancestors. Did no one in this family ever smile? I finally reached the top of the stairs, where Jeeves was waiting patiently for me to join him. I stood there a moment, quietly getting my breath back, and then looked him squarely in the eye.

"Where do you think the Colonel is, Jeeves?"

"I really couldn't say, sir. He's not in any of the places I would expect him to be. It's a mystery. And I really don't like mysteries."

"You're not really going to search the house again, are you?"

"No, sir," Jeeves said steadily. "There isn't any point. I checked every room, on every floor. That's what I'm here for. There isn't another living soul in this house, apart from Cook, of course, down in the kitchen. I suppose it is always possible Mister James could be concealing himself in one of the outbuildings. The tithe barn, or one of the cottages . . ."

I looked sternly at Jeeves. "What would he be doing, hiding out there? In this weather?"

He met my gaze unflinchingly. "I really couldn't say, sir. Unless, perhaps, he's waiting for you."

"But he has to know I'm here, by now."

"I would have said so, yes, sir."

"Then why hasn't he shown himself?"

"You would know that better than I, sir."

Some conversations, you just know aren't going to go anywhere useful. So I looked away, taking in the first floor of Belcourt Manor. Also designed on the grand scale, the long corridor stretched away into the distance, punctuated with yet more antique furnishings, along with displays of old-time weaponry, mounted with great care on ceremonial wall plaques. Reminders of old family martial history, no doubt, before the Belcourts settled down and became civilized. Scratch any old established family, and you'll find robber barons staring back at you. Tall, broad doors led off from the landing on both sides, standing quietly, firmly, closed.

"All the guests are staying on the first floor, sir," said Jeeves. "The upper two floors have been sealed off. No one lives in those rooms. Apparently, the upper floors became too expensive to maintain. These days, Belcourt Manor is effectively a house of just two floors."

"But you did check all the rooms on the upper floors?" I said.

"Of course, sir. I had to be sure all the shutters were securely locked, to keep the storm from breaking in. The house has enough problems with damp as it is. I had to get a special set of keys from Mister Belcourt. After Mrs. Belcourt reminded him where they were. The rooms themselves . . . I've never seen so many cobwebs in my life. The dust was thick and entirely undisturbed. No one has entered those rooms in years, sir. Least of all Mister James."

"Very good, Jeeves," I said. "Carry on."

The butler showed me to my room, situated right at the furthest end of the corridor. No number on the door, just a stylized portrait of a red rose. Jeeves unlocked the door for me, handed me the key, and then led me into the room.

"This is the Rose Room, sir. So called because of the roses on the wallpaper. All the rooms have their own flower motif. Bluebell, Tulip, Foxglove. And so on."

I looked around, doing my best to look as though I wasn't sure whether I was going to accept the room or not. You have to demonstrate your independence to butlers or they'll walk all over you. The room was big enough to be airy, but still pleasantly cosy. Nicely aged furnishings and fittings, some modernish prints on the walls. All of it easy enough on the eye. A large four-poster bed took up most of the space, with a mattress big enough for some serious fun and games. I wanted to jump on to it and bounce up and down, just to see the look on the butler's face, but I had my dignity to think of. My suitcase sat on the bed, open and empty. I looked at Jeeves.

"I have taken the liberty of unpacking for you, sir. Everything has been put away in its proper place."

"Good thing I didn't have time to pack any of my usual surprises," I said. "I wouldn't want to embarrass you."

"A gentleman's gentleman is never embarrassed, sir," said Jeeves. "Only, sometimes, terribly disappointed."

He showed me the door to the adjoining bathroom, and then made a point of indicating the open fire crackling cheerfully in the recessed fireplace.

"There is no central heating in Belcourt Manor, sir. Apparently Mister Belcourt's predecessors believed such things made you soft. When Mister Belcourt informed me you were on your way, I prepared a fire in here, to take the chill off your room. But I am afraid you will have to keep the fire going yourself. Top it up, when necessary. No staff, you see. They're all at home, with their families."

"But not you and the cook," I said.

Jeeves smiled, briefly. "Mister Belcourt does pay exceedingly good wages, sir. And we both do love our work."

"Ah," I said. "But what exactly is your work, Jeeves?"

"I am here to see that everything goes smoothly for Mister Belcourt's Christmas gathering, sir. Now, I have filled the coal scuttle and laid in a supply of freshly cut wood, to keep the fire going. There should be more than enough to see you through the night and well into the morning, but do feel free to help yourself to more from the coal bunker, which you will find outside the house, round the back. I'd make what you have last, if I were you, sir."

"I'm sure this will do fine," I said.

"I could arrange for a hot water bottle, if you feel the cold . . ."

"I don't," I said. "Tell me . . . You met the Colonel. What did you think of him?"

"A very impressive gentleman, sir. Very sharp. Very interested in everyone and everything. Just like you, sir."

"The Colonel invited me to come down here," I said carefully, "because he believed there was danger here. Some kind of threat . . . He didn't say what kind."

Jeeves considered that thoughtfully. "Danger to himself, or to everyone here?"

"He didn't say. And now, I can't ask him."

Jeeves stood in thought for a long moment, his dark face impassive, his eyes far away. "I will take this under advisement, sir. Now, unless you need me for anything else, I have to speak with Cook about dinner. I would advise you to keep your door locked, for as long as you stay in this house."

"I always do," I said.

Jeeves nodded and left the Rose Room, his back straight and his head erect. For a butler, he moved very much like a military man. I hefted the heavy old metal key he'd given me. It felt strong and solid. I hoped the lock was, too. Certainly the key made a satisfyingly loud sound as I turned it in the lock.

It didn't take me long to find my belongings, scattered through various levels of the massive chest of drawers. My things looked very small, and out of place, in such luxurious surroundings. Everything was neatly folded and arranged. Better than I usually managed. Of course, if I'd known a butler would be putting my things away, I'd have packed my good stuff. Though it had to be said: good was a relative term. I can't afford to wear clothes that would make me stand out.

My few toilet things had been neatly arranged on a handy side table, ready for use. They all looked very poor relation, set against the faded opulence of the Rose Room. I peered into the adjoining bathroom. It all appeared functional enough, if very last century. The bath looked big enough to swim laps in.

I sat down on the end of the four-poster bed, my feet swinging freely without touching the floor. I looked up at the ceiling, with its plaster decorations and single shaded electric light, and thought about the two empty floors of rooms above me. There's always something spooky about empty rooms that no one lives in any more. Packed full of dust and shadows and abandoned memories. Just ghosts of rooms, really. I did wonder whether I should go up and check them out for myself, just in case the Colonel had managed to avoid Jeeves and was hiding out in one of them. Could the danger here really be so great that he felt the need to hide away from everyone, in the dark and the quiet? It didn't seem likely. I'd never known the Colonel to be afraid of anything. There was the small problem of all the upstairs doors being locked, but he and I knew ways around that. And after all ... I only had Jeeves' word for it that he'd checked all the rooms. I had no reason to trust him.

Or any of the people down in the drawing room. I was here for the Colonel. No one else.

I shrugged angrily. I didn't want any of this. The people, the place, the situation. I hated not knowing what was going on, or what I was here for. The Colonel should have made contact with me the moment I arrived, if things really were as desperate as he implied. Since he hadn't, I had to assume it was because he couldn't. That he was in some way being prevented, perhaps even held captive. And the person responsible for that ... would have to be very strong and very experienced. The Colonel might be in his forties now, but he was still a first-class field agent in his own right, when the situation demanded. I'd seen him in action. He was fast and he was sneaky, and I would have bet on him against pretty much anyone I knew.

Since the Colonel wasn't here to tell me what to do, I'd just have to work it out for myself. Question all the guests, and mine hosts, and see what they had to say for themselves.

They weren't exactly short on secrets and their own precious little intrigues. They all had connections that they didn't want the others to know about. Alex Khan and Melanie Belcourt, for example. They both wanted Walter to retire from running his company, apparently for their own separate reasons . . . but did their relationship go deeper than that?

And I really wasn't happy that two of the people in this small gathering had known me before, in different parts of my past. Khan at Black Heir, in the eighties. And Diana in Paris, in sixty-nine. It could be a coincidence. Stranger things have happened, in my life. Or, it could all have been carefully arranged, to lure me into a trap. There are always people looking for me. Wanting to get their hands on me . . .

I sat on the end of the bed, swinging my feet idly, sinking comfortably into the deep deep mattress. Listening to the wind howl and the locked shutters rattle outside my window. There was something very comforting about being safe and warm and cosy inside, while bad weather prowled around outside, unable to get at me. I stared into the leaping flames of the banked fire at the other end of the room, listened to them crackle . . . The air was deliciously warm, and the bed was almost indecently comfortable. I wanted so very much to be able to just lie down and rest, to stretch out and relax, let the aches of the day's hard driving just slip away . . . but I didn't dare. I was too tired. I had to stay awake and alert until I figured out where the Colonel was and what the hell was really going on here at Belcourt Manor.

And then I had a dream that wasn't a dream.

Another place, another time. Far and far away, and close as yesterday. A raging sea, with waves big as mountains. Heavy dark purple waters slamming against a massive overbearing cliff, made up of smooth and almost organic shapes. A huge structure stood on top of the cliff, strange and overpowering. All metal slabs and shining surfaces, with vicious spikes and unnatural protrusions, following no pattern or purpose I could make any sense of. Some parts of the structure weren't there all of the time, fading or folding in and out, new parts replacing old in some terribly intricate endless cycle. The whole thing rose up and up, almost beyond bearing, on a scale beyond human acceptance. Towers blossomed like flowers as they stabbed the sky. Vivid piercing lights came and went, in explosions of colours.

And all of this under a bottle green sky, with a fierce white sun, and three small moons that went shooting across the cloudless heavens. There were sounds all around that I identify or understand, but were still horribly familiar for all that. A series of images flashed before my unblinking eyes: strange shapes, hauntingly familiar scenes—freakish, nightmarish, disturbing. A great Voice spoke my name . . . and it wasn't "Ishmael."

Something made me scream. Something made me feel sick. Something made me feel horribly lonely, and sad, for people and places lost.

The dream that was not a dream changed abruptly. Became something more recent. I was inside a place I immediately recognized, but could no longer remember the name of. As though its true name and nature had been concealed from me, hovering forever just on the tip of my mental tongue.

The interior of an artificial place. Not a building, but still a constructed thing. A shimmering phosphorescent glow squirmed up and down great curving walls, ridged like bone or coral, while complex machineries with more than three spatial dimensions rose up around me, doing things I couldn't understand or appreciate, but that I nevertheless knew were desperately important and significant. Things were happening all around me, with impossible speed. I was held in place, restrained, while terrible long needles plunged into me from every side, sinking in deep. Doing things to me. I felt no pain, but I could feel them working. And I couldn't look down. I wasn't allowed to look down, in this dream or memory. Because I wasn't supposed to see what I looked like.

A machine voice spoke to me, giving me information and instructions, and I couldn't understand any of it. I said something in return, and my voice didn't sound at all human.

I came back to myself lying full length on the bed, twitching and trembling, my face covered in a cold sweat. Exhausted, physically and mentally. Sometimes I think these intrusions are memories, and sometimes I think they're cover memories, to disguise something worse. They hit me out of nowhere, without warning, and they hit me hard. And I can't escape the feeling that somewhere deep inside, the old me is trying to tell the new me something. Trying desperately to warn me, about something I need to remember . . .

So. Time to tell the truth, at last. Or what I have come to believe is the truth.

I am an alien, passing for human. My starship fell out of the sky over South West England, back in 1963. It hit hard, digging a great hole in the ground. I no longer remember why we crashed, but I think something bad happened, high above the clouds, but under the stars. The rest of my crew were killed in the crash. I was the only survivor. I remember that much, even if I can't remember who or what the rest of my crew were. My ship's mechanisms remade me, rewrote my physical form right down to the DNA, so that I could appear human. So I could pass as one of you, unnoticed, undetected, until my ship's distress beacon could be answered by my own people. So they could come and find me, and pick me up, and take me home again.

The shape change is standard procedure, in an emergency. Because you must never know we walk among you.

But because my ship had crashed so very badly, the transformation mechanisms malfunctioned. They gave me a human body, but then they wiped most of my memories. I no longer know who or what I was, before the crash. I don't know where I came from. I remember staggering away from the crash site, out into my new world, overcome by human thoughts and senses. By the time I was back in control of myself I was miles away, lost and disoriented. I have no idea now where my ship crashed. No point even looking for it, even if I could retrace my steps to roughly the right area. The ship would have followed its standard procedures and buried itself deep underground, hidden behind powerful shields and protections.

Because we aren't supposed to be here. I remember that.

No rescue has ever come. After so many years, I doubt it ever will. Presumably the ship's distress beacon was also damaged in the crash.

I have been making my way alone on this Earth, passing for human, for over fifty years now. Never ageing, always looking exactly the same. The transformation machines did good work. Always moving on, hiding in plain sight, staying one step ahead of the human authorities. But it's become increasingly hard for me to stay under the radar, in this increasingly computerized world, with its ever-changing needs for confirmation of identity. So down the years I have had no choice but to work for many and various powerful subterranean agencies, in return for their protection. For the names and IDs they provide, backed up by all the necessary paperwork, to give me the appearance of a life, and a background.

I needed their protection because you can't be the kind of person I am, and do the kind of things I can do, without being noticed. I have moved from place to place and from organization to organization, down the years; and there are a lot of people out there looking for me. Because they want to interrogate me, or vivisect me. One of the reasons I joined Black Heir was to search their files on alien visitations, for some information on who or what I might be, but I never found anything useful. And of course I did feel safer on the inside, looking out . . . I did good work, searching out the aliens hiding among us. Because it takes one to know one.

Some of my jobs I liked more than others. I tried to do things I could be proud of. If I was going to be a man, I wanted to be a good man. So wherever I went, and whoever I worked for, or whoever I was supposed to be, there was always a line I wouldn't cross. Things I wouldn't do. And then it would be time for me to move on again. Become someone else again.

I've spent the last fifteen years working for the Colonel and his Organization. Doing good and necessary work. The longest I've ever stayed with one person, or one organization. The Colonel kept me busy and kept me protected. Because no one ever messed with the Colonel's people. I suppose . . . I should have asked more questions. But I trusted the Colonel, and I owed him so much . . .

There. My story, such as it is. An alien, passing for human. Of course, there is another explanation for all of this. I could be crazy. Completely loony-tunes, with a head full of hallucinations. Making up incredible stories to explain a simple case of amnesia. I have seriously considered this explanation, from time to time. But there still remain all the things I can do that normal people can't. The things I see and notice, that other people don't. And, I really don't age.

I pulled myself forward until I was sitting on the end of the bed again, and studied my reflection in the mirror on the dresser at the opposite end of the room. A very human face looked back at me, one that hasn't changed in the least since I first saw it in a mirror, in 1963.

I remembered Alex Khan from when we both worked for Black Heir, from 1982 to 1987. We'd seemed the same age, then. He was . . . intelligent, arrogant, very keen to get on. To succeed. He always saw his time in Black Heir as merely a stepping stone, on the way to inevitable greatness. But when he finally did leave it was just two steps ahead of being discovered and disgraced. Because he just couldn't wait. He had to go for the gold ring, and to hell with the consequences.

And I remembered Diana Helm, as she was then: a beautiful young Englishwoman, who gave up ballet to dance at the Crazy Horse, in Paris. A real scandal, in those far off days of 1969. We were lovers, for a while. I honestly hadn't recognized her at first in the drawing room. She'd changed so much, and I hadn't. We were happy together, for a while. I left her because she started asking too many questions about my past. Where was I from, who were my family . . . And she started to talk about our future, when I knew, even then, we couldn't have one. I hadn't learned to lie so easily, in those days. So I did what I always did when I felt threatened: I ran away. Didn't even leave her a note. After all, what could I say? *Sorry, I'm not what you thought I was?* I had to learn the hard way that I can never allow anyone to get close to me. That it's safer for everyone, if I stay alone.

So many people come and go in my life that I suppose I shouldn't be surprised if some of them reappear. Mostly they don't recognize me. When they think they do, it's easy enough for me to pass as my father, or grandfather. It's one of the reasons I keep moving—so they won't notice that they've aged but I haven't. I move on because I can't afford to look back. Because human beings have lives, with a beginning and middle and an ending, while I'm . . . just passing through.

Though I have to say, it did amuse the hell out of me that the Colonel's mother should turn out to be one of my old loves.

I've been tormented by the dreams, or flashbacks, or whatever the hell they are, all my human life. Glimpses of the world that was once mine. Of the ship that brought me here. The dreams rarely make any sense, and they've never been any help. I find it hard to hang on to them; they fade so quickly. I have tried writing them down immediately afterwards, but when I read back what I've written, it's always gibberish. I destroy the notes, immediately after reading. No sense in leaving ammunition behind for those who are always on my trail.

I had a sort of feeling that I might have visited Belcourt Manor before. Some of it did seem familiar. But I'm used to feeling that way. I've been to so many places down the years that the memories just jumble together. I've always found it easy to move on, to leave people and things and places behind. I can't afford to get attached, because it's so painful when I have to give it up.

I didn't change for dinner, because I didn't have any other clothes. I made an effort: splashed cold water in my face in the bathroom and pulled a comb through my hair. I studied my face in the mirror. *Who are you, really?* And then, I went downstairs to dinner.

✢ FOUR ✢
IT'S A COLDER WORLD
THAN YOU THINK

I WENT TRIPPING BACK down the stairs, making more noise than was strictly necessary and pulling faces at the family portraits. And then I came to a sudden halt at the foot of the stairs, where Alexander Khan had set himself to block my way. He stood his ground firmly, with a very serious face, so I stopped on the step above him and raised a single eyebrow. The best kinds of insult and arrogance are the ones your target can't legitimately take offence at.

Khan fixed me with his fiercest scowl. "I want to talk to you, Mister Jones."

"Well," I said cheerfully. "It's nice to want things."

"What?"

"What do you want, Khan? Speak!"

"Are you following me?" Khan said abruptly. "Have you come all the way down here, in this abysmal weather, just to pursue me? Won't you people ever leave me alone?"

I gave the matter some thought. "What are you talking about?"

"I look at you and I see a face from my past," said Khan. "A man I worked beside for the best part of five years. But that was some thirty years ago . . . so you can't be him. Who are you, really?"

"You have me confused with my father," I said firmly. "A man I never knew. I have, however, heard of Black Heir through my work for the Colonel. I know who they are and what they do . . . And I know that the first rule of Black Heir is: you do not talk about Black Heir."

"I've been out for far longer than I was in," said Khan. "But once they've got their hooks into you, you're never really free of them. I left the organization under something of a cloud. And seeing your face, so familiar . . . it brings back bad memories. The likeness is uncanny."

"So I'm told," I said. "I wouldn't know. Take it from me, Khan: I didn't come here for you."

Khan looked like he would have liked to say more, but a movement further down the gloomy hall caught his eye. He saw who it was and raised a hand in something like a wave. It was Melanie, standing at the far end of the hall. She didn't see me. She only had eyes for Khan. He looked quickly back at me.

"You'll have to excuse me, Ishmael. I must have a word with our hostess . . ."

He didn't look in the least bit furtive as he hurried down the hall to where Melanie was waiting. Not furtive at all. I was just getting ready to wander casually down the hall myself, to find out what it was those two needed to talk about so urgently, when I saw Walter and Jeeves standing together in an open doorway, some distance down the hall. They didn't even glance at Khan as he hurried past. They were far too wrapped up in their own business. What particularly interested me was that they didn't look in the least like master and servant. Jeeves looked a lot more like a soldier making a report to his superior officer. Which was ... interesting. So I stayed where I was and listened.

They thought they were safe, far away from anyone who might overhear their quiet words, but I can hear things at a far greater distance than most people. And no one notices me, unless I want them to.

"The house is secure," said Jeeves. "I've been up and down and back and forth till my feet ache, and the whole place is closed up tighter than a fly's arse. There's no sign of James anywhere. His belongings are still in his room, but his bed hasn't been slept in."

"I'm worried about James," said Walter. He was scowling so hard that it must have hurt his face, and he was wringing his bony hands together so tightly that the knuckles showed white. "He can't just have disappeared! He has to be somewhere!"

"Not in the house," Jeeves said flatly.

"He can't just have left!" said Walter. "Not after making such a fuss about turning up here this Christmas, after so many years away."

"His clothes are still here," said Jeeves.

"And then there's his man, Ishmael, turning up out of nowhere ... What do you make of him?"

"I took the opportunity to search through his belongings very thoroughly," said Jeeves. "Almost turned his suitcase inside out looking for hidden compartments ... His clothes are cheap and nasty, and his bits and pieces are distinctly downmarket—so bland as to be utterly characterless. No weapons, no interesting devices, no surprises at all. Nothing to suggest he's anything other than what he appears. But given that he always refers to James as the Colonel, and the practised way he answers every question without ever giving anything away ..."

"Yes," said Walter. "I know. He's too ordinary to be true. And no ordinary man could have made it all the way here from London, through this atrocious weather."

"Not in that piece of shit he was driving," said Jeeves.

"My son would never have ordinary people working for him. Why is he here, Jeeves? Why did my son want him here, so urgently?"

"We don't know for sure that this Ishmael Jones really is who he says he is," said Jeeves. "We only have his word for it. Surely your son would have told you that one of his people was on his way?"

"Perhaps he intended to," said Walter. "Before he disappeared. Ishmael is the sort of man I'd expect to find working for my son."

"I could always take him to one side," said Jeeves. "Beat some answers out of him."

"No!" Walter said sharply. "No. Just . . . keep an eye on him."

"What do you want me to do—about James?"

"You've done all you can." Walter looked down at his hands and seemed surprised to find them wrung so tightly together. He pulled them apart with an effort. He looked older, frailer. "We'll just have to hope James turns up. Eh? Yes . . . And he'd better have a bloody good explanation when he does!"

They both went their separate ways, disappearing into the depths of the great old house. I looked quickly around for Khan and Melanie, but they were gone. Either their little chat was already at an end, or they'd decided to continue it somewhere more private. Pity . . . But I did spy Diana and Sylvia, standing before the front door. Diana hauled it open, straining hard with both hands to get the heavy weight moving, and then the two women stood side by side, staring out the open doorway at the thick falling snow. Diana hugged herself tightly and shivered. They thought themselves alone and unobserved, and free to speak freely; so again, I took the opportunity to listen in.

"I had hoped the storm would have died down by now," said Diana, "so we could leave. But look at it! Awful weather . . . Worse, if anything. I can't even tell which of those snowy burial mounds is our car."

"Why do you want to leave?" said Sylvia. "Aren't you having a good time? Dropping a barbed bon mot here and a home truth there; sticking it to Walter and making little Mel squirm?"

"I don't seem to have the stomach for it, this year," said Diana. "Sometimes reliving the past feels more like picking at a scab. Makes me feel old . . . And I hate that. You know what, Sylvia? It isn't that, not really . . . It was seeing that delightful young boy, Ishmael. He reminds me so much of my dear Adam, sweet folly of my misspent youth. I never thought to see his face again . . . I wonder where Adam is, now . . ."

Sylvia closed the door firmly and turned to Diana. "You need a nice lie down, dear, before dinner. Get some rest, get your strength back, and work on some really catty comments to throw at Mel over dessert. Come along. I'll see you to your room."

"I wish James was here," Diana said fretfully as the two women came back down the hall, heading for the stairs. "I was so looking forward to seeing my son again, after all these years . . ."

"I know, dear," said Sylvia. "I know."

She helped Diana up the stairs like a nurse supporting an invalid charge. They didn't see me at the foot of the stairs, standing in the shadows. I stayed put, leaning back against the wall, thinking. The damage I do to people's lives, without even trying.

Finally, I headed for the drawing room. I pushed open the

door and then stopped abruptly in the doorway, as I realized I'd just walked in on a blazing row. Penny and Roger were standing face to face in the middle of the room, hands clenched into fists, so caught up in their quarrel that they didn't even know I was there. So of course I remained where I was, and watched and listened with great interest.

"Stop shouting at me!" said Penny.

"I have to!" said Roger. "It's the only way I can get you to listen to me!"

Penny made an exasperated sound and made to leave the drawing room. Roger immediately moved to block her way. Penny looked at him dangerously. "Roger, darling, get the hell out of my way right now, or I swear to God I will kick you so hard in the groinal area that your balls will eventually come down somewhere in Scotland!"

"What balls?" Roger said bitterly. "You cut them off when you threw me over, for no good reason."

"Don't be dramatic, Roger. It doesn't suit you."

"You're not going anywhere till we've talked this out!" said Roger. "You think I want this? You think this is the way I want it to be between us? I hate this! We used to be so happy together . . . You don't know how miserable I've been since you walked out on me . . ."

"You don't have to be miserable," said Penny, her voice softening despite herself. "Just admit it's over. Let it go, and move on. Find someone else."

"Like you have?" said Roger.

"What are you talking about?" said Penny.

"I saw you. I saw you staring at that Ishmael character . . ."

"Oh, for God's sake!"

"You never did explain why you broke off our engagement. Or why you won't give me another chance! I can change, I know I can! You know I still love you, Penny . . ."

"No, you don't, Roger," Penny said firmly. "You want me. That's different."

"I can be whatever you want me to be," said Roger, not even trying to hide the desperation in his voice. "Just tell me what you want . . ."

"I will not discuss this any further," said Penny. "I have said all I'm going to say. And if you're wise, you'll leave it at that."

"I could make you want me again," said Roger, drawing himself up to his full height and doing his best to look commanding. "There are things I could do, people I know . . . You have no idea of what I'm capable of. No idea at all of how the real world works."

"And you have no idea of how a real woman works," said Penny. "Or you wouldn't be wasting my time and yours with this nonsense. I am not the kind of woman you're used to, the kind you can buy or intimidate. Now get out of my sight, Roger! Before I forget the few things I still like about you."

Roger turned abruptly and started away from her. He almost bumped into me, still standing in the doorway. He started to apologize, and then recognized who I was. His face reddened as he realized I must have heard everything.

"Eavesdropping?" he snarled. "About what I'd expect from your sort. Hear anything good? You'd better be careful, Jones. The mood I'm in, I could easily punch your head in."

"No," I said. "You couldn't."

And there must have been something in my voice, or my eyes, because Roger hesitated, and then barged right past me. And kept going. I heard him stomping up the stairs, heading back to his room, slamming his feet down like a child in a tantrum who wants everyone to know how upset he is.

I carefully closed the door behind me. Penny was standing with her back to the fire, her arms tightly folded, glaring angrily at nothing in particular. Her face was pale, apart from two angry red blotches on her cheeks. She looked at me suddenly, almost defiantly.

"You mustn't mind Roger. He's finally found something he really wants that he can't have, and he isn't used to that. He doesn't know how to deal with it."

"Some things are worth fighting for," I said.

"He wouldn't know how," said Penny. She looked at me, consideringly. "You look like you might know how to fight for someone you wanted."

"I don't do that any more," I said. "I am a man alone. I live for my job."

"Yes..." said Penny. "Working for the Colonel, dear missing stepbrother James."

"Yes," I said.

Our eyes met, and I felt a definite spark in the air. And all I could think was: *No. I can't. This is no time to be making an old mistake.*

Penny moved slowly forward to stand before me. "James is Daddy's only son, by his first marriage to Diana. I am Daddy's only daughter, from his second marriage to Melanie, Mummy dearest. I inherit everything; James gets nothing. Mummy insisted, right after I was born. She made ever such a fuss until Daddy agreed to change his will in my favour. I have never been consulted in the matter. But that's Mummy for you—she's spent most of her life doing good for me, from a distance. And that, right there, is all you need to know about this family."

"How did the Colonel feel about all this?" I said.

"Didn't give a damn, as I understand it," said Penny. "You see, I've never met my mysterious stepbrother. James left home years before I came along. Left, and never came back. He's always maintained a strict distance between his life and that of his family. You must know him better than us…Do you know why he left, Ishmael?"

"I only work for the Colonel," I said. "He sends me places, and I do things. Good things, mostly. Things that need doing. I've been with him fifteen years, and he never mentioned his family once."

"Is he a good man?" said Penny. She seemed honestly curious.

"I would say so, yes."

"But you're not going to tell me what you do, or what he does?"

"Sorry," I said. "It's more than your life's worth."

"A man of many secrets," said Penny, admiringly. "Do you work for Intelligence?"

"Not as far as I know," I said.

We shared a smile and, without either of us having to say anything, tacitly agreed to change the subject.

"There was so much excitement when James announced he'd be coming home for Christmas," said Penny. "For the first time in God knows how many years. No warning. Just a telephone call out of the blue, yesterday morning. I'd never seen Daddy so animated…Stomping up and down, waving his arms around, so happy and so full of life…And all I could think was: he never gets that happy about me coming home. But then, James has always meant more to him than I ever could. I may be Daddy's little girl, but you know how it is, with fathers and sons."

"Not really," I said, but she wasn't listening.

"It's hard to compete with the perfect memory of an absent brother. Mummy…wasn't nearly so happy at the news. But she knew better than to try and talk Daddy out of it. Some things Daddy just won't be moved on."

"How about the others?" I said as she paused for breath.

"How did they feel about the Colonel joining the gathering this year?"

"Mostly curious," said Penny. "Quite keen to see this mysterious long-lost prodigal son for themselves. Diana, on the other hand . . . I have to say, I may be wrong, but she didn't seem nearly as happy at the thought of seeing her long missing son again. Anyway, James arrived here late last night. After we'd all got tired of waiting up and gone to bed. Daddy stayed up, of course. So he was there to greet James. Apparently they talked for ages, and then James retired to his room. Tired out after his long drive, I suppose."

"So no one here has seen the Colonel, except for your father?" I said. "And that was late last night."

"You're worried about him, aren't you?" said Penny.

"Yes," I said. "Something's not right. I can feel it. The Colonel can take care of himself against most things, but . . . Do you have any idea why he stayed away for so long? Was there a row?"

"No one knows," said Penny. "Except Daddy, and he won't talk about it. But there was no disguising how pleased he was, just at the thought of James coming home at last. Mummy wasn't pleased. She's always been worried Daddy might change his mind and disinherit me in favour of his firstborn, James."

"But you're not worried," I said.

"No . . . I'm not. How can you tell?"

"I see many things," I said. "I can also tell . . . you don't give a damn about your father's money."

"Well, no," said Penny. "I have my own life. And my own money. I work in London, in publishing. And I'm very happy there, thank you. Mummy shouldn't worry so much . . . Daddy would make sure she was looked after, whatever happened. Just like he did with Diana. But Mummy wants *all this* . . . The Manor and the grounds and everything. Being Lady of the Manor and queen of the local scene. She just loves all that."

"And you don't."

"Frankly, darling, I couldn't give a rat's arse for all . . . *this*."

I wouldn't have thought it possible to get so much contempt into one word. Penny's face cleared, and she smiled brightly at me.

"I was looking forward to meeting James. My invisible half-brother. You know, he always sent me a birthday card and a Christmas card. Every year without fail, since I was a little girl. Never missed once. That was nice of him. He didn't have to do that, for a little stepsister he never even met."

"You said the Colonel only spoke to your father," I said. "But Jeeves said he spoke to him."

"I didn't know that," said Penny. "Why? Does it matter?"

"I don't know," I said. "Is Jeeves your usual butler?"

"Hell, no!" Penny said immediately. "He creeps the hell out of me! I have to fight down the urge to run every time I see him coming. Daddy couldn't get any of the usual servants to stay over this Christmas. Had to go to some agency. For a while it looked like we were going to have to fend for ourselves. I was quite looking forward to seeing that . . . And then Jeeves turned up at the very last minute, with Cook in tow, and saved the day. He is . . . very efficient."

"So you've never met Jeeves before."

"No. Is that significant?"

"Beats me," I said. "I'm still getting the feel for this place and this family."

"And how do you feel?" said Penny. "About . . . us?"

"I'm worried that the Colonel has disappeared so completely," I said. "Jeeves seems very certain he isn't anywhere in the house."

"Then let's go outside and look for him!" Penny said brightly. "We can take a walk through the grounds, see if he's hiding anywhere."

"In this weather?" I said.

"Oh, we'll be fine!" said Penny. "Long as we bundle up properly. Come on, it'll be an adventure!"

"I have had enough of those, in my time," I said.

"I could always ask Roger," said Penny.

I sighed, quietly. "I cannot allow you to inflict such a penance on yourself. All right, let us go for a stroll and brave the sub-zero temperatures together. Who knows, maybe we'll bump into a penguin."

"You only get penguins in the Antarctic," Penny said crushingly. "Though I did hear something rather interesting about polar bears, on some documentary, just the other day. Apparently, when they're sneaking up on someone, across the snowy wastes, the polar bear always raises one arm up across his face. Because his nose is jet black and would stand out against the white background!"

"Something to bear in mind, while we're out in the snow," I said solemnly. "Though actually, that's not why they do it. Polar bears always raise one arm across their face because they're pretending to be Batman. Great fans of Adam West, the polar bears."

Penny giggled, despite herself. "Oh, you! Come on, let's get you properly attired for the great outdoors."

"Very well," I said. "But I reserve the right to head back to the house, at speed, if certain important parts of me start dropping off."

Penny led me all the way down the hall, to an intimidatingly large cupboard by the front door. Big enough to hold a political gathering in, while swinging a whole bunch of endangered species in an entirely uninhibited manner, and absolutely stuffed full of dozens of fur coats, along with a huge and varied selection of fur hats, gloves, and really heavy boots. No skis or snowshoes, but then, you can't have everything.

"Who do all these belong to?" I said. "Can we really just take what we want?"

"That's what they're for," Penny said patiently. "For Daddy's guests, as required. You've never been to a country house before, have you? Try this one on. It looks your size."

"It looks like someone skinned a polar bear," I said. "And a big one, at that. Does Greenpeace know about this cupboard?"

"This cupboard probably pre-dates Greenpeace," said Penny.

I took off my jacket, hung it carefully on a nearby hanger, and tried on a few fur coats for size.

Penny looked me over, with a considering eye. "Nice body . . ."

"I can't take any credit for it," I said. "It's what I was given."

"At least you've looked after it," said Penny.

"Clean living and a vegetable diet . . . are two things I've always avoided," I said solemnly. "Can't help feeling there's a connection."

It took a while, but we both finally found something we liked and, half-buried under fur coats, hats, gloves and really heavy boots, we looked each other over critically. Penny took in the tentative way I'd set a Russian fur hat on my head and shook her own head, more in sorrow than anger. She took a firm hold on the hat with both hands and pulled it down hard, until it settled just above my eyes.

"There," she said, stepping back. "That's better."

"Shoot me now," I said. "Before anyone sees me."

"You look very stylish!"

"I do not do the style thing."

"You do now, unless you want your brains to freeze inside your head. It's cold out there!"

"I had noticed."

We left the cupboard and approached the front door. Weighed down by our big furs, we didn't so much walk, as waddle. I pulled the door open, and we stood together in the doorway, looking out on a pristine white world. The harsh cold hit my face like a slap. Penny squeaked loudly and shuddered, despite her many layers of clothing. I didn't.

A light fog had descended since I arrived, pearly grey mists hanging heavily on the air, cutting off the long view. But the snow had stopped falling, and the wind had quietened down. The outside scene was all peace and quiet, and eerily serene, as though the whole world was waiting for something to begin. I stepped carefully forward, and my heavy boots sank deep into the snow. Penny followed quickly after me, slamming the front door shut behind her.

I took my time, looking around. Snow-covered lawns stretched away in every direction, entirely clean and unmarked, until they disappeared into the flat grey mists. White shapes of covered cars crouched in front of us, while indistinct buildings stretched away to either side of the Manor. Certain vague shapes further away might have been trees or hedges. Winter had laid her hand heavily across Belcourt land, as though trying to wipe out every mark Humanity had made on the landscape. The air was savagely cold, searing my lungs every time I took a breath. Penny huddled in beside me, making quiet noises of distress with every breath, looking around her with wide startled eyes, like a child taken to see Santa Claus's grotto for the first time.

And then she grinned at me, delighted with her winter wonderland, and I couldn't help but grin back.

"If you see a sleigh with reindeer, grab the presents and run," I said.

"The elves would take you down before you managed ten paces," said Penny. "This way..."

She led the way forward, stomping clumsily through the deep snow, and I strode easily along beside her, kicking the snow out of my way. The grey wall of fog receded before us, reluctantly revealing more and more of the snow-covered grounds. It was getting to be late in the afternoon, and an ominous twilight was descending. There wasn't a sound anywhere, apart from the crisp crunching of our boots in the snow. Penny looked this way and that, sometimes grabbing on to my arm for support. I let her.

"I grew up in these gardens," she said breathlessly, and just a bit giddily from all the effort. "I remember running wild in the gardens, as a small child. I used to make a real mess of the ceremonial flower beds, convinced I was helping. No one ever said anything. I was an indulged child, then. See those great shapes, there, just looming out of the fog? Topiary creatures, cut out of hedges. Looking at them now, buried under the snow, you'd never know what they were supposed to be. I can only tell because I recognize the locations. That one is a giant bunny, that is a lion and a unicorn, and that's a giant cock. Well done, you didn't go for the obvious comment."

"I wouldn't dare," I said.

And then I stopped abruptly and looked back at the Manor. I could still make the whole thing out, even through the mists. I stared at the house steadily, for a long moment.

Penny looked at the house, and then at me. "What? What is it?"

"I thought . . . I saw a light," I said. "Shining out of one of the windows on the top floor. Just for a moment. As though someone inside had opened the shutters, to look out."

Penny stared dubiously at the top floor. "There's no one up there, Ishmael. All those rooms are locked up and sealed off."

"I know," I said. "But I'm sure I saw the same thing when I first arrived here. As though someone was taking a look at me. Taking a specific interest in me."

"You think someone in the house is watching you?" said Penny.

"Yes," I said. "I wonder why."

Penny sniffed loudly. "If you ask me, it's probably Roger. Spying on us. Let's give him something to look at!"

She grabbed me by the shoulders and kissed me hard. I stood very still. Her mouth was warm and kind on mine, and her body was a comfort and a promise. Penny stepped back, looked at me for a moment, and then turned and waved cheerfully at the manor house.

"Get a good eyeful, Roger?"

There was no light at any of the windows, not the slightest movement at any of the shutters.

Penny turned back to me. "I don't normally throw myself at people, Ishmael. It's just . . . there's something different about you."

"Yes," I said. "There is."

"I have to say, I usually expect more reaction from a man when I stick my tongue halfway down his throat."

"I hardly know you," I said steadily. "And I will be leaving here, once I've finished my business with the Colonel."

"So?" said Penny. "Carp that diem, that's what I always say. Don't you like me?"

"I haven't decided yet," I said.

She looked at me. I don't think she was used to such plain speaking. "Is there ... somebody else?" she said, finally.

"No," I said. "There hasn't been anyone else for a long time now. Love ... is for other people."

"You know," said Penny, "for someone who's only a few years older than me, you do talk like an old man, sometimes."

"I get that a lot," I said. "As a wise man once said: it's not the years, it's the mileage. Now, tell me about the other buildings."

"You're sure that's what you want to talk about?"

"Yes."

"You're a mystery, Ishmael Jones," said Penny.

"I get that a lot too," I said.

We walked on. Penny didn't try to hold my arm any longer. She pointed out the terraced row of Victorian cottages, set out on one side of the manor house, and the medieval tithe barn on the other. Just great dark shapes now, looming out of the thickening fog. Again, no lights anywhere, and not a sound to be heard.

"All the cottages are locked and boarded up for the winter," said Penny.

"No signs of habitation," I said.

"Daddy rents them out as guest cottages, from spring to autumn," said Penny. "The weather's always too harsh, come winter."

"And the tithe barn?" I said.

"Oh, that goes way back. Fourteenth century, if I remember right. Certainly it was here long before the manor house. Just a big old barn, originally, for storing the village's grain. And then, more recently, for storing heavy farm machinery. If you're thinking James could be hiding out in there, forget it. No doors, you see, just two great openings, front and back. Open to the elements . . . He'd be frozen solid, if he was in there."

"Think I'll take a look anyway," I said.

Penny shrugged, making a good show of indifference. I led the way, slamming my boots through the thick snow. Penny had to struggle to keep up. Our boots sank in deep, making loud crunching noises, as though warning the barn we were on our way. The front opening turned out to be an arch ten feet high and almost as wide. Great drifts of snow had blown through, covering large areas of the heavily ridged stone floor. I had to climb up and over the main drift to get inside. Penny made hard going of it, so I reached back, grabbed one arm, and hauled her up and over. She let out a loud squeak of surprise at how strong I was, and hung on to me with both hands till she got her breath back. I let her. I knew it wasn't fair to encourage her, but I'm not always as strong as I should be.

Inside, the tithe barn was just a huge open space, deep and dark and gloomy, with long shafts of grim grey light falling through slit windows high up on the bare stone walls. Rough stone, thick and solid, rising up to a high-raftered wooden ceiling. Just a place to store things. The only way the Colonel could have survived any time in here would have been to build an igloo, and I didn't see one anywhere. I looked carefully into the shadows, but nothing looked back. Great hulking shapes took up most of one end of the barn: ancient farm machinery, under drooping tarpaulins.

"Ugly old place, isn't it?" said Penny. "Daddy would love to tear it all down and improve the view, but officially this is a listed building. Part of our great English architectural heritage. So we can't touch it. Even if it is butt ugly and half as useful. Even though one good fire would do millions of pounds of improvement. Honestly, darling, just because a thing's stood around for a few years doesn't automatically make it a thing of beauty and a joy forever."

I went back to the front opening to stare out over the still and silent world. Cold and white and pearly grey. Penny came to stand beside me.

"How very peaceful," she said, after a while. "Such a shame it won't last."

"No," I said. "It won't. I can feel the storm building, all around us. Piling on the pressure till it breaks, and then the wind will hit us like a battering ram, and the snow will come down like the wrath of God."

"You're not the most cheerful person I've ever met," said Penny. She put her head right back, to stare up at the iron grey sky past the rim of her fur hat, and then she looked at me. "Can you really feel a storm coming?"

"Yes," I said. "It's a gift. But we've still got some time. Tell me about your family, Penny. The Colonel's family. He never told me anything about you."

"If you like," said Penny. "I don't mind. If you're hoping for dirt, I'm afraid there isn't any. Or, at least, nothing interesting. The Belcourts have lived in the manor house for generations, though Daddy will probably be the last to live here. He's going to have to sell off the Manor soon, even if he doesn't want to admit it. I don't think he'll really care all that much. He's only hanging on now out of a sense of family duty. Mummy's the one who's desperate to stay on. If it hadn't been for her, Daddy would have sold up and moved on long ago. To somewhere cheaper, and warmer. Daddy could use the money to prop up his business. That's why Alex is here."

"What about you?" I said. "This is supposed to be your inheritance. How do you feel about selling Belcourt Manor?"

"I can't honestly say I've any real fondness for the old

place," said Penny. She stood staring out into the mists, her hands thrust deep into her pockets, her eyes far away. "And I'd hate to have the expense of running all this. The Manor's upper floors were abandoned when I was a kid. I used to go exploring up there, even though it was strictly forbidden. Well, probably because it was strictly forbidden. I was always a wilful child. I used to steal the keys and unlock rooms at random, just to see what was in there. Searching for treasure and enjoying jumping at shadows. Pulling open drawers and peeking under the dust-sheets, making a mess... Eventually Mummy got tired of that, and all the other wilful things I did, and when shouting at me didn't work, I was sent away.

"I spent the rest of my childhood at boarding school and my adolescence at a very proper finishing school in Grenoble, Switzerland. From which I gained a first-class education, a posh accent, and a deep and abiding hatred for all forms of authority. I only ever got to come home for the holidays. Like being sent down to Hell, and then allowed brief trips back to Heaven. Just so you could appreciate how bad Hell was."

She turned her head, to look at me. "You're really very easy to talk to, Ishmael. You know that?"

"Yes," I said. "Was school really that bad?"

"No... But it's the principle that counts!" She looked back at the snowy expanse. "I loved the grounds here, and the luxury of the house, but I would have loved anywhere that wasn't school. With all its petty rules, and regulations... What were we talking about? Oh yes... The family. The Colonel's family..."

"Yes," I said.

"Daddy mostly gives in to Mummy, to keep the peace. He divorced Diana because she started looking her age, and he wanted a beautiful wife at his side. He met Mummy at a sales conference, where she was tottering around on high heels, handing out gourmet nibbles from a tray, while wearing hardly anything at all. Really, I've seen the photos. It's a wonder she didn't catch a chill. Daddy took a shine to her and brought her home with him. And just like that, Diana was on her way. Replaced by a newer model. With a good enough settlement that she wouldn't fight it. She's always invited back for Christmas, and she always turns up. Daddy seems happy enough to see her. Mummy, less so, though she's always polite. Mummy is still very wary of Diana, even though she won Daddy away from her. Heavy lies the head that bears the tiara . . .

"Mummy's never felt secure here. You see, she married into wealth and position. Never had any of her own. That's why she was so keen for me to go away to boarding school, and then finishing school. So I could have all the advantages Mummy never had. No one ever asked me what I wanted. I think I would rather have had a mother. And a father." She paused there, as though waiting for a comment. But I didn't have one.

"What about the guests?" I said, finally.

"Roger is a bore," Penny said flatly. "Don't know what I ever saw in him. I think perhaps . . . He was just my way out of the family. Cut my links, once and for all, by marrying someone I knew they couldn't stand. If I had any conscience I'd do something absolutely beastly to the poor boy, so he'd go away and not want me any more. But it's so hard to be rotten to him. Like kicking a puppy.

"Alexander Khan . . . gets on my nerves, big time. Always has . . . on all the occasions he's invited himself here to discuss business with Daddy. Which usually seems to consist of shouting sessions in private. Alex has always cared more about the business than Daddy has. He only ever turns up here when he wants more money for this great new scheme or that. I don't like the way he looks at me or Mummy. I keep my distance. He's been hovering around Roger all this weekend. Don't ask me why.

"And then, there's dear little Sylvia. Seems a decent enough sort. Diana collects good-looking companions to remind herself of what she used to look like before her face wrinkled up into a road map. She says having bright young things around her helps her feel young again. I say she leeches off their youth and energy . . . Sylvia's just the latest in a long line, and she won't be the last, even if Sylvia hasn't realized that yet. She's more fun than some I've known, from previous Christmas gatherings. And fun's always in short supply, this time of year."

"You don't care for Christmas?"

"Christmas is fine. It's the family gatherings that get on my tits. Trapped here for days on end, with people I hardly know or care about. For me, Christmas is just something to get through. Though it's not as if I've anywhere else to go. Or anyone else to be with . . ."

"Why do you keep coming back?" I said.

"Because it's family," Penny said tiredly. "Family obligations, and all that. The blood that calls, and the ties that bind. You know how it is . . ."

"No," I said. "Not really. I have no family. There's only ever been me."

Penny looked quickly at me. "Oh Ishmael, I'm so sorry. And I've just been prattling on . . . Are you an orphan?"

"Something like that," I said. "The Colonel . . . James . . . is the closest I've ever had."

"To a family?"

"To a father," I said.

I hadn't realized I was going to say that, until I heard

myself saying it. I stopped short, thinking. Trying to work out what I felt. Penny smiled, slipped her arm through mine, and cuddled up against me. I should have pushed her away. I knew it wasn't fair, to her or to me, to give her any encouragement. As soon as I found the Colonel, and dealt with whatever business he had for me here, I would be on my way again. I'm always leaving. It's easier on everyone else that way. Because they're going to get old, and I won't. Because I can never tell anyone the truth about me. Because they wouldn't love me, if they knew I wasn't human. And because . . . I'm afraid. Afraid I might not be what I think I am. That my memories, or flashbacks, might be just a cover, to hide something awful. I made a firm decision long ago to walk alone, and live alone, because that was safer for everyone. I don't want to hurt anyone.

I walk on the dark side of the road.

I quietly disengaged my arm from hers, kicked my way through the piled-up snow drift, and strode out of the tithe barn and into the unnaturally still air. I headed past the Manor, towards the row of Victorian cottages on the other side. Penny came hurrying after me, muttering baby swear words under her breath as she trudged through the deep snow as quickly as she could. She stumbled along at my side, glancing at me from time to time in a puzzled sort of way, but said nothing. Perhaps she sensed my mood, even if she didn't understand it. She moved forward to take the lead, and I let her. This was her home, after all. The sound of our footsteps, punching through the snow, seemed very small in the face of such a great open snowscape. Gleaming white expanses stretched away before us, heading off into the distance beyond the cottages, until they disappeared into the iron grey fog.

"OK," said Penny, after a while. "This is just a bit odd, and not a little freaky . . ."

"What is?" I said, looking quickly about me.

"Look at the snow behind us. What do you see? Our footsteps. A long line, from the Manor's front door to the tithe barn, and then more, coming back. Now what do you see ahead of us? Nothing! The snow ahead is perfect, unmarked, for as far as I can see. You'd expect something... bird tracks, animal tracks...fox, stoat, badger. But there's nothing. That's not right, Ishmael. Unless, maybe it's just too cold for anything to be out and about..."

"Could be," I said. "I've been places where the air gets so cold, birds just freeze on the wing and drop dead out of the sky."

Penny looked at me. "You've lived, haven't you?"

I smiled. "You have no idea."

We came at last to the long-terraced row of Victorian cottages. Squat and square buildings, built from a creamy stone, with bay windows and neatly slanting roofs. Probably tiled, under the snow. All of them dark and still and silent, as though huddling together for warmth and support against the cold. Penny looked them up and down, and sniffed loudly.

"Pleasant enough, I suppose. Even charming, if your tastes run that way. They always look to me like they should be on the cover of some really twee jigsaw puzzle. Nothing too demanding. That big one standing on its own: that's GravelStone Cottage. Originally intended for the Manor's head gardener and his family. The others were for the extensive gardening staff. Took a lot of people to look after these grounds, in the days before the ride-on mower. The other servants lived in the manor house itself, so they could always be on call... But, these days, the gardening people are supplied by an outside agency, and the few house staff prefer to come in from outside. So Daddy rents the cottages out."

She paused, so she could lean in confidentially. "Daddy needs the money. The family fortunes aren't what they were. Daddy used to run the family business, and well enough from what I hear . . . but as he got older, he just found it all too much of a chore. He backed off and let the Board make all the decisions. They haven't done as well. Particularly since they started listening to Alexander Khan. He speaks for the Board now. And I'm pretty sure he's only here now because he's trying to talk Daddy into selling off some of our land, to provide liquid cash for the company. I mean, I don't mind! It's not like we use it for anything. But Daddy won't want to. Like the house, the land has been in Belcourt hands for generations. Alex is trying to get to Daddy through Mummy. They think I haven't noticed. Hah!"

That last word came out harshly, with real anger behind it. I didn't say anything. I did wonder why Roger hadn't spoken to Penny about the money Khan wanted him to put into the company. It seemed like the kind of thing Roger would enjoy holding over her. To put pressure on her . . . Maybe the young man had principles, after all. People can always surprise you.

Penny led me on, past the row of cottages and round the end, so we could move out into the great white wilderness of the open grounds. There were a few dark stick-figure trees, too thin for the snow to cling to . . . and great lumps and mounds, here and there. Buried flower gardens, old moss-flecked statues buried up to their waists, pagodas and gazebos, and snow, snow, everywhere.

Penny stopped suddenly and looked about her. "We have to be careful, Ishmael. There's a big pond here somewhere. Covered with thick ice, I'm sure, with snow on top; but even so, I don't think we want to go walking across it. Come around this way, and we should be safe enough."

"You have your own pond?" I said as we circled around.

"Full of trout, in the summer," said Penny. "And of course there's a swimming pool, just up beyond the orange grove."

"Oh, well," I said. "If I had an orange grove, that's where I'd put a swimming pool."

Penny laughed. "It's another world, isn't it?"

We ended up walking between two great rows of louring snow-covered topiary shapes. I found them disturbing; their very vagueness suggested all sorts of unpleasant possibilities. Sometimes great clumps of snow would fall away from them as we passed, plunging to the ground, shaken off by the vibrations of our heavy footsteps. Penny would always jump. I didn't.

"I used to love these topiary animals, as a child," said Penny, glancing quickly about her. "Not so much, now. It's like there could be a whole new shape, hidden under the snow. Monsters, hiding in plain sight."

"Yes," I said. "I know what you mean."

Penny stopped and scowled about her, into the thickening mists. "The main flower gardens should be around here somewhere, but I'm damned if I could show you where. They're just . . . gone. Vanished into the snow. I really don't like this, Ishmael . . . feeling lost, in familiar surroundings. Like you can't trust anything."

"Yes," I said. "I know what you mean."

Penny shuddered suddenly, even inside her heavy fur coat. "Dear God, I'm freezing! Aren't you freezing? Maybe this wasn't such a great idea, after all."

"Then let's go back," I said.

"Oh, bless you! I've been dying to say that for ages, but didn't know how to without sounding like a complete wuss."

"The Colonel definitely isn't in any of the outbuildings," I said. "And there's nowhere else he could be, out here, so we might as well go back."

"Let's go," said Penny. "Somewhere back at the Manor, a nice hot drink is calling my name, in a loud and compelling voice."

She stomped back through the snow, heading for home, and I strode along beside her.

I could feel the storm building. Growing, gathering its strength. I would have preferred to hurry, to get safe inside the house before the storm hit, but I couldn't leave Penny behind. So I allowed her to set the pace and filled the time looking about me. And it was only by chance I saw the snowman, hidden behind one of the great topiary shapes. I stopped and pointed it out to Penny, and she squealed with delight like a child, clapping her gloved hands together. So of course we had to go over and take a look. It was just a rough shape—man-sized, though something less than a man's height—but with no pieces of coal or carrot to make a face, and no scarf wrapped around the thick neck.

"I wonder who made it?" said Penny. "I mean, why come all the way out here, in this awful cold, and then make such a half-assed job of it?"

I stood very still, looking steadily at the rough snow shape. "Penny, I smell blood."

She looked at me, not sure how to take that. "Really?"

"Yes," I said. "Blood. Something bad has happened here."

I gouged great chunks out of the snowman's side, throwing them away. And a human arm fell out, hanging stiffly from the snowman. The hand was frozen solid, perfectly colourless. Penny didn't scream, but her eyes were very wide. I pulled the snowman apart with savage speed, ripping great handfuls of snow away. It took more than human strength, but Penny didn't notice.

Inside the snowman was the body of James Belcourt. My Colonel. Dead, for some time. He'd been left sitting cross-legged on the ground, and then covered with snow, shaped to look like a snowman. So no one would suspect. I stood back, not even breathing hard, brushing snow from my gloves. Looking at what someone had done to my Colonel. And right then my heart was colder than anything in that winter garden.

"Not a bad idea," I said. "The body wouldn't have reappeared until the snow melted, and by then the killer expected to be long gone. But the storm set in, sealing off the Manor from the rest of the world. And the killer was trapped here."

"You mean . . . you think one of the people staying at the Manor is the killer?" said Penny. Her voice was steady enough, but here eyes were still very wide.

"Yes," I said. "That's what I think. Don't you?"

She didn't know what to say. I knelt down before the body, to stare into the Colonel's unblinking eyes.

"All the time I was looking for you, here you were, waiting for me to find you. Came really close to missing you, Colonel. Sorry. This probably would have worked, if I hadn't smelled the blood." And then I stopped and looked the body over carefully. "No obvious wounds. No damage to the body, apart from what looks like a ring of dried blood round the throat. Strangled? Garrotted? And no blood underneath you . . . So you weren't killed here, Colonel. You were killed somewhere else and dumped here."

"I'm really very sorry, Ishmael," said Penny, tentatively. "You came all this way, just to find him dead. What will you do now?"

"Avenge him," I said.

I took the Colonel's body in my arms and hugged him tightly. The body was hard and unyielding in my arms. I never once held him when he was alive. But he had been closer to me than anyone, in his own way.

After a while Penny knelt down beside me and put a hand on my shoulder, saying something, trying to comfort me, but I didn't hear what she said. I wasn't listening. The Colonel had been taken away from me, and I was alone again. I'd never felt so cold.

Someone would pay for this. Pay in blood and horror.

I took a firm grip on the body and started to lift it up. It came free from the frozen ground with a lurch, and Colonel's head fell off. Penny made a brief sound and fell back a few paces. I put the body back down and looked at the head. Someone had taken the head clean off, leaving a ragged wound at the neck stump. And then, they had replaced the head, quite neatly. I studied the pale pink and grey neck wound carefully. It was a savage, ragged tear. Far worse than you'd expect from a sword, or an axe. This looked more as though the head had been sawed off. I reached down and picked up the Colonel's head. The face seemed to stare reproachfully up at me.

You got here too late, Ishmael.

❖ FIVE ❖
THE POINTING FINGER
OF SUSPICION

SNOW BEGAN FALLING AGAIN. Great fat white flakes, coming down so hard that even I had trouble seeing the way ahead. The storm was coming, and it was going to be a monster. The temperature was already plummeting to the kind of cold that kills. I could cope with that, for a while, but Penny couldn't. I had to get her back to the manor house, as quickly as possible.

I picked up the Colonel's body and slung it over one shoulder. He was still frozen solid in his cross-legged stance, but I managed. I held his head under my other arm. A bit undignified, but the Colonel wouldn't have minded. He was always a very practical man.

I headed back to the manor house, with Penny trudging along beside me. She looked straight ahead, so she wouldn't have to look at the body. I pressed on, driving my feet deep into the snow, to give me enough traction to keep me moving forward. It wasn't long before I realized Penny was falling behind, unable to keep up. She didn't have my strength, and the bitter cold was leeching the energy right out of her. I moved to walk directly in front of her, so she could use my body as a windbreak. That helped her make better time.

Finding our way back was easy enough; all I had to do was follow our footsteps. And by the time enough snow had fallen to cover them, the great house was already looming out of the mists, right ahead of us. Penny made a harsh sound of relief and plunged past me, forcing her way through the snow with all the strength that adrenalin and desperation could provide. She scrambled up to the front door, tried the handle, and the door wouldn't open.

Penny looked back at me. "It's locked! Someone's locked the door!"

She tried the heavy iron knocker, but it was frozen to the door, and she couldn't budge it. She beat on the door with her fist, but the thick glove soaked up most of the sound. Penny ripped her gloves off, and then cried out despite herself as the bitter cold seared her bare skin. She hammered on the door with both fists, calling out as loudly as she could. No one answered.

"Get out of the way, Penny," I said. "I'll kick the door in."

"Don't be stupid!" she snapped, not looking round. "Look at the size and weight of the door! You couldn't budge it! Nothing human could."

I was pretty sure I could kick the door right off its hinges if I got annoyed enough, but even as Penny was speaking the door swung suddenly open, and Jeeves looked out. He saw the body in my arms and fell back. Penny plunged past him, and I followed close behind.

Jeeves slammed the door shut the moment Penny and I were inside. The sudden warmth of the hallway was a blessing, and the heavy wooden door shut off the howl of the rising storm. The manor house had been built to keep the world and all its problems outside. Penny leaned against the wall, her eyes closed. Her face was dangerously pale, and she was shuddering violently. I wasn't. I put the Colonel down, set his head in his lap, and then stretched slowly.

Penny's eyes snapped open, and she glared at Jeeves. "Who locked the bloody door?"

"I'm sure I don't know, miss," said Jeeves. "But you really shouldn't have gone outside without telling anyone. If I hadn't happened to be in the hall..."

"We would have frozen to death," I said. "And no one would have noticed till it was far too late. Whoever locked that door knew what they were doing."

Jeeves looked at the headless body, sitting cross-legged and quietly melting into the thick carpeting. He didn't seem particularly upset, or affected. "Mister James... Dead, all this time, and we never knew it."

"Someone knew," I said.

And then people came running down the hall to join us, to see what was happening, attracted by our raised voices. Walter and Melanie emerged from a side door, while Roger and Khan came out of the drawing room. Diana and Sylvia came hurrying down the stairs. They all ended up standing together in the hall, packed tight into a small crowd of anxious faces, staring at the Colonel. The severed head in his lap drew most of their attention. I looked from face to face, but everyone appeared equally shocked and horrified. Except for Jeeves, who seemed to be taking everything in his stride and was studying everyone else as closely as I was.

Walter stepped forward, leaning heavily on his walking stick, jerking his arm free from Melanie's grasp. He reached out a shaking hand to touch James' face, and then his hand dropped away. Walter seemed to collapse in on himself, suddenly so much older and frailer. Melanie was quickly there to take hold of him and give him her strength to lean on. She gave all her attention to Walter, didn't look at the Colonel at all.

Walter looked at me, his eyes full of tears. "It can't be James," he said. "I can't have lost my son. Not like this. Not so soon after getting him back . . ."

"I'm sorry," I said.

Diana stepped slowly forward, her gaze fixed on the Colonel's frozen face. "What have they done to you, James? I wanted so much to see you again, but not like this. Oh Walter, our baby's dead . . ." She turned to the man who used to be her husband, to comfort him, but Melanie was already there, blocking the way. Diana took in the cold implacable look on her replacement's face and turned away. Sylvia was quickly there, to hold and comfort her friend.

I turned to Jeeves, as he seemed to be the only one who still had all his wits about him. "Jeeves! Where can I put the body? It needs to be somewhere safe and secure and out of the way. With a door we can lock."

"Of course, sir. There is a side room down here, on the left, only used for storage now."

"Show me," I said.

Jeeves started down the hall, and I picked the Colonel up. Everyone fell back, to give me plenty of room. I went after Jeeves. He stopped before one particular door, produced a large key ring with many oversized keys, and unlocked the door. He pushed it all the way open, and I carried the Colonel through. The room was dark and gloomy, and distinctly chilly after the warmth of the hall. It was full of piled-up old furniture and other junk. There was a table to one side, so I put the Colonel down on that. The body was still locked in its crosslegged position. I settled it carefully in place, and then took the head out of the lap and put it back where it belonged. The frost on the face was starting to melt, running down the impassive features like so many slow tears.

"Sorry about this, Colonel," I said quietly. "I'll come back when your body's had time to thaw and lay you out more respectfully. I know you're usually very firm about not interfering with evidence or crime scenes, but I couldn't leave you outside. Alone. In the cold and the dark. Why am I here, Colonel? What did you bring me here to do? Was the danger aimed at you, all along, or were you killed trying to protect one of your family? I promise you, I will get to the truth of all this, Colonel . . . James."

I left the room without looking back.

I stood thoughtfully in the hall as Jeeves locked the door. It was all very still, very quiet. I could just hear the murmur of the storm outside.

"Who else has a key to this room, Jeeves?"

"No one, sir. I have the only key. I am in charge of all the keys to this house."

"Then you hang on to them, and don't let them out of your sight. Don't let anyone else take them. No one is to go into this room until the police get here. For any reason."

"I feel I should point out, sir, that I work for Mister Belcourt," Jeeves said carefully. "But since those are very sensible instructions, I have no problem following them. Mister Belcourt . . . seems too upset to take charge, for the moment."

I went back to join the others, who were still standing close together in the hall, looking at the spot where the Colonel's body had been. A large patch of melted snow was soaking into the carpet.

Diana emerged from the drawing room, carrying two mugs of hot steaming liquid. She gave one to Penny, who made low murmurs of contentment as she warmed her hands on the mug, and then gave the other to me. She smiled weakly. "It's just the hot toddy, I'm afraid. All I could lay my hands on, at short notice. You need something to warm you up."

"Yes," I said. "Thank you, Diana."

I sniffed at the dark steaming liquid, winced internally, and then knocked the stuff back in several quick gulps. A hearty glow coursed down my throat and built a fire in my stomach. Good stuff, in its own way. Penny tried to do the same, and then yelped as she all but scalded her mouth. I hadn't realized it was that hot. I kept drinking, at a slower pace, until I'd finished it all, and then handed the mug back to Diana. Penny sipped doggedly at her toddy, glaring balefully at me over the rim of her mug. Colour was slowly coming back into her face, and the hands holding her mug weren't shaking anywhere near as badly.

"How could you drink this stuff so fast?" said Penny. "It's practically boiling!"

"It was hot," I said. "We needed hot. And it doesn't actually taste that bad."

"Yes, it does," Penny said firmly.

"Well," I said. "I've tasted worse."

"I'd hate to think when," said Penny.

"Drink your nice toddy," I said. "You need the heat."

Walter stepped forward. He'd used the time to pull himself together again, and as head of the house he wanted answers. He fixed me with a fierce gaze. "What happened out there? Who did that to my son?"

While I was still considering how best to say what I knew, and what I suspected, Penny stepped in. She explained the circumstances behind our finding the snowman and what was inside it. She did a pretty good job, sticking to the facts even when they clearly upset her and the people listening. She didn't mention my smelling blood, so I didn't either.

Walter nodded slowly, struggling to take it all in. This kind of thing just didn't happen, in his world. "We must call the police," he said firmly. "The killer could still be around here, somewhere."

He hadn't made the deduction yet: that the killer almost certainly had to be someone in the house. Given the weather, there was nowhere else they could be. When I looked around, it was clear to me everyone else had got it. Slowly dawning suspicions showed in all their faces. Except Jeeves, who seemed to be thinking hard.

"Excuse me, Mister Belcourt," he said. "Unfortunately, I have to inform you that the landlines are down. I discovered that some time back. The storm, presumably."

Everyone immediately thrust their hands into their pockets, digging for cellphones. Melanie got there first, but Walter snatched the phone out of her hand the moment she'd tapped in the emergency code. He was head of the house, so he had to take command.

"Hello? Give me the police! This is an emergency . . . Come on, come on . . . Ah! Yes! I wish to report a murder! What? Oh yes, I am Walter Belcourt, of Belcourt Manor. My son has been killed!"

I could hear the voice at the other end quite clearly, even if the others couldn't. So as they all watched impatiently, I just leant back against the wall and quietly listened in as the emergency operator put Walter through to the local police. Their response, though understandable, wasn't what Walter wanted to hear.

"I'm sorry, sir," said a polite, overworked voice, "but there's nothing we can do for the moment. We can't get to you. It's the storm, you see. No one's seen anything like it. All the roads are blocked. Major, and minor. My entire force is out, stretched dangerously thin, doing what they can. I can't get anyone to you until the weather's calmed down."

"But my son has been murdered!" said Walter.

"Yes, sir, I understand that. I am sorry for your loss. But my men would probably be killed just trying to get to you! The conditions are impossible."

"Then get some snowploughs on the job!" said Walter.

"They're all occupied, fighting to keep the main roads open, sir," said the voice. "We have to concentrate our resources where they can do the most good. Where they can save the most lives."

"Don't you know who you're talking to, man? Don't you know who I am? This is Walter Belcourt!"

"I am aware of that, sir, yes. I understand this must be very disturbing for you. For the moment, touch nothing, and try not to disturb the crime scene. We will get out to you as soon as we can."

The phone went dead. Walter looked at it incredulously, and then thrust it back into Melanie's hand.

"Well?" said Diana. "What did the police say? When are they coming?"

"No one's coming!" Walter snapped. "We're on our own . . . He hung up on me! On *me*! I'll have his guts for this . . ."

"But what did they say?" said Khan. "Why isn't anyone coming?"

"Because of the weather, you damned fool!" said Walter. His face was dangerously flushed.

"How long before they can get to us?" said Melanie.

"They don't know," said Walter. He suddenly sounded very tired. "My son is dead, and no one's doing anything."

"Excuse me, sir," said Jeeves. "I was listening to the radio, down in the kitchen with Cook. According to the latest weather reports, the storm will be getting worse before it gets better. It is expected to last all the way through the evening and into the night, and possibly well into tomorrow morning."

"We're cut off!" said Melanie, her voice rising sharply. "We're on our own!"

"Hell with this," said Khan. "I'm not staying here! I'm leaving! Right now . . ."

"Damn right," said Roger. "I'll take my chances on the roads."

Diana looked to Sylvia, who nodded quickly. "We'll be safer on the roads than trapped here in this house with a murderer."

They were all moving towards the front door when Jeeves moved forward, to block their way. His solid presence was enough to bring them all to a sudden halt.

"Get out of the way, man!" said Khan. "We're leaving, and no one's going to stop us!"

"I'm afraid you can't leave," said Jeeves. And there was something in the way he said it that gave them all pause. I studied Jeeves thoughtfully. He was becoming more interesting by the moment.

Surprisingly, Roger was the first to challenge the butler. "Who the hell do you think you are?" he said angrily. "Who are you to tell us what we can and can't do?"

"Oh, don't be such a drip, Roger," said Penny.

"You stay out of this, Penny," said Roger, reddening despite himself.

"It is not my place to give you orders, sir," said Jeeves, in his most calm and reasonable tone. "It is, rather, a matter of unfortunate circumstances. Your cars have all been parked outside the house for some time now, in sub-zero temperatures. Being buried under a thick layer of snow may have helped to insulate them . . . but even if you could get your engines to start, the drive is completely blocked with snow. The outside roads will undoubtedly be even worse. Local radio was quite firm on the subject: no one should venture out in the storm, or try to travel anywhere, until the weather improves."

I could see the resolution going out of Khan and Roger's faces as they thought about it. Sylvia still looked ready to have a go, but Diana was holding on to her companion's arm with both hands and shaking her head.

"Jeeves is right," I said. "I had to struggle to get up the drive, and that was hours ago."

"Then we'll walk," said Khan, drawing himself up to his full height. Doing his best to convince himself. "As long as we dress up right, and step it out . . ."

"Don't be a damned fool, Alex," said Walter. His voice was just a growl, openly contemptuous. "It's more than four miles to the nearest village. Across fields with no landmarks. You can't follow the roads, because they'll have disappeared under the snow. You'd freeze to death."

"You see?" said Melanie, wringing her hands together. "I was right! We're trapped here. With a killer hiding among us!" She turned to Walter, expecting him to comfort her, but he was just staring at nothing, struggling with his thoughts. He'd been through too many shocks in a short period, and I could see the concentration fading in and out in his face.

"Why would anyone want to kill my son?" he said, querulously.

One by one, everyone turned to look at me. All I could do was shrug and shake my head. There was nothing I could say that would help.

"Did James have . . . enemies?" said Khan.

"Everyone has enemies," I said. "Question is, did he have enemies here?"

"What are you saying?" said Khan.

"You can't really believe one of us wanted the man dead!" said Roger.

"Why not?" I said.

I looked around. People were clinging to each other, comforting one another as best they could. Melanie clung determinedly on to Walter, who was pulling himself back together through sheer force of will because he was damned if he would let his son down. Diana and Sylvia huddled together like frightened children, drawing strength from each other. Roger had a protective arm across Penny's shoulders, holding her close, glaring around as though he'd fight anyone who dared threaten her. She let him, because he needed to do it. Khan stood alone, scowling thoughtfully. He didn't seem too bothered by the Colonel's sudden death, but then, he wouldn't. He'd worked for Black Heir. And finally there was Jeeves, standing alone, calm and poised as always, looking around at the others in the same way I was. Looking for a killer's eyes in a familiar face. He caught me staring at him and just nodded, briefly. There was a sober, professional air to the man in a hallway where hysteria was hanging dangerously close on the air, just looking for a way in.

"What are we going to do?" said Melanie, in a voice quite a bit higher than it needed to be.

"We have a murderer among us," Penny said steadily. "And we have no choice but to find him ourselves. It's the only way to be safe. We have to find him before he can kill again, maybe kill all of us, to cover his tracks. We can do this! It's not like he can go anywhere; he's as trapped in this house as the rest of us!"

I smiled at her admiringly. Good to see someone keeping

their head. Everyone else was just waiting for somebody to take the lead. It was clear none of them liked the idea that someone they knew was a murderer.

I looked at Walter. "Help is a long way off. How secure are we here?"

Walter nodded briskly, coming back to himself now he had a chance to take charge. "Yes! Of course... Well, we're safe enough from the storm in here. The outer walls are good thick stone, built to keep out the cold. As long as we keep the fires going, we should be snug as a bug in a rug. The pipes are all lagged... and we have our own generator, for electricity! And of course we have a hell of a lot of food and drink laid in, for Christmas. Enough to keep us going for days. And we have weapons!"

He looked meaningfully to Jeeves, who nodded and stood up a little straighter. And just like that, he didn't look like a butler any more. He held himself differently, in the experienced military manner I'd seen before. His servility was gone, like the act it always was, replaced by a cold-eyed professionalism.

"Ladies and gentlemen, I am not a butler. I was hired by Mister Belcourt to act as one for this weekend, while also serving as his personal bodyguard. My job is to keep people alive, and I'm very good at it. And like all bodyguards, I am armed."

He brought out his hidden gun and showed it to everyone. He held the Smith & Wesson .45 with an easy, practised familiarity. Everyone looked at the gun, and then looked at Jeeves. They didn't seem too sure as to whether the man with the gun made them feel safer, or not. And then they all looked at each other, as though trying to decide who else might be pretending to be something they weren't. Most of them looked at me with open suspicion.

"Why did you hire a bodyguard, Walter?" said Melanie. She sounded honestly puzzled. "You never said anything to me about needing a bodyguard!"

"I didn't want you to worry, dear," said Walter, patting her hand absently. "It was just for the holidays. All businessmen have enemies—you know that."

"But why now, Daddy?" said Penny.

Walter didn't answer her directly, but his eyes did seem to linger on Khan for a moment. "There are more weapons in the house, for those who feel the need," Walter said loudly. "Old family weapons. Look around you! Swords and axes and pikes. Easy enough to get down, and still in good enough shape to scare any villain into keeping his distance! Eh?"

We all looked at the old weapons on their wall plaques, but no one made any move to take one. It seemed no one felt the need ... just yet.

"So!" said Walter. "We're perfectly safe in here from the storm, and we're not helpless! We can look after ourselves."

"It also means our hidden killer has access to an endless supply of killing tools," I said.

Khan looked at me sharply. "You really believe one of us killed James?"

"Who else is there?" I said.

Sylvia suddenly stabbed an accusing finger at me. Her raised voice was sharp, even spiteful. "Everything was fine here until you arrived! Come on, people, he's the only one here that none of us knows! Does anyone know him from before?"

"He found James' body!" said Penny.

"Is that supposed to clear him?" said Roger.

"If he was the murderer, he only had to leave his kill hidden," Penny said coldly, throwing off Roger's protective arm.

"And given the state of the body, James must have been dead for some time," said Jeeves. "Long before Ishmael turned up."

"He could have been . . . outside, skulking around," said Khan. "Killed James, and then hid outside, before making his appearance."

"Not in this weather, he couldn't," said Jeeves. "No, I would have to say that in my professional opinion, Ishmael is the least likely suspect."

"But isn't that who the killer always turns out to be, in murder mysteries?" said Diana, with a short, bitter laugh. "I feel like a character in an Agatha Christie novel! Which is never good for a minor character . . ."

"I am not a minor character!" Melanie said immediately. "Walter, tell that woman I am not a minor character!"

"I never read any of the novels," said Penny. "Though I did follow most of the stories on television . . ."

"Same here," I said. "Which Miss Marple did you prefer? I always had a soft spot for Geraldine McEwan, myself."

"She was far too nice," said Penny.

"Yes," I said. "That's what I liked about her."

Jeeves cleared his throat meaningfully, and we all turned to look at him. "If we could keep to the matter at hand . . . Ishmael, you had time to study James' body. How do you think he was killed?"

"You all saw the severed head," I said. "It looked to me like his head had been sawed off."

Walter flinched. Everyone reacted, even Jeeves.

"You can't just say things like that!" protested Melanie. She pressed a hand to her mouth, as though to keep from being sick.

"Why not?" I said. "That's what happened. There were no other obvious wounds. It seems likely he was drugged, or otherwise incapacitated, and then his head was cut off afterwards. Much more likely than a fight. The Colonel was quite capable of looking out for himself. I can't see why the killer felt the need to cut off the head . . . Normally, that's done to help prevent identification . . . But here, the head was left with the body. Strange . . ."

"I still want to know: who locked the front door?" Penny said loudly.

"What?" said Walter. "What are you talking about, girl?"

"When Ishmael and I came back from our walk, with James' body, the front door was locked!" said Penny. "If Jeeves hadn't heard us yelling and let us in . . ."

"We could have died," I said.

No one admitted to locking the door.

"Wait a minute!" said Walter. "I've just thought of something! The killer could be hiding in one of the outbuildings! In one of the guest cottages!"

"We already looked at the cottages, Daddy," said Penny. "We didn't see anyone."

"But we only looked inside the tithe barn," I said. "We didn't go inside any of the cottages. There were no lights on, no obvious signs of occupation or forced entry . . . but the cottages should certainly be searched at some point. When the weather permits."

"I will do that, if it needs doing," Jeeves said immediately. "I am a professional bodyguard. And I have a gun."

"But you work for Walter," I said. "Who, I regret to say, could be a suspect. Who knows what orders you're following? I worked for the Colonel, which means I am the only one here with no motive to want him dead."

"How do we know that?" said Khan, his voice rising. "We have no idea what your real relationship with James was like! A lot of people have good reason to want their boss dead.

What did you do for the Colonel? What exactly is your job, Ishmael?"

"I protect the innocent and punish the guilty," I said.

"Oh, that's not vague at all," said Roger. "Who are you really, Ishmael?"

"If you find out," I said, "let me know."

Melanie turned abruptly to Jeeves. "Lock all the doors, front and back! And make sure all the windows and shutters are properly secure! I don't want anyone outside getting into the house!"

"I have already done that," said Jeeves. "Well . . . do it again!" said Melanie.

Walter nodded to Jeeves. "Probably best to check. If only to reassure people . . . And you'd better go down to the kitchen and tell Cook what's going on."

"Of course, sir," said Jeeves. He strode off down the hallway, disappearing into the dark depths of the house. Everyone looked at everyone else, trying to decide whether they felt safer or not, now the man with the gun was gone.

Walter just sent his bodyguard away, I thought. *Leaving him unprotected. And Jeeves didn't even argue. I just missed something . . . What did I miss?*

"I think we should all go to our own rooms, and lock the doors, and barricade ourselves in, and wait till the police arrive!" said Melanie.

"No," I said immediately. "Not a good idea. Being on your own is the best way to get picked off. The killer could go quietly from room to room, kill everyone, and then just leave."

"That's a horrible thought!" said Sylvia.

"What do you suggest, Ishmael?" said Penny.

"We should all stay together," I said. "In one room, with one easily defended door. Where we can all watch and protect each other."

Everyone seemed to like the sound of that. Safety in numbers is always a comfort.

"Wait! I just thought!" said Sylvia. "The murderer could already be gone! I mean, if he killed James out in the garden, he might never have come inside the house. He could have murdered James, hidden the body, and then left the gardens by . . . whatever way he got in! Why would he hang around? The snow would cover up whatever tracks he left . . ."

"She's got a point," said Walter. "Good thinking, girl!"

They all began to smile, and relax, for the first time. Everyone liked the sound of this new idea. They wanted to believe it. Because it meant the killer was gone, so they didn't have to worry any more . . . and because it meant one of them didn't have to be a killer, after all.

Khan looked at me, scowling thoughtfully. "James did have enemies. Someone could have followed him here."

"Yes," I said. I was about to point out that the Colonel couldn't have been killed where he was found, because there was no blood pool, but I decided to keep that to myself. Let the killer think themselves safe.

"I think we should have dinner as planned," Walter said loudly. "And talk things through. Don't you, eh? All of you? I think we'll all feel a lot better with some good hot food and drink inside us."

They were all nodding and smiling. I was quietly amazed they could contemplate just sitting down to dinner, so soon after a sudden violent death. But I said nothing. Let the killer think suspicion had passed. I'd still be watching.

✥ SIX ✥
PREDATORS AND PREY ALL DRINK FROM THE SAME POOL

WALTER AND MELANIE led the way down the hall, and we all just followed on behind. As though it was just another dinner, and just another day, and no one had died who mattered. Roger was still sticking close to Penny, who didn't have the heart to brush him off. Khan was right behind them, trying to attract Roger's attention so they could continue their conversation. To his credit, Roger was having none of it. Not as long as he thought Penny needed him. Everyone was all talking loudly and cheerfully, as though they could drive back the dark if they only made enough noise. Diana and Sylvia walked together, apparently inseparable, until Diana stopped abruptly and looked back at me, bringing up the rear. She gestured for me to wait, and then smiled apologetically at Sylvia.

"You go on ahead, dear," said Diana. "I need to talk privately with this young man."

Sylvia glowered at me, openly suspicious. "Are you sure, Diana? I could hang around, at a respectful distance, just so you're not left alone with him . . ."

"No, you go on, Sylvia," said Diana, and there was enough authority in her voice that Sylvia just shrugged quickly, turned, and walked on.

Diana came forward, to stand before me. She had to tilt her head back, to look up at me. And in her old face, I could see a young face I used to know. She stared at me with something like wonder. "You look just like the young man I used to know, back in Paris."

"But that was 1969," I said gently. "All those years ago. So it couldn't have been me, could it? That would have to be my grandfather, Adam."

"Yes," said Diana. "That was his name. You look like him, sound like him, move like him. Every time I look at you, something you say or do brings back an old memory. Like the Ghost of Christmas Past, when the world and I were both so very much younger." She reached up to touch my face, with a trembling old hand. I stood still, and let her, doing my best to keep my smile nothing more than polite and respectful. Her fingertips trailed across my face, like the hand of a blind woman searching for truth.

"My dear Adam," she said. "In Paris, in the spring. Such a time to be alive. But mostly what I remember now was how badly I treated him. I was young and foolish, and I thought I had the world at my feet. I told him to his face that my career had to come first. That I was one of the leading dancers of my generation, and I had a duty to pursue my art. And then I was surprised when he walked out on me. I never saw him again. So I could never tell him how wrong I'd been, and how sorry I was. Could I tell you, instead?"

"I'm sure he knew, then," I said gently. "And I'm sure he knows now. But yes, you can tell me. If you like."

"I'm so sorry, Adam," she said, her voice cracking as old unshed tears glistened in her eyes.

"It's all right, Diana," I said. I took her in my arms and held her. And she clung to me like a drowning woman.

After a while, I gently pushed her away from me. "Take my arm," I said. "And I'll lead you into dinner."

"Thank you, Ishmael," she said. "Sometimes, as you get older, you have to take your comforts where you can find them. My son is gone, my first love is gone, and all that's left is some old woman whose face I don't even recognize in the mirror. Getting old . . . is all about leaving things behind."

"That's not getting old, girl," I said. "That's just life."

She laughed, briefly. "You sound just like him."

She slipped an arm through mine, and I led her down the hallway. She was smiling.

Of course I remembered her, from Paris, in the spring, when we were both so very young. I'd only been human six years then, and I was still learning what that was. Diana taught me everything I needed to know about love; about joy and happiness and shared good times. About the importance of caring more for someone else than for yourself. I didn't leave Diana because of her career. I left because I couldn't be who and what she needed me to be. Because I couldn't grow old alongside her.

I remembered Diana, dancing. Like the Goddess of Dance come down to blaze among mere mortals. I thought . . . She doesn't need me. She needs a good man. I hoped she'd find one, after I was gone. Instead, she found Walter Belcourt, which didn't last, and then apparently a succession of cheerful young women like Sylvia. Who were never meant to last. I wondered how long it had been since Diana last danced, throwing her body across a lit stage like the music itself come to life. And then curtsying deeply to an audience driven to its feet by wild appreciation.

Throwing flowers and cheering themselves hoarse, and pounding their hands together till they ached.

Of course I remembered Diana, in that wonderful year, with the best films and the best songs ever. Of course I remembered being young, and in love. But what would be the point of saying anything? What could I say that wouldn't be cruel?

We came at last to the dining hall door, and there was Walter, waiting for us, with Sylvia at his side. He fixed me with a stern look.

"Just need a quick word with you, Ishmael," he said briskly. "You go on in, Diana my dear. I kept Sylvia here with me to walk you in, so you wouldn't have to be on your own, even for a moment."

"How very kind of you, Walter," said Diana, disengaging her arm from mine. "If you'd been this thoughtful when we were married, we might still be together. I was just talking to Ishmael about my old dancing days. You never did see me dance, did you, Walter?"

"No," he said. "But I am told, you were a wonder to behold."

She was. Oh, she was.

Walter pushed open the dining hall door, and Diana and Sylvia went in together. Walter shut the door, very firmly, shutting off a brief clamour of raised voices from within. And then he hesitated, not sure where to start.

"What is it, Walter?" I said, as kindly as I could.

"We need to talk," said Walter, but still he hesitated.

"Tell me," I said. "Why did you bring in Jeeves as a bodyguard for this particular weekend gathering? Were you expecting trouble?"

Walter nodded, slowly. "Not much gets past you, does it, boy? I've had bodyguards before, that neither Diana or

Melanie needed to know about. But this is the first time I felt the need for an armed guard so close at hand. I hired Jeeves after Alex told me there had been a series of threats made against the company. More serious threats than usual. The company has been having cash flow problems, of late, and we had no choice but to lay off a whole bunch of people. The Board made the decision, of course, but I went along. These things happen . . . You do what you have to do, to keep the company going. We would have hired them all back, as soon as things improved . . . Or at least, I like to think we would.

"Anyway, Alex brought these latest threats to my attention because they were death threats. You destroyed my life so I'll destroy yours . . . Aimed not just at me, but my family as well. Nasty stuff . . . Alex turned them over to the police, of course, but they couldn't offer much in the way of reassurance, or protection. So I felt it best to err on the side of caution.

"Jeeves isn't just here to look after me. He's here to protect Melanie and Diana and Penny. I didn't know James would be here too . . . I didn't tell Melanie, because I knew she'd only be upset. I didn't tell Diana, because I knew she wouldn't take it seriously. And I didn't tell Penny . . . because she would only have insisted she could take care of herself. I wanted them protected. It isn't the first time I've lied to them, to keep them safe. And in the end, it turns out the threat wasn't to any of them, after all. The bastard went after my son, James."

"You still think this is aimed primarily at you, rather than the Colonel?" I said.

Walter reached into an inside pocket with an unsteady hand and brought out an envelope with familiar handwriting on the outside. He hefted the envelope in his hand, as though it was something precious that he didn't want to give up.

"James left a letter with me, to give to you as soon as you arrived. It was the very first thing he did, yesterday evening.

Before he even said hello. I told him he could give it to you himself, but there was something in his eyes . . . He didn't look scared; more, resigned. I should have pressed him for details . . . but there were so many things I wanted to say to him, so many things I needed to talk to him about. So we sat in my study, together, and we talked for hours and hours. Just the two of us. He couldn't tell me anything about his work, of course, and I wasn't really interested. This was all . . . father and son stuff. I wanted to be sure he was happy, content in his life. That he was living the kind of life he wanted. He said he was. I like to think we made our peace . . . I'm glad we had that chance, at least."

"He couldn't tell you about his work," I said. "Who he was, what he did. But if he could have, you would have been proud of him."

"Of course I was proud of him!" said Walter. "I was his father . . ." His voice cracked on that last word, and he thrust the sealed envelope at me.

I took it from him and studied the inscription on the outside. Just my name, in the Colonel's immaculate hand. I'd seen it before, on so many sealed orders. I looked up, to see Walter gazing at me expectantly.

I just looked back, until it became clear to him that I wasn't going to open the envelope until I was alone.

"Security," I said.

"Of course," said Walter. "I understand."

"I will tell you what it says, later," I said. "If there's anything in it you need to know. It's probably just my instructions. Explaining why he called me here, and what I'm supposed to be doing."

Walter nodded, reluctantly. He turned to the closed dining hall door, hesitated, looked back. "Will you be all right here, on your own?"

"I'm always on my own," I said. "And I'm always all right."
Walter nodded again, trying to look like he understood. He
pushed the door open, and once more there was a brief
uproar of raised voices from inside, before the door shut
them off again. I put my back against the door, so I could
keep an eye on the empty hallway, and then I opened the
envelope.

It wasn't a long letter. Just a hurried scrawl, rather than
the Colonel's usual perfect penmanship. Wouldn't surprise
me if he wrote it in his car, before he got out and entered
Belcourt Manor. One last piece of insurance.

As I read it, I could hear the Colonel's voice in my head.
Calm and assured, even in the face of danger. Because he was
the Colonel.

*Ishmael, watch your back. I have returned to my old home
to face a very real danger, because my family is at risk. I stayed
away all these years, distanced myself from my family, so that
my work wouldn't endanger them. But now, everything has
changed. A horror has come to Belcourt Manor. I don't know
if I can stop it, if I can protect my family. If it turns out I can't,
I must ask you to do it for me. I can't even tell you what I think
the danger is, because I have no proof, and I can't risk pointing
you in the wrong direction. It is possible that I am wrong. And
if I am, then we'll just have a jolly Christmas together. But
that's not the way I'd bet. Whatever happens, Ishmael, protect
my family.*

And that was it. Not even a signature. Just one last note,
from a man who believed he was going to his death and went
willingly. Because he had always been a man who believed
in duty. And in one last act of love for his family. I read
through the letter again, looking for some clue as to what
kind of danger I'd been brought here to fight. *A horror has
come to Belcourt Manor . . .*

That suggested a danger from my world, not from Walter and his business. From the hidden world, and the dark side of the road. I had to wonder: how bad was this danger that a man as experienced in dealing with bad things as the Colonel could fall to it so easily? A man who'd shut down many a monstrous trouble in his time? I'd worked with him in the field on several occasions, seen him in action. The Colonel always led the way, because he was the best of us.

I remembered the Murder Generals, the Dark Lady from Under the Hill, the Queen in Waiting and the Cathedral in Flames, and the High Orbit Ghosts. They all threatened the world, in their time, until the Colonel and I put them down.

But I'd seen nothing at Belcourt Manor to suggest the touch of Outside Forces. Could the Colonel's death really be nothing more than a disgruntled ex-employee? Sawing off the Colonel's head spoke to human cruelty, to making a vicious point . . . I couldn't rule that out. But I couldn't believe the Colonel would call me in for anything so straightforward. No, this had to be linked to the Colonel's past. All the enemies he made, all across the world, doing the Organization's business.

Except I would have sworn an oath they were all dead. The Colonel never did believe in leaving loose ends.

I slipped the letter carefully back in its envelope and tucked it securely away in an inside pocket. And then I pushed open the door and went in to dinner.

They were all sitting around one end of a really long table, in the grand old dining hall of Belcourt Manor. The room was huge, vast, overpowering. Big enough to play cricket in, with a high arched ceiling you couldn't have reached with a stepladder. A great fire burned fiercely, in a massive stone fireplace. Two hanging chandeliers shed fierce electric light from one end of the dining hall to the other. The shutters covering the two huge windows at the far end were so heavy, I couldn't hear even a murmur from the storm outside. The room was in a state of denial, like the people inside it.

Everyone at the table made a point of not looking up as I entered. They all seemed very preoccupied, though the plates set out in front of them were all conspicuously empty. I slammed the door, on general principles, and strolled forward.

Walter sat at the head of the table, with Melanie seated at his right hand and Diana at his left. The Lord of the Manor, with his Ladies. Sylvia sat next to Diana, and Khan sat next to Melanie. Roger next to Khan, and opposite him, Penny next to Sylvia. I pulled out a chair and sat down next to Penny. She shot me a quick, grateful smile, before going back to not listening to what Roger was saying to her.

I settled myself comfortably, removed the gleaming white napkin from its engraved silver ring, flipped the cloth out and dropped it into my lap. I don't need napkins; I never drop anything. But it's all part of fitting in.

The china set out before me was really quite impressive, and I'm not easily impressed. Old pieces, much used, probably going back generations. The layers of cutlery spreading out from my plate didn't intimidate me in the least. I have travelled through every country in the world, doing good, or something very like it, and learned all their customs. All you had to do here was start at the outside and work your way in, course by course. At least no one at Belcourt Manor was going to object if I ate with my left hand.

The long dining table had obviously been intended to seat a much larger gathering, from the days when the Belcourts were a much larger family. Or perhaps they were just bigger people in those days. Walter's Christmas gathering didn't even fill up half the table. The tablecloth was gleaming white samite, with burning candelabra set at regular intervals. The candle flames burned straight up, not bothered by even a breath of a draught. It was all very calm and dignified, and not a Christmas cracker was in sight. I've never cared for such things. I won't read out stupid jokes, I won't play with stupid toys, and I absolutely refuse to wear stupid paper hats. It's not about dignity, it's about self-respect.

Still no promise of any food, so I looked around the room.

The walls boasted yet more family portraits, more weapons on display, and the odd souvenir or relic from the Belcourt family's military past. Flags and banners, handwritten proclamations preserved under glass, silver snuffboxes and bejewelled bits and bobs. The loot of history. I made a mental note to steal something small and valuable before I left the house, just on general principles. And without quite seeming to, I looked at everyone seated round the table, and watched their faces as I listened in on their conversations.

Penny sat back in her chair and stared at nothing, toying vaguely with her napkin ring, making vague noises of interest in response to Roger's desperate attempts to make conversation.

"Everything's going to be all right, Penny," the young man said earnestly. "You're not to worry. I'll look after you. I know it must have been a hell of a shock . . . finding James like that." He paused, to look dubiously at me. I made sure I just happened to be looking somewhere else.

Roger sniffed loudly, possibly without even realizing he was doing it, and turned back to Penny. "I would never let anything happen to you, Penny. You do know that, don't you?"

Penny smiled at Roger, giving him her full attention for the first time. "Yes, I know that, Roger. I never doubted it. Every now and again I remember what it was I saw in you. A crisis always brings out the best in you. Such a shame it takes so much to make you interesting. Tell me something, Roger..."

"Of course, darling. Ask me anything."

"What's going on, between you and Alexander? Come on, he's been hanging around you all weekend, badgering you like a love-struck stalker. What does he want from you?"

Surprisingly, Roger grinned easily. "What does he always want? Money, of course. He thinks he can get it out of me. He thinks he can pressure me. He thinks he can get me something I want."

"What?" said Penny.

"You, of course! But alas, I know better. So, dear old Alex ... can sit on it and rotate."

I left the two young people to smile at each other and switched my attention to Alexander Khan, talking earnestly with Melanie. They were smiling into each other's eyes and ignoring everyone else.

"I'm sure you're right, my dear," said Khan. "Whatever danger there might have been is quite definitely past. The killer is gone, and we are all perfectly safe. It's always possible James brought the danger with him, as a result of whatever he was up to. But now the murderer's got what he wanted, he's undoubtedly long gone."

"Did you know James at all?" said Melanie. "Only sometimes, the way you say his name, I get the distinct impression—"

"I knew of him," Khan said quickly. "He had a reputation... in a field I was once involved in. But I never met the man."

"Or Ishmael?" said Melanie.

"No, that was his father. Daniel. Just one of those strange coincidences, I suppose, that the son of my old colleague should work for Walter's son. But then, life is full of strange connections. Like us."

"Hush," said Melanie, still smiling. "Not in front of Walter."

"He's not listening."

"You can never tell with Walter."

"But we will meet, later?"

"Oh, of course. Later," said Melanie. And they went back to smiling into each other's eyes.

I let my concentration move on, to Diana and Sylvia. Not surprisingly, Sylvia was doing most of the talking. Chattering cheerfully about previous Christmas parties she'd attended, at other great houses. Shamelessly name-dropping minor celebrities, past lovers and important business connections. Diana just nodded, here and there and not always in time, lost in her own memories.

Sylvia finally gave up. "Honestly, darling! Here I am, treating you to my very best gossip, and you're miles away! Whatever is the matter, dear?"

"My son is dead," said Diana. "My only child. I never wanted another, until it was far too late." She smiled sadly at Sylvia. "And so I make do, with my dear young companions. My substitute children. Don't get too attached to me, dear. I'm a terrible mother."

And all this time Walter sat alone at the head of his table, lord of all he surveyed, saying nothing, looking at no one. Except, perhaps, at his great family hall. Such a large room, with so few present to enjoy it. Walter was the end of his family history, and he knew it. He had grown old, in an old house. And soon, he wouldn't even have that. Because he had done well, but not well enough. It's a hard thing, to know that soon you will have no choice but to sell your family inheritance for a few last years of comfort.

And then all the conversation broke off abruptly, and everyone looked around as the door slammed open and in came Cook, pushing a large and heavily laden trolley ahead of her. There was a sudden marvellous smell of hot food, and everyone perked up. Jeeves followed Cook in.

"Ah, Mrs. Bridges!" said Walter loudly. "Dinner, at last!"

"You're lucky to have it!" snapped Cook. A small fierce blonde woman in her late twenties, in a stylized Victorian cook's outfit, she scowled around the dining table, sparing no one. Her hair was short and spiky, her face red with sweat and exertion, and her gaze was full of an uncomplicated fury. She slammed to a halt, leaning on her trolley while she got her breath back, and looked very much like she would enjoy spitting in the food. Right in front of us.

"Here's your dinner!" she said loudly. "On time! And it's *Ms.* Bridges, thank you very much. Leilah Bridges, and don't you forget it! I have produced this entire dinner on my own, without any staff or support, under conditions I wouldn't wish on a deceased dog! That nasty old shit-hole downstairs is the most old-fashioned and inefficient kitchen I have ever had the misfortune to work in. And I've been around!"

"It's true," murmured Jeeves. "She has."

"So here's your dinner!" said Cook. "Eat it while it's hot! I'll serve the soup, and then I'm out of here. You can help yourselves to the other courses from the trolley, because I'm not coming back. And yes, there is afters. Plum duff, on the bottom shelf. Hope you like your custard thick and lumpy, because that's how I like it, so that's how I make it. All right?"

No one dared answer. Cook prowled round the table, shoving the trolley in front of her with sudden bursts of ill-tempered strength, ladling generous amounts of soup into bowls and then slamming them down in front of people, most of whom were wise enough to just sit well back in their chairs and let her get on with it. Khan made the mistake of asking what kind of soup it was, and she slammed the bowl down in front of him so hard, the contents actually jumped up into the air for a moment.

Cook fixed Khan with an openly mutinous glare. "Can't you smell it? That is Mulligatawny! Beef curry soup! Get it down you; it's good for what ails you. Don't poke at it like that! It's supposed to have bits in it!"

She finished her rounds, abandoned the trolley and headed straight for the open door. She paused there, to glare back at us one last time. "I could have been at home with my family, safe and sound and stuffed full of good food, but no! I am trapped here in this decrepit old dump, with a murderer lurking in the shadows, and all hell breaking loose outside. I'm only here because I was tempted by the money. I should be getting a bonus! I should be getting danger money! Right, I am out of here. I am going straight back to my kitchen, where I want everyone to know I have a really big cleaver and a complete willingness to use it!"

"It's true," said Jeeves. "She has."

"Hold everything," I said.

All eyes turned to me. To my surprise, Cook calmed down immediately and studied me with cool, thoughtful eyes.

I nodded at the soup in front of me. "It looks fine," I said. "And it smells delicious. But given that one of us has already been murdered, almost certainly after being drugged . . . I can't help wondering how much we can trust whatever is put in front of us."

Everyone looked at their soup.

I smiled at Cook. "No offence to you, Ms. Bridges, but anyone could have sneaked down to your kitchen and . . . interfered with the food. So I have to wonder, do we need a food taster?"

Jeeves moved in beside me, took up my soup spoon, stirred the soup thoroughly, and then raised a spoonful to his mouth. He knocked it back, without a single emotion crossing his face, licked his lips, and then dropped my spoon back into the bowl.

"Delicious," he said.

I picked up the spoon, polished it carefully with my napkin, and then smiled around the table. "Well," I said. "Good enough for me! Bon appétit, everyone."

Cook said, "*Hah!*" in a loud and carrying voice, and stomped away. Jeeves went after her, shutting the door quietly but firmly behind them.

"So," said Penny. "That's Cook . . . Where on earth did you find her, Daddy?"

"Same place that gave us Jeeves," said Walter. "Apparently they come as a package . . . Does anyone want me to say grace?"

He looked hopefully down the table, but he'd left it too late. We'd all had a long hard day, and we were all of us extremely hungry. In fact, most of us had started the soup before he'd finished his first sentence. Nothing stimulates the appetite like an unexpected proximity to death. So we all tucked in. The food was excellent, and everyone gave it their full attention. But even the best food couldn't stop these people from talking for long, not when they all had so much they wanted to say. After a little surreptitious prompting from Khan, Melanie started the ball rolling.

"Walter!"

"Yes, dear?" he said immediately. "Have I forgotten something?"

"I demand to know why you felt the need to bring an armed bodyguard into our house, masquerading as a butler!"

Walter looked at Khan, who just shrugged. Walter patted Melanie's hand comfortingly. "Just being cautious, my dear. Alex drew my attention to some rather worrying hate mail, aimed at me and the company, so I decided we would all be a lot safer with a professional security expert on hand. I think you'll all agree, Jeeves has proved a first-class butler . . ."

"The Colonel is still dead," I said, and Walter had no reply to that. I looked at Khan. "So, Alex. As head of the company these days, you must have known about Jeeves all along?"

"No," said Khan. "I didn't. Walter didn't see fit to inform me."

He glared at Walter, who met his gaze unflinchingly. "I don't have to tell you everything, Alex. I am still capable of making my own decisions."

"Is that why my James is dead?" Diana said loudly. "Was he killed because of these threats to you and your damned company? Are you responsible for our son's death?"

Walter looked at her, helplessly, and then looked at me. I nodded, took the envelope out of my pocket, removed the letter, and read out the contents to the whole company. And then I passed the letter down the table, so everyone could look at it for themselves. To see I wasn't exaggerating. So I could look at them, looking at the Colonel's last words. Because I felt the need to stir things up a little. They were all clearly intrigued by the letter's contents, but they also seemed equally surprised and equally baffled. The letter went up the table and down the other side, and ended up with Roger, who didn't want to give it up until he'd had his say. Penny cut him off with a hard look and kept on glaring at him until he reluctantly handed the letter back to me. I put it away again.

"I think the time for secrets is past," said Khan, not looking at anyone in particular. "We need to know, we have a right to know, just what the hell is going on here. And exactly what it is you and the Colonel do, Mister Jones, that has brought this . . . horror, here."

"Damn right!" said Roger.

"I'm sorry," I said, trying to sound like I was. "I could tell you, but then I'd have to nuke the house from orbit, just to be sure. You could say, I was the Colonel's Jeeves. I solved problems for him. Protecting those who needed protecting from bad things, and putting the hard word on people who deserved it. Except, unlike Jeeves, I don't carry a gun. Never have. Don't believe in them. Now, I hate to rain on everyone's parade, but I can't let you hide behind a false sense of security any longer."

I explained to them why the Colonel simply couldn't have been killed where Penny and I found him. That the lack of blood made it clear it was a body dump. And that the murderer was almost certainly sitting right there at the table, hiding in plain sight, hoping to go unnoticed till the storm passed and they could make their escape.

"Only, that isn't going to happen," I said. "Because I will find the killer first."

"And put the hard word on him?" said Penny.

"He killed my Colonel," I said. And something in my voice made everyone at the table shiver, just for a moment.

"Why didn't you tell us all this before?" said Khan.

"Because you weren't ready to hear it," I said.

People were looking back and forth around the table, staring into familiar faces, looking for something out of place. They all seemed to accept my logic, even if none of them were happy about it. Here and there, hands moved a little closer to the knives by their plates, as though feeling the need for something like a weapon. Everyone was eyeing up everyone else and wondering if they could take them. Or outrun them.

"So," I said, and everyone's eyes snapped back to me. I did my best to smile reassuringly. "It's time to establish who has an alibi. See if we can rule anyone out. Where were you all, when the Colonel was murdered?"

"But . . . we don't know when James was killed, do we?" said Melanie.

I looked at Walter. "You said the Colonel arrived here very late, last night. Can you remember what time it was when he finally retired to his room?"

"Half-past two in the a.m.," said Walter, very firmly. "I remember, because James pointed out how long we'd been talking, and we both laughed. We would have gone on, but we were both tired out. If I'd known it was the last time I would ever talk with him . . . Anyway, I escorted him upstairs. I'd put him back in his old room, the Tiger Lily."

"We only have your word for it that that's the right time," said Roger, bullishly.

"Really, Roger!" said Penny. "You can't call Daddy a liar to his face! I won't have it!"

"Assume, for the moment, that Walter's memory is correct," I said. "That means the Colonel had to be murdered some time after two thirty a.m., and before four thirty p.m., when Penny and I found the body. Which is a hell of a gap, complicated by the frozen state of the body. He had to have been there for some time before we found him, to have frozen so solidly. Everyone, think hard. Do any of you remember anyone here going missing, during that period? As in, unaccounted for? Not being where you would expect them to be?"

I looked up and down the table, where everyone was busy looking at everyone else. They would all have liked to accuse someone, either to pay off some old score, or just to make themselves feel better . . . but none of them felt justified in pointing the finger, just yet.

"I was with Walter," Melanie said finally.

"And I was with Sylvia," said Diana.

"I've spent most of the day talking business with Walter, or Roger," said Khan.

"And Roger's been hanging around me pretty much nonstop," said Penny.

She didn't sound particularly happy about that. Roger started to bristle, remembered where he was, and subsided again.

"We have to be realistic," Walter said heavily. "Any one of us could have slipped away, for perfectly justifiable reasons... Disappeared for a while, without anyone noticing or thinking twice about it. How could we know what was going to be significant and what wasn't? It's a big house, and we've all been coming and going. None of us has an alibi that's worth a damn."

"We've locked the killer inside the house with us," said Khan. And no one had anything else to say, after that.

I wished the Colonel was there. He was always so much better at this sort of thing than I ever was.

For want of anything better to do, we all started eating again. Course after course. Partly to keep us occupied, mainly because no one wanted to go anywhere. There might be a killer in the room, but there was still safety in numbers. We ate everything on the trolley, including the plum duff and custard, which was actually quite tasty, and drank a lot of tea and coffee. We talked of various things, in brittle artificial tones, looking for hidden meanings in everyone's words. Circling around the subject no one wanted to discuss, but which we couldn't stop thinking about. I was still thinking hard and getting nowhere, when Melanie suddenly stood up.

"Walter needs his rest," she said firmly. "Look at him, nodding off in his chair. He needs to lie down properly, or he won't be able to get up at all tomorrow."

"I'm too tired to argue with you," said Walter. He allowed Melanie to help him to his feet, leaning heavily on her for support. And then he stopped and looked at me. "You did say ... you thought we should all stick together."

"Yes," I said. "The company may be uncomfortable, but it's still the safest way to go. If you really do need to lie down, we could always bring in a couch ..."

"Nonsense!" said Melanie. "Walter and I have our bedroom here on the ground floor, these days. Just down the hall. You'll have no trouble hearing me yell if we need you."

"When did you move downstairs, Daddy?" said Penny, frowning. "You've had the same room on the first floor since you were a boy."

"The view's better down here," growled Walter, avoiding her gaze.

"He can't handle the stairs any more," said Melanie. "Another good reason why you need to lie down and get your rest, dear."

"She's right," said Walter. He smiled at her. "You always know what's best for me. That is why I keep you around, isn't it, dear?"

"Of course, Walter. Because I'm always right. Now come along."

They headed for the dining hall door, Walter leaning heavily on his walking stick and on Melanie. He was too tired now even to try and hide how tired he was. Everyone else started getting to their feet.

I stood up, to face them. "This really isn't a good idea," I said.

"No one else has been killed since James," said Sylvia, just a bit testily. "I don't see any reason why we should see ourselves as targets. Murderers don't kill for no reason. You need your rest too, Diana. You get some sleep, and I'll stand guard over you. Well actually, I'll sit guard over you. I've got some magazines."

"She's right," Diana said to me. "We've all had a long hard day, and we can't hope to defend ourselves or protect each other if we're too tired to keep our eyes open. We're only on the first floor, after all. And I can probably scream louder than Melanie, if I have to."

"Dear Diana," murmured Melanie, still guiding Walter to the door. "Always so competitive..."

"I think I'll feel safer in my own room, with the door locked and a chair jammed up against it," said Khan. "I suggest we all get what sleep we can, recharge our batteries, and then reconvene tomorrow morning in the drawing room."

"Someone should send word down to Jeeves, in the kitchen," said Penny. "He can stand guard in the hallway, with his gun."

"You trust the one man we know for sure isn't who he said he was?" I said. "The one man in the house with a weapon?"

"The Colonel wasn't shot," said Penny. "And right now, I don't trust anyone."

She just happened to be looking at me when she said that.

"I'll walk you to your room, darling," said Roger.

"I can look after myself!" she said, a little more sharply than was necessary.

And just like that, they were all heading for the door. There was nothing I could say or do to stop them separating, so I just shrugged mentally and went after them. Maybe if they did split up, someone would seize the opportunity to do something stupid, or revealing. Or incriminating.

At the last moment, Penny hung back at the doorway and gestured for me to come forward so we could speak quietly.

"You can't bully them into doing the sensible thing,

Ishmael. They all need time to themselves, to talk and think in private. A chance to play the blame game and decide who they trust. It's scary to be on your own, but it's even scarier to be stuck in a room with a hidden killer. What do you think is really going on here, Ishmael? Was James the real target, or was he just a way to get at Daddy?"

"The killer must have seen the Colonel as a threat, to kill him first," I said. "Beyond that, I have no idea. It could be anyone."

"Including me?" said Penny.

"Of course not," I lied.

❖ SEVEN ❖
PEOPLE COME AND GO

I TOOK MY TIME CLIMBING the long winding staircase to the next floor. Partly because I had a lot of thinking to do, but mostly because I wanted to give the others time to get ahead of me. I didn't want anyone at my back. In fact, by the time I got to the top of the stairs, I was alone on the landing. Everyone else had hurried inside their rooms, and all the doors were firmly closed. It was very quiet.

I strolled down the corridor, all the way to my far-off room, and stopped before the door. I looked at the stylized image of the red rose, and then leaned forward and listened carefully. I couldn't hear anything inside the room. Couldn't smell anything, either. But I still had a feeling of being watched, so I took my time getting my key out of my pocket, and then looked quickly back down the corridor. No less than four doors that had been closed were now cracked open just a little, so people could peer out. The doors all slammed shut in a hurry as they saw me looking, like so many firecrackers going off. I smiled, unlocked my door, and then sent the door flying inwards with a push of one finger. It swung all the way back to crash against the inside wall, with a satisfyingly loud noise. The room inside was very dark, very still, very quiet.

I reached inside and found the light switch. A pleasant yellow glow filled the room, showing it to be completely empty. I remained where I was, in the doorway, looking in. I didn't feel at all embarrassed, or even self-conscious, at taking these necessary precautions. Being so very careful, all the time, is what has kept me alive all these years. I listened, carefully. I could hear people moving about in their rooms, further down the corridor. I could even hear them talking, quietly and far away. Muffled, as though underwater. It all seemed peaceful enough, nothing worrying or out of the ordinary, so I entered my room.

I shut the door firmly, but didn't lock it. I had a distinct feeling people would be coming to talk with me. To say things they wouldn't or couldn't say to someone they actually knew. To tell me things in private that they would never dare say in public. People have always found it easy to talk to me, perhaps because they can sense I won't be so quick to judge them.

I looked around my room. The yellow light was warm and comforting and easy on the eyes. The rose-patterned wallpaper somewhat less so. The fire was still crackling cheerfully in the fireplace. I went over to it and studied the flames thoughtfully. Jeeves had been very firm that I needed to tend the thing, to keep it from going out. I knew you had to feed it coal, regularly, but not too much or you'd smother the fire and it would go out. But beyond that . . . I took a piece of coal from the scuttle, dropped it on to the fire, considered the effect, and then added another piece. That should do, for a while.

I did some more looking around. Everything was just as

I'd left it. No one had entered my room. If they had, I would have seen their footprints in the thick carpet. Smelt their perfume, or their aftershave, or just their scent. My battered old suitcase was still sitting on the bed. I picked it up, carried it over to the massive oak cupboard, opened the door sharply, and when I was sure there was no one hiding inside it, I put the case in and shut the door again. And then, I sat on the edge of the bed, to do some thinking. I didn't change into pyjamas, because I don't wear such things, and I didn't lie down on the bed because I had no intention of sleeping. I didn't sit in one of the oversized chairs provided, because that was where people would expect to find me.

I'm not really a detective. Usually, by the time I arrive on the scene all that stuff has already been taken care of. The Colonel's people will have worked out what and where and when, and will usually have a pretty good idea as to who and why. The Colonel gives me a name, or an identity, and then it's up to me to track them down and take all necessary measures. On those occasions when I am called in to solve a mystery, it's because the local field agents have run dry and the Colonel is depending on me to pick up the slack because I have a knack for the unusual. And even then, the Colonel will have amassed a really thick file for me to read on the way in, to bring me up to speed.

Belcourt Manor gave every indication of being both a murder and a mystery, which might or might not be connected. *A horror has come to Belcourt Manor . . .* It wasn't like the Colonel to be so dramatic. Why couldn't he just say what he meant? Did he expect his letter to fall into enemy hands? Did he expect his father to open it, and hadn't wanted him upset? What could be so horrific that the Colonel didn't even want to hint at it?

Questions without answers. Best to stick to the situation

at hand. Work it through. Who killed the Colonel, and why? And why kill him in such an extreme manner? So far, it seemed I was faced with two main possibilities. One, the Colonel was killed by the horror. Whoever or whatever that might turn out to be. Or two, he was killed by whoever sent the death threats to Walter. I sat up a little straighter as a third possibility suggested itself. That this was the result of something out of the past. The Colonel's past. The trailing end of some old investigation, something missed or overlooked at the time.

The one thing the Colonel had feared the most: that his family might be punished for the life he'd led.

The Colonel and I had worked a number of cases together. Usually, I was left to run my assignments alone. I preferred it that way. If only because it meant there would be fewer questions to answer afterwards. But sometimes the Colonel would just turn up. Not to take charge, and not because he didn't trust me to do things properly, but because he was interested. Like the Case of the Trans-Siberian Underground Railway. I had no trouble remembering that one.

It started with people going missing, and then turning up again hundreds of miles away from where they should have been. I followed the clues, and the Colonel followed me, and we ended up going underground, into the deep dark places of the Earth. I could still remember running through endless caverns, miles and miles beneath the surface of a country that doesn't even exist any more. Following the long silver railway lines as they stretched away into the darkness, only illuminated by the phosphorescent glow of a blue moss growing in thick mats on the curving walls. Some said, if you ate or smoked the blue moss it would blow the doors of perception in your mind clean off their hinges. I wasn't tempted.

I just kept running, following the tracks and the trail of blood left by the horrible laughing thing ahead of me. The Colonel stuck close at my side, just about managing to keep up. I could hear his lungs labouring as he struggled. I couldn't afford to slow down, for fear the Damned Thing would get away. And then, there was what was coming after us . . . Every now and again, the Colonel would turn and fire his machine pistol back down the tracks to slow our pursuers down. I never did learn the name of the local agent they'd already killed, drowning out his screams with their awful piping laughter.

The Colonel emptied his machine pistol and hurried after me, fumbling in his pockets for another magazine. And then he made a tutting sound, and shrugged easily, as he realized he'd run out of ammunition. He didn't say anything, just ran along beside me, trusting me to catch the villain and find us a way out.

And then, there was the Appalling Affair of Roger Styles.

Just a small fishing village, tucked away in some forgotten part of the Cornish coastline, where the locals still took their boats out every day, whatever the weather. The Colonel told me to book into the village's one and only hotel, and inquire about the fishing. I did sort of hope it might be my long-delayed vacation time. I should have known better.

The moment I started my innocent inquiries, the hotel owner couldn't wait to bend my ear over all the troubles the village had been having. Fishing boats going out, and never coming back. Nothing left for Search and Rescue to find, not even bits of wreckage or a body floating in the water. Fishermen told of seeing things, shining white, down in the very depths of the sea. Things big as churches or cathedrals, or bigger still. Some of the fishermen were afraid to go out, and it takes a lot to scare a Cornish fisherman. And then there was Roger Styles. The man who was not a man, and never wanted to be.

The Colonel set himself up as bait. Sitting there on the old wooden bench, on top of the cliff, looking out to sea for hours on end, with only an improving book for company. Sitting there till the sun went down, waiting for Styles to come and get him. To shut him up, because of all the things the Colonel had been saying so loudly in the local tavern. I was there too, hidden and waiting. The Colonel sat at his ease, the bait in his own trap, trusting me to do whatever might be necessary. To take Styles down and save the Colonel's life.

And, of course, there was the last case we worked together, in deepest, darkest Peru. In that horrible hidden city on the Plateau of Leng. A cruel place and a cruel people—if you could even call them people. The roots of their family tree didn't lie in the earth, but in the stars. The buildings in that city were older than human civilization, huge and blocky, actually unnerving to look at for too long. Their aesthetics hadn't been meant for human eyes. Everything seemed to lean at some unnatural angle, and their proportions didn't add up to any whole my mind could accept.

There were windows that showed shifting views of other places, some of them beyond human comprehension. The Colonel vomited every time he looked into a window, so he stopped looking. I couldn't bring myself to stop, because every now and again I thought I glimpsed something... familiar.

I remembered the Colonel kneeling in an open square, concentrating on the terrible thing he'd brought with him. I stood guard, while he programmed the nuclear device and set the timer. We weren't taking any chances with the awful people of Leng.

I remembered them all. Old cases, old faces; moments from a past filled with thrilling incidents. I could have sworn we hadn't left a single loose thread anywhere.

I felt suddenly tired and old. With the Colonel gone, there was a tremendous gap in my life. Every time I remembered I'd never speak to him again, it was like someone kicked me in the gut. I hadn't realized how attached I'd become to the man, down the years. All the things we'd seen, and all the things we'd experienced, that we could never talk about to anyone else. I never told him my secret, but sometimes I thought he knew. He never brought it up, and I never volunteered. Probably each of us thought we were protecting the other. The Colonel had given my human life a sense of purpose, of direction. He made me believe that the work I was doing mattered. That I mattered.

What was I going to do now?

I made myself concentrate on the situation. If the killer really was one of the people here at Belcourt Manor, what motive could they have for killing the Colonel? Some things had become clear, even in the short time I'd been here. Khan and Melanie were either having an affair, or about to start one. Suppose Khan wanted Walter dead, so he could marry Melanie and take control of the company that apparently meant so much to him . . . Yes. I could see Khan doing that. He'd worked for Black Heir. You learned to do the cold, hard, necessary thing if you wanted to get on at Black Heir. It wasn't a place for a man with a conscience.

And then there was Melanie herself. Did she want Walter dead, for her own reasons? Could she be playing Lady Macbeth to Khan, urging him on to remove the only obstacle in their way? If the Colonel had overheard something, noticed something he wasn't meant to, tried to protect his father . . . Yes. I could see that happening.

Next, Diana. Who had already told me how much she missed living at the Manor and all that went with it. What would she do to get her old life back? Did she perhaps plot to kill Melanie, so she could remarry Walter? The girl I remembered from Paris would never have been capable of doing anything so cold-hearted, let alone kill her own son, but Paris was a long time ago. People change.

Roger wanted Penny—that was obvious to anyone with an eye or an ear. What would he be prepared to do to get her? And then, there was Sylvia. Could she have acquired a taste for the good life, travelling with Diana? Could she be running some scheme to grab some of that good life for herself?

Bringing up the rear, as the least likely suspect and therefore not to be ruled out: Walter himself. Besieged on so many sides. If he decided someone else's death would make his little world safer and more secure . . . he was quite capable of ordering any number of things done. Especially if he thought Khan was after his wife . . . Or could it be that Walter had never really wanted his son to come home? Had there been some terrible, unspoken insult, never forgiven by either side? Could Walter have killed his own son for daring to come home again?

Was that why Jeeves was here? An ex-soldier, maybe even an assassin, posing as a butler, hiding in plain sight? No one else knew him from before . . . Could Walter have sent the death threats himself, to justify Jeeves' presence?

Everyone at Belcourt Manor had motives for murder, but none for killing the Colonel. Unless he just . . . got in the way. No one had expected him to turn up here when they were making their plans. Perhaps someone just saw him as an obstacle to be removed. But the manner of the Colonel's death still disturbed me. Why saw the man's head off? There seemed every indication it had been done after he was murdered. There had to be a reason. Sawing a man's head off is hard work. Takes a fair amount of time, too. The Colonel must have been drugged first, to keep him from fighting back. There was no other way an experienced man like the Colonel could have been taken down... There was no shortage of opportunities for someone to drop a little something into all the food and drink available. The Colonel couldn't have refused any of the seasonable fare, for fear of raising suspicions.

There was a knock at the door. Solid, authoritative, even peremptory. So I just sat there on the end of my bed, letting them wait, until I finally said, "Come in." The door swung open immediately, and Alexander Khan strode in, acting like he owned the place and was already thinking of evicting me. I'd thought he'd be my first visitor, given that he was the most likely person to be on his own, because there was no way Melanie was going to leave Walter on his own. Khan closed the door carefully behind him, and then looked quickly round my room, as though he wanted to make sure I hadn't been given a better room than him. He took his time before he looked at me, and when he did, it was almost defiantly.

"We need to talk," he said.

"What's the matter?" I said. "Annoyed you can't be with Melanie?"

"That is not what I came here to talk about!" said Khan.

"You knew who the Colonel was, knew what he was, from your time at Black Heir," I said.

"I'd heard of the Colonel, of course, but I never knew he was Walter's son until he turned up here," said Khan. "I never met him before in my life. But he knew me. He made a point of talking to me, away from everyone else. Told me he knew why I'd had to leave Black Heir."

"Because you stole alien technology from their vaults," I said. "To buy your way into Walter's company."

"I was never a thief!" said Khan. "I was Prometheus, stealing fire from alien gods to give to Humanity! It wasn't fair for Black Heir to keep all those wonders locked up, benefiting nobody!" He stopped and looked at me for a moment. "How did you know... Did your father tell you?"

"No," I said. "I never knew him. But I did read the Colonel's files on everyone here, before I set out."

I've always been able to lie convincingly, without benefit of rehearsal. Part of the job. Part of staying alive.

"Of course you know," said Khan, his shoulders slumping just a little. "Everyone knows. Even Black Heir."

"They know you stole from them?"

"Of course! They knew what I was going to do before I did it. They encouraged me... In return, I gave them some of my shares in Walter's company. Outside money that they could use to fund things they weren't officially supposed to do. You really think I could have stayed alive all these years, if Black Heir had still wanted my head?" He stopped again, looked at me squarely. "Did you ever work with Black Heir, on any of your missions for the Colonel?"

"You know I can't talk about that," I said. "Why are you still so concerned about Black Heir? You don't work for them any more."

"You're never really free of them," said Khan. "Look! This isn't what I came here to talk about!"

"So talk," I said. "Who do you think killed the Colonel?"

"James was never the target," said Khan. "Walter was always the real target. I think James just overheard something he wasn't supposed to, or got in the way."

"Spit it out," I said. "Who do you think wanted Walter dead?"

"Isn't it obvious?" said Khan. "It's Roger! Has to be Roger. Because he wants Penny, and he thinks she is only turning him down because her Daddy disapproves. Behind that boyish facade, Roger is a very dangerous and single-minded young man."

I let that accusation hang on the air for a while and considered Khan thoughtfully. "Are you sure you're not just saying that because Roger isn't going to give you the money you want from him?" I said finally.

"You have been keeping your eyes and ears open," said Khan. "Watch Roger. That's all I've got to say."

"And you and Melanie?" I said. "Just good friends?"

"Can't stand the woman," Khan said briskly. "But she is my best way to influence Walter, so . . . I will do whatever I have to do, to keep the company from going under."

He turned quickly, hauled the door open and left my room, not quite slamming the door behind him. He'd said rather more than he'd probably meant to, in return for as little as I could give him. A useful enough first conversation. No real surprises, and a few things confirmed.

I sat on the edge of my bed, leaning forward just a bit as I listened to Khan walk quickly back down the corridor to his room. He didn't stop along the way to talk to anyone else. I heard his door shut. There was a pause, and then I heard more footsteps, moving slowly and steadily up and down the corridor. Which was odd, because I hadn't heard a door open. The footsteps went this way and that, stopping at one door after another, but no one knocked, or opened a door. And then the footsteps just . . . stopped. I couldn't hear anything. I got up off the bed and moved quietly over to my door. I opened it slowly, not making a breath of sound, and looked out into the corridor. There was no one there. The whole length of the corridor was completely empty. Someone had walked up and down and then just ... disappeared. I sniffed at the air and couldn't smell anything. Which was odd. I closed my door and went back to sit on my bed.

I'd barely had time to settle down and start thinking again, when I heard new footsteps approach my door. There was a quick, impatient knock, and then the door flew open before I even had a chance to invite anyone in. Penny came tripping into my room, beaming happily, only just remembering to shut the door behind her. I started to get up, and she immediately waved for me to sit down again. So I did.

Penny paced restlessly back and forth before me, speaking so impatiently that the words all but tumbled over each other. She had a lot she wanted to say. "I waited as long as I could!" she said. "But I just had to come and talk to you! Isn't this exciting? I mean, an actual murder! And terribly sad, of course, because your friend is dead, after all. Don't think I don't feel that, because I do, but ... This is just the most exciting thing that's ever happened to me! So, I'm just bursting with theories and suspicions, and I had to talk to someone about them, and you're the only one here who isn't a suspect."

"You couldn't talk to Roger?" I said, just to make a point.

"Don't be silly, darling. Roger has many good qualities, though I'd never tell him that to his face, but a fully functioning brain isn't one of them. If he ever needs anything difficult or distasteful doing, he has people to do that for him. And as for spotting a murderer, unless the killer was wearing a black and white striped jersey, a black domino mask, and a hat with *Killer!* written on it, Roger wouldn't recognize him."

"So who do you think killed the Colonel?" I said.

Penny stopped pacing and threw herself into the nearest heavily padded chair. It didn't budge an inch under the impact. Penny crossed her legs and waggled the top one fiercely. "There are so many secrets in this house, in this family; I really don't know where to start, darling."

"Try," I said.

"James was definitely Diana's son," said Penny. "But I'm not at all sure Daddy was his father. I've heard a great many rumours, from people in a position to know, that Daddy married Diana when she was already pregnant with another man's child."

"I didn't know that," I said. "Though the Colonel could be a real bastard, when the need arose..."

"Ishmael!" said Penny, putting a shocked hand to her mouth. "What a thing to say! Here I am trying to spare your feelings by being discreet..."

"Sorry," I said. "We all grieve in our own ways."

"Yes, well..." said Penny. But she was too full of things she needed to say to stay shocked for long. "Then there's the letter James left for you. I mean: A horror has come to Belcourt! What do you think he meant by that?"

"Too many possibilities," I said.

"Then there's Alex Khan, of course. Running after Mummy like a dog in heat." Penny shuddered delicately. "They think they're being so discreet... But if Alex really thinks he can get to Daddy through Mummy, he's in for a rude awakening. Mummy's always been a lot smarter than most people realize. She'd never do anything to endanger her meal ticket. You don't think Daddy just 'happened' to bump into her at that grubby little sales conference, did you? She put a lot of hard planning into getting that job and choosing just the right outfit to attract some rich old fool. When she set her cap at Daddy, he didn't stand a chance."

"And you know all this because...?" I said.

Penny grinned. "People really shouldn't keep diaries. And

certainly not ones with such fragile locks. I know all I need to know about Mummy dearest."

She paused for the first time, to look around my room. "I don't think I've been in here for years. There aren't usually enough people at these little gatherings to fill all the guest rooms. You must never forget, Ishmael, Mummy wants all of this, more than anything. The house, and everything that goes with it. I think it's possible she would kill to keep it. If she thought Daddy was going to sell it, after all . . . If she thought Alex was trying to take control of everything away from Daddy . . . and if poor James got caught in the middle . . . I think it's entirely possible Mummy could commit murder. To protect her interests."

"You're being very hard on your parents," I said.

"They should have been better parents," said Penny. "You might have noticed, my family isn't a real family. As such."

"I wouldn't know," I said.

Penny sat forward in her chair, immediately contrite. "Oh, of course! You said you were an orphan."

"Something like that," I said.

Penny frowned. "Sometimes I think . . . Daddy never let himself get close to me, for fear I'd go away and leave him, like James. You've no idea how much that hurt Daddy. He couldn't bear to go through it again."

"The Colonel had his reasons for staying away," I said. "You saw what he said in his letter."

Penny waited, until it became clear I wasn't going to say any more, and then she just sniffed, loudly. "You're much better off without a family, darling. They do so complicate things. Mummy, for example, was never really interested in children. She only had me to make sure of hanging on to Daddy. I don't think I want to talk about my parents any more."

"All right," I said. "What do you want to talk about?"

"Well, there's Alex, obviously. The man who sold his soul, for a company that was never his and almost certainly never will be. Who knows to what lengths desperation could drive such a man? But, my best bet would have to be Sylvia."

"Really?" I said. "Why?"

"Oh, come on, darling, do try and keep up. She's the only one here we don't know anything about! She's from outside the family and nothing to do with Daddy's business. Who is Sylvia, really? Just another sweet-smiling gold-digger, with Diana as her latest meal ticket? Or . . . did she deliberately ingratiate herself with Diana, in order to get herself invited here? Could she, in fact, be responsible for the death threats? Perhaps she was married to someone Daddy fired, who then committed suicide, so Sylvia swore to make Daddy pay, and—"

"You're reaching, now," I said.

"I know!" said Penny. "Isn't it fun?"

We both looked round sharply, at a sudden knock on my door.

Penny was up and out of her chair in a moment. "I don't want anyone to know I was here!" she hissed.

"Hide in the cupboard," I said.

"What?" Penny looked at the massive oak cupboard on the other side of the room. "In there? Are you serious?"

"It always works in bedroom farces," I said reasonably. "Would you expect someone to be hiding in someone else's cupboard?"

"Well, no, but . . ."

"I was always a big fan of the Brian Rix farces," I said. "He understood the importance of a cupboard. Go on, get in there!"

Penny hurried over to the cupboard and opened one of

the doors. There was more than enough space for Penny to hide in. She stepped carefully inside, shot me a quick glare, and then pulled the door almost but not completely shut.

"Come in!" I said brightly.

The door opened, and Roger slouched in. He pushed the door shut behind him, peered around, and then glowered at me.

"You took your time, leaving me standing around out there. Don't want the others to get the idea I'm sneaking around behind their backs."

"Even though you are," I said.

He scowled miserably, looked down at his shoes, and then straightened up to face me squarely. "Have you heard someone moving about, in the corridor? Just . . . walking up and down?"

"Yes," I said. "But when I looked, there was nobody there."

"I knew I heard someone!" said Roger. "Far too much sneaking around going on in this house. Look, I need to talk to you. Man to man. Can't talk to the others. This family of Penny's has secrets like a dog has fleas. Can't start a conversation without tripping over something you're not supposed to talk about. They think they're so good at hiding things . . . They should have grown up with my family."

"What were they like?" I said.

"Evolution in action," said Roger. "Survival of the fittest, and trample the weakest underfoot. Everyone out for themselves and scrambling all over each other to get ahead. I figured out early on that I couldn't compete. Wasn't hard enough, or self-centred enough. So I just retreated into the background and did my best not to be noticed. And now every single one of them, every brother and sister and aunt and uncle and cousin, hates my guts. Because I'm the one who inherited everything!"

He grinned broadly. "Oh, that put the cat among the pigeons! Mum and Dad died in a car crash, and the will left everything to me. Not even a bequest to anyone else, despite all those years they'd spent trying to crawl up Mum and Dad's arses. I think the will was my parents' last act of revenge, on a family they couldn't stand..." He stopped and looked at me. "You know, you're remarkably easy to talk to."

"I get that a lot," I said.

"Anyway! That isn't what I'm here to talk about. I want to talk about the murder!"

"All right," I said. "Who do you think killed the Colonel?"

"Spoilt for choice, old man!" said Roger. "James was the only one in this family that Walter really cared about. Harsh though that is. And, James was the only one here who couldn't be bought or pressured or used to get at Walter. So of course he had to go. He should never have come back. All he did was put himself in the line of fire." Roger smiled broadly again. "See? I'm a lot smarter than most people think. I notice things. I learned to fade into the background, so the rest of my family wouldn't notice me, but that's the best way to see what's really going on. Walter is the key to all this. Alex wants Walter's company and his wife. Diana wants Walter, so she can have her old life back. Don't ask me about Sylvia, though... Haven't a clue what she really wants. Far too cheerful and charming and everybody's friend for my liking. It's not natural. People like that are always after something. When I look at her, I see a professional at work. But what kind of professional..."

"And Penny?" I said.

"Only one here who's worth a damn," Roger said steadily. "That's what I wanted to talk to you about. I want to protect her, but I'm not sure I can. Not sure I know how. It seems to me... that if we have got a killer trapped in this house, they're going to strike again. That's what killers do, isn't it? And I think ... the next victim could be Penny. Don't ask me why I think that; I just do, all right? I can't be with her all the time; she won't let me. So I'm asking you to help. Help me watch her, protect her. If you have any idea how much I feel for her, you know how hard this is for me. I don't know you, don't even like you much, but I'm forced to turn to you. Because there's no one else here I can trust. Still, even while you're watching and protecting Penny, you keep your distance. Because she's mine. And don't you ever forget that."

He swept out of my room, only remembering not to slam my door shut at the last moment.

Penny immediately stepped out of the cupboard, smiling and shaking her head at the same time. "Isn't that just typical of the man? He can be so sweet, and then ... so infuriating! I don't need him, or you, to protect me! I can look after myself!"

"Never doubted it for a moment," I said.

"I never knew all that stuff about his family ... Poor dear. They sound perfectly awful. It does explain a lot about him, though, doesn't it?"

"Explains a lot," I said, "but not necessarily all. What does a man do, when he finally gets all the money he needs to do everything he's ever dreamed of ... and then finds he can't have the one thing he really wants?"

"You are not seriously putting Roger forward as a suspect?" said Penny. "He wouldn't hurt a fly!"

"They're always the ones you have to watch," I said. "How was the cupboard?"

Penny wrinkled her nose. "Full of mothballs."

"I didn't know moths had—"

There was another knock at the door. I looked at Penny, and she nodded resignedly.

"I know, back in the cupboard."

I waited till Penny was safely hidden again, and then invited in my next visitor. Who turned out to be Sylvia, looking as glamorous as ever. She swayed into my room quite elegantly, as though entering a fashionable salon. She waited for me to get up, and then graciously pretended not to notice when I didn't. She didn't sit. She struck a pose before me and fixed me with a cool, thoughtful stare.

"Ishmael, I have a proposition to put to you."

"Oh yes?" I said. "I am flattered."

"Down, boy. I am being entirely serious here. I think we should leave this place. Just bundle up, walk out of the house, and go."

"Really?" I said. "Just like that?"

"Why not?" said Sylvia. "What have we got to lose? Horrible place, Belcourt Manor. Wish I'd never come here. It's not like we'd be leaving behind anything that mattered. We're not family, or friends, or business partners. I only came here to attend a party! A pleasant Christmas gathering. Good times, with convivial spirits, that's what I was promised! Not a nightmare like this, where no one trusts anyone. With a killer who could be sneaking up behind us at any time. No, I want out of here. I don't feel safe in this house. If the cars really aren't an option, we'll just have to walk. I'm not an idiot; I can hear the blizzard outside, just like you. But if we prepare ourselves properly and strike out across the fields . . . Look, I don't want to do this on my own. But with you beside me, I think we could make it to the next village, and safety. What do you say?"

"I'm not going anywhere," I said. "Not until I know who killed my Colonel."

Sylvia sighed and threw a dramatic glance Heavenwards. "Why are the good men always so stubborn? Are you sure I can't tempt you?"

"No," I said.

"So, it would appear I'm staying after all," said Sylvia. "You were the only one I thought might have the guts to make a break for it. Ah well." She turned to leave.

"Wait a moment," I said quickly. "Who do you think the killer is?"

"Haven't a clue," she said. "I don't know these people. I barely know Diana. I'd better get back to her. I only popped out for a moment, while she was sleeping. I don't want her to wake up alone."

"But you would have left her here, if I'd agreed to go with you," I said.

"It's all about survival, sweetie," said Sylvia. "I've always been able to do what's necessary, to survive."

"Tell me," I said. "Have you heard someone walking up and down, in the corridor?"

She looked at me sharply. "I wasn't sure . . . I thought I might be imagining it. Have you seen anyone?"

"No," I said.

Sylvia shrugged, bestowed one last dazzling smile on me, and left, shutting the door very quietly behind her.

Penny was immediately out of the cupboard again. "What a cow! Ready to just go charging off and abandon Diana, and leave everyone here trapped in the house with a killer! After everything Diana's done for her! And after everyone here went out of their way to make her feel at home! Survival . . . Yes, I know her type! I really must remember to say something especially catty and cutting to her over breakfast tomorrow. Look, I have to go, Ishmael. Before anyone else turns up."

"Keep your door locked," I said.

"Are you kidding? Of course I'm going to lock my door! I won't be able to sleep tonight. I'm going to jam a chair up against the door, and then sit up all night with a really absorbing book. While keeping a poker from the fireplace close at hand at all times!"

And with one last quick smile, she was gone. My room seemed so much quieter, and emptier, without her.

I sat and thought, about everything I'd learned so far. I might not be a detective, but everyone else seemed to be going out of their way to help. They all had their own theories and suspicions, their own secrets and surprises, and a need to place the blame squarely on somebody else. I was now in possession of some interesting background information I hadn't been aware of before, which helped me to understand these people better. But nothing particularly useful. I was still no closer to understanding who had killed the Colonel and why.

There was another knock. I looked at the door. I was getting just a bit tired of visitors. I had to struggle for a moment, to think who was left.

"Come in," I said.

The door opened, and Melanie stepped inside. She shut the door quickly and gave me a brief, preoccupied smile.

"I can't stay long," she said. "Or Walter will miss me. I've only just got him settled; I don't want him to wake up and find me gone. I've got Jeeves standing outside his door, with his gun at the ready . . . I really believed he was just a replacement butler! And a sight better than some we've had . . . You know, you could stand up when a lady enters your room . . ."

"I'm tired," I said. "What do you want, Melanie?"

"I never knew James. Your Colonel. He was Walter's son, from long before my time. James belonged to Walter's life with Diana, and I always stopped listening whenever he started to talk about that. Until he learned not to. I think you should keep a careful eye on Diana. I think she wants my Walter back. And the house, of course. And everything that goes with it. She still thinks of this house as hers. And I believe she'd do anything, absolutely anything, to get what she wants."

"Does that remind you of anyone?" I said.

"No," said Melanie. "Should it?"

She didn't seem to get the inference, so I moved on. "Do you really think Diana would murder her own son?"

"I don't know what to think," said Melanie. "Nothing in this house makes sense any more..."

"How do you feel about Alexander Khan?" I said bluntly.

Melanie was immediately defensive. "How do you mean?"

"Do you see him as a suspect?" I said.

"Oh, I see," said Melanie. "Well, I don't know... I wish Walter had never invited any of these people. We should have celebrated Christmas alone, just the two of us, like I wanted. Everything was going fine until all these people turned up! Excitement like this is very bad for Walter... I won't have him upset! He needs his peace and quiet."

"Why did you come to see me?" I said.

"To warn you about Diana," Melanie said firmly.

"That's it?" I said.

"Isn't that enough?" said Melanie.

She turned her back on me and strode out, closing the door behind her very firmly, as though to cut off any comment I might make. I wasn't sure what to make of Melanie. Could any woman really be as self-centered as she appeared to be? Perhaps only a woman that self-centered could carry out a murder right in the middle of a family gathering. She did seem very protective of Walter; if she saw him threatened by James' return... Or saw her own position with Walter threatened by James and Diana ... I was still thinking my way through that, when there was another knock at my door.

Before I could say anything, the door burst open and Jeeves and Cook strode in together. Cook kept a watchful eye on me, while Jeeves peered back out into the corridor, to check no one was watching. He closed the door, and then the two of them took up a position side by side before me, shoulder to shoulder, as though they belonged together. The tall black butler and the short blonde cook. Except they no longer looked like a butler or a cook. They looked a lot more like soldiers.

"Good evening," I said. "Do come in. No doubt you're wondering why I summoned you here ..."

"Flippancy will get you nowhere," said Jeeves. "It's time for the truth to come out."

"I'm all in favour of that," I said.

"Leilah and I are a husband and wife security team," said Jeeves. "We were hired to provide security for Mister Walter Belcourt, for this weekend get-together. Things seem to have got a little out of hand."

"So we thought it was time we asked you a few leading questions," said Leilah. She produced a small handgun from her Victorian cook's outfit and aimed it at me. She looked like she knew how to use a gun. I sat very still.

"Leilah and I always work together on assignments," said Jeeves. "One obviously, the other less so."

"We're here to interrogate you," said Leilah.

"Is that so?" I said. "Why me in particular?"

"You're the outsider," said Leilah. "No one here knows you. You claim to work for the deceased James Belcourt, but we only have your word for that. I'll bet you don't even have a Security ID, do you?"

"No," I said. "The Organization I work for doesn't officially exist. People who need to know, know who we are."

"Well," said Leilah. "You would say that, wouldn't you?"

"You can see why you make such a good suspect," said Jeeves.

"Of course," I said. "I'm sure I'd do the same, in your shoes. Those are your shoes, aren't they? Good. What can I do for you?"

"He's being flippant again," said Leilah.

"Ask the questions," said Jeeves.

"Ask away," I said.

"You can start by telling us everything about yourself," said Leilah. "Who you really are, who you really work for, and what you're really doing here. Everything we need to know, to protect our client. You talk, and we'll tell you when to stop."

"And if I don't care to do that?" I said.

Leilah grinned nastily. "Then I will beat it out of you. I'm really very good at that. Ask Jeeves."

I looked at him. "You'd let her do that to me? A possibly entirely innocent bystander?"

"Let her?" said Jeeves. "I plan to stand well back to avoid getting blood on me, take notes and cheer her on as necessary. We're not police, we're not government, and the only rules we follow are our own. That's how we get results."

Leilah waggled her gun at me, in a meaningful manner. "Start talking."

I came up off the end of the bed in a rush, slapped the gun out of Leilah's hand, grabbed her by the front of her cook's outfit, and threw her on to the bed. She hit it with enough force to drive the breath out of her. Jeeves was already going for his gun as I closed in on him. I grabbed his arm with one hand and squeezed the muscle until he groaned with agony.

All the strength went out of his hand, and the gun dropped from his nerveless fingers. I caught it, and then grabbed Jeeves by the front of his butler's outfit and threw him on to the bed, next to Leilah, who was only just getting her breath back. I picked up her gun from the floor, and then stood at the end of the bed, training both guns on their previous owners. I wasn't even breathing hard. Jeeves and Leilah glared at me from the bed and didn't move a muscle.

"Damn," said Jeeves. "You're fast. And very well-trained. All right, I'm convinced. To be able to take us down that easily, you must work for the Organization."

"And, I am not a suspect," I said.

Leilah scowled at me. "You can say anything you like while you're covering us with our own guns. But you're still a suspect. It would take someone as cold-blooded and expertly trained as an Organization agent to kill James Belcourt in such an extreme way."

"I thought we'd agreed I couldn't have been here when the Colonel was killed?" I said.

Jeeves did his best to shrug, while lying on his back. "The cold changes everything. Who knows when he was killed, really?"

"Fair enough," I said. I tossed both their guns back to them, and they caught them expertly, out of mid air.

"Please get up off my bed," I said. "You make the place look untidy."

Jeeves and Leilah rolled off different sides of the bed and were immediately on their feet again, each with a gun in hand aimed at me. I raised an eyebrow. Jeeves and Leilah looked at each other, as though each was hoping the other would have some idea what to do. In the end, they both shrugged more or less simultaneously and put their guns away.

Leilah looked at me defiantly. "I suppose you expect us to trust you, just because you've given us our guns back?"

"I don't trust anyone in this house," I said. "And neither should you. Tell me, before you go. Who do you think killed the Colonel?"

"We only care about that as it pertains to protecting our client," said Jeeves. "Are you sure the attack on the son is connected to the father?"

"Don't you think that?" I said.

"I strongly suggest you stay in your room until morning," said Jeeves. "And lock your door. I've managed to contact my people, and they're hoping to have someone here by tomorrow. Leilah and I will spend the night standing guard in the hallway. Perfectly ready to open fire on anything that moves that isn't us."

"I was surprised to see both of you up here," I said. "Leaving poor Walter unattended."

"Melanie has the door locked," said Leilah. "And with the whole place shut down, we can hear anybody moving about."

"Really?" I said. "You weren't my first visitors tonight. I've spoken to several people, and they all reported hearing someone moving about up here, in the corridor. But whenever someone went to look, there was never anybody to be seen."

Jeeves and Leilah looked at each other. "Have you seen anyone moving about up here, Ishmael?" said Jeeves.

"No," I said. "But I've heard someone."

"It's an old house," said Jeeves. "Maybe it's haunted."

Leilah winced. "Don't. I hate ghosts."

They left together, and I locked the door behind them. And then I went and sat in the most comfortable-looking chair and thought hard for a long time.

Some time later, my head snapped up. I sniffed the air and

was up on my feet in a moment. I hurried over to my door, unlocked it, and hauled it open. I sniffed the air again. The next door but one to mine opened, and Penny looked out. She hadn't changed out of her day clothes, and she had a heavy iron poker in her hand.

"Oh, it's you!" she said. "I thought I heard someone on the move, and this time I heard a door opening, so I thought I'd take a look. What's wrong? Why are you looking like that?"

"Can you smell anything?" I said. "Like meat burning?"

Penny sniffed hard, and then shook her head. She looked at me doubtfully. "We're a long way from the kitchens, Ishmael."

And then we both looked round sharply as a horrible scream sounded from the far end of the corridor, by the stairs. Penny and I ran towards it.

✦ EIGHT ✦
BLOOD WILL HAVE BLOOD

PENNY AND I were halfway down the corridor when another door swung suddenly open, and Alexander Khan looked out. He was wearing a stylish and very colourful dressing gown, entirely ordinary slippers, and a confused look on his face. His normally slicked-back hair was all over the place. He'd clearly managed to get some sleep and was only half awake now.

"What's going on?" he said roughly. "Did I hear ... Did somebody scream?"

I didn't have the time to answer him, and Penny didn't seem inclined to. We ran on down the corridor. Khan stumbled after us. Jeeves and Leilah were already pounding up the stairs, gun in hand, their faces professionally focused. They reached the top of the stairs just as Penny and I got to the end of the corridor. A quick glance back past them showed me Walter and Melanie, standing together at the foot of the stairs in matching battered old dressing gowns. Walter was demanding to know what was going on, his voice loud but his eyes vague, while Melanie did her best to hush and comfort him. Walter would have none of it. He started up the stairs, moving as quickly as he could, leaning heavily on his walking stick. Melanie followed him up, if only because she didn't want to be left on her own.

And finally, I looked at the door at the end of the corridor. Sylvia was staring through the open doorway into a room full of darkness, her face full of horror. She turned abruptly to look at me with wide shocked eyes. She'd stopped screaming now, but probably only because she had both hands pressed to her mouth. I took a moment to look her over, to make sure she was unharmed. Sylvia was wearing an expensive silk wrap, but no curlers in her hair or cream on her face. She didn't look like she'd been sleeping. She gestured frantically at the room before her, unable to force the words out. I took her by the shoulders and moved her gently to one side. She stumbled and almost fell, but Penny was there to catch her and hold her up as I peered through the dark opening.

"Stay with her, Penny," I said.

"Hell with that," said Penny. She checked Sylvia could stand unsupported, and then moved quickly forward to stand beside me, peering into the dark beyond the doorway. Light falling in from the corridor didn't travel far.

Jeeves and Leilah finally arrived.

"Stay where you are!" I said sharply. "You need to keep everyone else out of this room. We can't risk contaminating a crime scene." I turned to Penny. "Whose room is this? Who's in there?"

"This is Roger's room," she said steadily. "He invited me in, earlier, but I didn't want to go. This isn't going to be good, is it?"

"No," I said.

"Is Roger dead, do you think?"

"It seems likely," I said. "Someone in this room is dead. I can tell."

The light was off in Roger's room, and with the shutters closed over the window there was no interior light at all. Just the darkness, hiding something, like a child with a nasty secret. I could smell burnt meat, clearer than ever. I could hear flames crackling, quietly, but there was no light from the room's fireplace.

Penny crowded in beside me, but made no move to push past me. "I can smell something burning now," she said quietly. "Where's the light switch?"

I reached inside the doorway and fumbled around till I found the switch. I turned the light on, and Penny cried out, despite herself.

A blackened, charred body sat in a chair by the cold fireplace, facing the door. The body's clothes had mostly burned away, and the exposed flesh was scorched and cracked. The face was an unrecognizable mess. Teeth gleamed whitely in the ragged mouth. The eyes were gone. I moved quickly forward into the room, ripped the top blanket off the bed, and threw it over the body. I pressed down hard, but I already knew it was too late. I heard bones crack, from where I pressed down too hard. I let go of the blanket and stepped back.

"I'm sorry," I said to Penny.

She swallowed hard. Her face was pale, but when she finally spoke her voice was steady. "This is Roger's room, but can we be sure that's him?"

"Good point," I said. "It's getting so I don't trust anything in this house."

I pulled back one side of the blanket, just enough to uncover the charred right hand. A little smoke rose up. I found a gold signet ring, huge and flashy. I showed it to Penny, and she nodded quickly.

"Yes. I know that ring. He was so proud of it, always so keen to show it off, and I was always rude about it because it was ugly. That's Roger." She stopped talking and shook her head briefly, her mouth compressed into a flat line, and then she looked unflinchingly at the body. "I won't cry now. Not when there's so much that needs to be done. I'll cry later, when there's time. I promise you, Roger." She looked angrily at me. "Who would want to kill Roger, of all people? He isn't important, not like your Colonel. I don't think Roger had an enemy in the world."

"He did say everyone in his family hated him," I said carefully.

"Well, yes, but they're not here," said Penny. "And why would any of them want to kill James?"

"I don't know," I said. "I can't see any obvious connection between the two murders. It doesn't make sense."

Jeeves leaned in through the doorway, looked at the body, and scowled. "Did I hear right, that's Roger?"

"Yes," said Penny. "He's dead."

She went back out into the corridor, Jeeves moving quickly to get out of her way. I went after her and stood in the doorway, blocking it off.

"Roger's dead," Penny announced loudly. "The killer set him on fire."

A small crowd had gathered together in the corridor. They all made sounds of horror and distress, and huddled together. Everyone present seemed honestly shocked by the news. Khan was comforting Sylvia, who was weeping quietly against his chest. She looked like a child who'd just discovered how harsh and cruel the world can be. Khan looked lost and bewildered, even as he patted Sylvia's shoulder automatically. Jeeves and Leilah stood close together, their guns in their hands. Neither of them seemed sure what to do. Walter and Melanie had finally made it up the stairs to join the rest of us. Walter was breathing hard, and the colour in his face wasn't healthy. He leaned heavily on his walking stick and on Melanie's arm. She looked wildly about her, as though expecting to be attacked at any moment.

"I can't believe it," said Walter. "Two of my guests dead, in my own home . . . First James, and now Roger? What the hell is going on? Somebody tell me what's going on!"

"Hush, dear," said Melanie. "For God's sake."

Walter seemed to realize for the first time how upset his wife was, and he patted her hand, on his arm.

I stepped forward, to address Sylvia, who was still leaning heavily on Alexander Khan. "I know you're upset, Sylvia, but I have to ask you some questions. How did you happen to be here?"

Sylvia slowly turned away from Khan to answer me. Her voice was higher than usual, but still reasonably steady. Tears ran down her face, though she didn't seem to notice.

"I heard those footsteps again. Just . . . walking up and down, going nowhere. But this time when they stopped, I heard a door open. And I thought: that's different. So I went to my door and stood there and listened for a while. No voices, and I didn't hear the door close. So I unlocked my door and looked out. I couldn't see anyone, but I didn't want to think I was just imagining things, so I stepped out into the corridor. And that's when I realized Roger's door was standing open. So I came down here, to see what was going on. I knew I shouldn't, I knew it wasn't a sensible thing to do, but . . . I couldn't seem to help myself. I had to know . . . And then I looked in through the door . . . And saw Roger—" She broke off, unable to go on.

Khan took her in his arms again. He glared at me over her shoulder. "Can't this wait?"

"I suppose so," I said. "It's not as if any of us are going anywhere." I looked round at the others. "No one is to go into this room. We finally have an actual crime scene, and I don't want anything disturbed. We never did find out where the Colonel was killed, but it seems clear Roger died right here."

Jeeves and Leilah nodded, reluctantly. "All right," said Jeeves. "We'll talk to these people, while you check out the state of the room and the body. You probably have more experience with dead bodies, anyway."

"Excuse me," said Melanie. "Can I just ask, why is Cook carrying a gun?"

I left Jeeves to explain and went back into Roger's room. Penny was immediately right there, with me.

"I know he was your friend," I said. "But I have to examine the body pretty thoroughly. You don't have to . . ."

"Try and keep me out," said Penny. "I want to know everything. I need to know."

"If you have to throw up, go out into the corridor to do it," I said, as kindly as I could.

I removed the blanket from the body in the chair and tossed it back on to the bed. Penny swallowed hard, but didn't turn away as I looked the body over. The charred remains were still smoking, here and there, but the flames were all out. The body was sitting upright, and apparently relaxed, in the chair. Nothing to indicate any movement while he burned. For all the damage the fire had done, it didn't seem to have consumed much of the body. And then I looked round sharply as Penny made a noise behind me.

She had both hands over her mouth and nose, to keep out the smell. From the expression on her face, that wasn't working too well. She saw me watching her and waved one hand impatiently, for me to continue. I studied the body carefully from top to bottom, leaning in close where necessary, careful to touch nothing. The smell didn't bother me. Or the state of the body.

"I suppose you're about to say you've seen worse," said Penny.

"Yes," I said. "I have."

"Working for the Colonel? For dear mysterious stepbrother James? Exactly what kind of work did you do for that man, Ishmael?"

"Ask me later," I said. "For now, just accept I'm the best chance for revenge that Roger's got."

The more I looked, the more convinced I became Roger hadn't died from the fire. He'd been killed in his chair, and then set on fire to destroy the evidence. To cover up what had actually happened to him. And so far, it was working. I couldn't see an obvious death wound anywhere.

"The fire happened after the murder," I said to Penny. "Presumably to hide the method. So I have to assume that's significant, in some way. Or informative. Perhaps when we know how Roger was killed, the manner of it will point to one person in particular."

Jeeves leaned in through the doorway. "Hate to interrupt the deep thinking," he said, "but I really think Leilah and I need to come in and see what's happened for ourselves."

"Of course," I said. "Tell everyone else to stay put, though. Professionals only for the moment."

"And me," said Penny.

Jeeves and Leilah stepped cautiously into Roger's room, wrinkling their noses as the smell hit them. They'd both put their guns away.

"No sign of any struggle," I said. "And nothing to indicate he was killed somewhere else and his body dumped here. I would say Roger died sitting in his chair."

"Sylvia found the door open," said Jeeves. "Roger would

have had his door locked . . . so he must have opened it to let his killer in."

"Why would he open the door to anyone, under these circumstances?" said Leilah.

"He knew his visitor," I said. "And felt safe inviting them in."

Jeeves looked at Penny. "He would have opened his door to you, Miss Belcourt. When he might not have to anyone else."

"I'm a suspect?" said Penny.

"Everyone's a suspect," said Leilah.

"Ishmael!" said Penny. "Say something!"

"Everyone's a suspect," I said.

"That's not what I was hoping for," said Penny.

"Everyone in this house is a suspect," I said. "Including Jeeves and Leilah."

"Well," said Penny. "That's better. I suppose."

"At least now we know for sure the murderer is still in this house," said Jeeves. "Leilah and I did a complete tour of the Manor. Checked all the doors and windows. Everything's secure."

"The doors and shutters aren't just locked, they're bolted," said Leilah. "You can pick a lock, or force it, and not leave a trace, if you're a professional. But no one gets past a bolt. I'm a great believer in bolts." She moved over to check the room's single shuttered window and nodded quickly. "Told you. The only way in is through the door."

"But . . . why is he sitting in his chair?" I said.

"To make it look like a case of spontaneous combustion?" said Leilah.

We all stopped what we were doing, to stare at her in pretty much the same way.

Leilah glared defiantly back at us. "Well it could be! Come on, we've all seen stranger things!"

"I haven't," said Penny.

"You have now," I said. "But no, there was nothing spontaneous about this. Roger was deliberately set alight."

"How?" said Jeeves. "The fire's out in the fireplace. What could the murderer have used to set a man on fire so completely? I mean, Roger was burning from head to foot. Some kind of accelerant?"

I looked at him, almost pityingly. "You could say that . . . Get closer to the body. What else can you smell, apart from the expected?"

Jeeves and Leilah looked at each other, leaned in and sniffed hard, and then recoiled quickly, coughing hard.

I took pity on them. "The killer doused the body in brandy. See the empty bottle, standing by the fireplace? Soaked him in the stuff, from head to toe. That's why the clothing went up so quickly and completely. It would only take a match to set it off, then just stand well back, and let the body burn. And it's clear this was done after Roger was already dead. Because no one would have sat quietly in their chair and burned."

"Hell no," said Jeeves, shuddering suddenly. "He'd have been running round the room, screaming his head off, banging into the furniture, throwing off hot fat and setting fire to the furnishings . . ."

He stopped then and looked apologetically at Penny, who just nodded quickly. Leilah hit Jeeves hard on the arm. He shrugged quickly.

"Could there be a connection?" Leilah said slowly. "In how both the bodies were treated? Cold for James, heat for Roger? Could this be some . . . elemental thing?"

"Serial killers do like to send messages," said Jeeves.

"Can we call him a serial, with only two killings?" said Leilah.

"You think he's going to stop at two?" said Jeeves.

Leilah looked at Penny. "He . . . or she."

"Yes . . ." said Jeeves. He turned the full force of his natural authority on Penny. "Do you have an alibi, Miss Belcourt?"

"How the hell should I know?" said Penny, entirely unfazed. "We don't know when Roger died, do we?"

"No one has an alibi," I said. "Just like the Colonel."

And then I stopped and looked thoughtfully at the floor. "Hold everything . . . Someone else was quite definitely in this room. I can see footprints in the carpeting."

Jeeves and Leilah looked at each other, and then at the carpet. In the end, they had to get down on their hands and knees and study the carpet close up, before they finally nodded agreement. They got back on to their feet again, helping each other considerately, and then looked at me.

"You have really good eyes," said Jeeves.

"You're weird," said Leilah.

"At the very least," I said. "Comes with the territory. No marks of spiked heels, to indicate a woman, just flat imprints. Basic slippers. From the size, it could be male or female."

"So, not really helpful after all," said Leilah.

Jeeves hushed her. "Is there anything else we've missed, Ishmael?"

"Yes . . ." I said. "I can smell something else in this room, something out of place. Apart from the obvious. Under the burnt meat, and the brandy, I can smell blood."

"You can smell blood?" said Leilah. "What the hell are you, part bloodhound?"

"He smelled blood before," said Penny. "Just before we found James' body, hidden inside the snowman."

"What kind of training does the Organization give you people?" said Jeeves.

Leilah looked at Jeeves. "You believe him?"

"He's been right about everything else, so far," said Jeeves.

"I think you should take the others downstairs," I said. "This floor doesn't feel safe. Take them down, fill them in on the situation, or at least as much as you think wise, while Penny and I finish looking the scene over. I would suggest you hole up in the drawing room. Just the one door, easily defended, and there's food and drink. Should be safe enough for the time being."

"I don't think I'll ever feel safe again," said Penny. She glanced at the body. "Or hungry again. Ever."

Leilah looked at me bullishly. "We don't take orders from you! We only answer to the client. Why should we be the ones who have to guard the sheep?"

"Because you've got guns," I said.

"And because that's our job, Leilah," said Jeeves. "We don't solve murders, we protect the client. Right?"

"Still say he's weird," muttered Leilah.

They left the room, and I heard them speak politely and persuasively to the people in the corridor. And then they all went downstairs, Jeeves and Leilah in the lead, followed by Khan and Sylvia, and finally Walter and Melanie. I turned back to the body. Penny was staring into the ruined face.

"I wanted to be free of him," she said. "But not like this. He wasn't a bad sort, you know. Not really. He just fell in love with the wrong woman. He should have found someone who might have been . . . kinder to him."

She turned abruptly and walked out of the room. She stood outside, breathing deeply of the somewhat fresher air. I went out to join her, and then hesitated in the doorway, looking back. I couldn't help feeling I was missing something. Some important detail . . .

I went to shut and lock the door and found the key was still in the lock, on the inside of the door. So the killer . . . left it there? And left the door open, so the body could be discovered? Why would the killer do that, after going to such pains to hide the Colonel's body? Or, could it be that the killer was in such a hurry that they didn't have time to lock the door? Suggesting...what? That the killer murdered Roger almost immediately after being admitted into his room? Why the rush? And how would the killer have overpowered Roger so quickly? Roger wasn't what I would have called a fighter, but surely he would have put up some kind of struggle...Unless he was caught completely by surprise...Or drugged.

I reined in my thoughts. Far too many questions, and hardly any answers.

I locked the door and slipped the key into my pocket. I didn't want anyone else having access to the body until I'd had time to think some more. I moved over to join Penny. She was still breathing deeply, but a healthier colour had come back into her face. She looked at me squarely.

"You don't think I killed Roger, do you, Ishmael?"

"I can't see any reason why you would," I said.

"That's not what I asked," said Penny.

"I don't believe you are capable of such an act," I said.

Penny smiled. "Thank you."

She hugged me suddenly. I let her.

"Of course," I said, "I have been known to be wrong about people."

"It was a lovely moment," Penny said into my shoulder. "Don't spoil it."

"Sorry," I said.

After a while she let go of me and stood back. She smiled brightly. "Since you and I are the only people in this house we can trust, I think we should work together to solve the mystery and identify the killer. We both have good reason to bring this bastard down. I want to avenge Roger, and you want to avenge James. Your Colonel."

"Why do you trust me?" I said. "You barely know me."

"I don't know," said Penny. "I just do. Sometimes you only have to look at someone and you know."

"Yes," I said. "I know."

And then I looked around the corridor sharply. "Hold it! Hold everything! I knew I'd missed something . . . Where's Diana? She wasn't here before, with all the others."

"You're right!" said Penny. "She wasn't here, and I never noticed . . . Why didn't I notice? And why didn't she show up with the others? Oh, wait a minute. Sylvia could have given Diana something, to help her sleep."

"Then why did Sylvia go downstairs with the others, leaving Diana on her own up here, dead to the world in her room, and not say anything?"

"Shock?" said Penny. "Finding Roger like that must have—"

"Why didn't we notice Diana wasn't with the others?" I said. "Something's very wrong here. Which is Diana's room?"

"Daddy put her in the Primrose Room," said Penny. "Diana always insists on the same room, every year."

She led the way. The door to Diana's room was closed, and when I tried the handle it was locked. Penny rapped loudly on the door and called Diana's name. There was no response. I sniffed at the air.

"Blood," I said. "I can smell blood."

"Through a closed door?" said Penny.

I smashed in the door, with one hard shove of my hand. The lock exploded, and the door was blasted right off its hinges. It fell forward into the room, measuring its length on the carpeted floor.

Penny looked at me. "OK, I am now seriously impressed."

"All part of the training," I said.

"Really?"

"No."

The room was in darkness. I found the light switch and turned it on. Penny wanted to rush in, but I gestured for her to hold back. I stepped cautiously inside, and then stopped. The bed was empty, all the bedclothes perfectly in place. Nothing to show anyone had slept in it. The room was still and quiet. I could smell Diana's perfume, half hidden under half a dozen other smells. She was here, somewhere. I moved forward, following the scent across the room, with Penny sticking close at my side. I ended up standing before the fireplace. It was a lot bigger than the one in my room. Someone had piled the fire high with coal, and it was burning fiercely, throwing off a lot of heat. I dropped down on one knee, thrust both my hands into the fire and pulled it apart, hauling out the burning coals and scattering them across the grate. It only took me a few moments.

Penny watched all this from a safe distance, only moving occasionally to kick a burning coal back into the grate, if it rolled too far and tried to set light to the carpet. With the fire gone, I forced myself into the grate and looked up the wide chimney. The smell of Diana's perfume was suddenly stronger.

Penny made a sudden shocked sound. "Ishmael, no! She can't be..."

I forced my shoulders into the chimney gap, reached up into the dark, and found a single dangling hand. I took a firm hold and pulled Diana's body down out of the chimney and into the grate. She'd been pushed a fair way up and packed in tight, which spoke of a great deal of strength from the killer. But I was stronger and more determined.

I backed away, hauling Diana's body out of the grate. Penny fell back, making shocked noises as I laid Diana out on the carpet. Exposure to heat and smoke had seriously distorted the skin, but it was still Diana. I recognized the clothes and the perfume. I sat on the floor beside the body.

Penny crouched down beside me. "Ishmael, let me see your hands."

"They're fine."

"They can't be; you just pulled a fire apart. Let me see how badly you're burned."

"They're fine!" I showed her my hands. They were flushed red, but not burnt.

"I don't understand," said Penny.

"Concentrate on what's important," I said. "Diana's dead." Penny looked at me dubiously, and then gave her attention to the body. "It's just like the old Edgar Allan Poe story," she said. "*The Murders in the Rue Morgue*! But in that story the killer turned out to be an orangutan. No. I can't believe that ... Are you sure that's Diana? I mean, the face is ..."

"It's her," I said. "I know her. Her clothes, her perfume, her body. I know everything about her."

I gathered Diana up in my arms and held her close, rocking her back and forth, like a parent with a sleeping child. I didn't cry, but there must have been something in my face, because Penny knelt in close beside me. She didn't try to touch me, didn't say anything, just stayed with me, giving me what comfort she could with her presence. Diana felt light, almost weightless in my arms, as though everything that mattered of her was gone.

"You should have seen her dance, Penny," I said finally. "When she was young and talented and so full of life. Featured dancer at the Crazy Horse, in Paris. When she moved on that stage ... she was a wonder to behold."

"What?" said Penny. "I'm sorry, Ishmael, I don't understand."

"She didn't deserve to die like this," I said.

"Neither did Roger, or James," said Penny.

I stood up, still carrying the body effortlessly in my arms, and moved across the room to lay Diana out respectfully on the bed. I crossed her hands on her chest. Mercifully, her eyes were shut.

Penny hovered beside me. "Why did the murderer do this?" she said. "Why kill poor old defenceless Diana? She didn't have any money, or... And why is the killer doing these awful things to the bodies?"

"So many questions," I said. "Why didn't Sylvia notice Diana was missing?"

"I suppose... all she could think of was Roger and the terrible thing that had been done to him," said Penny.

"Could Diana have been killed after Sylvia left the room?" I said slowly. "Could Diana have been murdered here, while we were all distracted with Roger?" I looked at Penny. "Did you notice anyone missing from the group, at any time?"

"No," said Penny. "I was totally focused on what had been done to Roger. Anyone could have come and gone..."

"Same here," I said. "And again, look around the room. No sign of any struggle. No overturned furniture, not even any scuff marks on the carpet. As though the murderer just... killed Diana, and then stuffed her straight up the chimney. All in a few moments..."

"But why put her up there?" said Penny, almost desperately. "Why stoke up the fire afterwards? Why saw off James' head and set Roger on fire? Why do all this, after they were already dead!"

"Assuming there is a reason," I said, slowly. "Not just some psychotic, sending a message that only makes sense to them... Why did the killer need to go to such lengths with the bodies? All of them hidden, disfigured... Yes! That's it!

All the bodies were damaged, disfigured, to hide some specific injury to the bodies! Snow, fire, heat and smoke ... To hide the true method of murder! I've smelt the same thing at all three bodies, Penny: blood. But there's never been a trace of spilled blood, anywhere near the bodies. So where did all the blood go?"

I leaned over the bed and examined Diana's body up close. It took a while, but finally I found what I was looking for. Teeth marks, on her throat. Right over the main veins. And not just pin pricks, or a pair of puncture marks: a full set of human-sized teeth, sunk deep into the meat. Heat and smoke damage would have disguised and hidden the marks from a cursory examination. And after two or three days stuck up that chimney, you'd have needed a full autopsy to uncover the wounds. I straightened up and stood a while, thinking. Penny looked at me anxiously.

"What do all three bodies have in common?" I said finally. "Marks of violence, but no blood spilled. Because there was no blood left to spill ..."

I turned and ran out of Diana's room, all the way back down the corridor. Penny sprinted after me, trying to keep up. I didn't stop to unlock Roger's door, just kicked it off its hinges and burst in. I leant over the chair and pushed the burned head back to expose the neck, ignoring the loud cracking from the bones. Now I knew what to look for I soon found teeth marks, disguised by the burns. I pointed them out to Penny, but she didn't want to get that close.

"All right!" she said, just a bit breathlessly. "I'll take your word for it. Teeth marks on the necks. The killer bit them. What for, to leave his mark?"

"Not as such," I said.

I let go of Roger's head and stepped back from the body. I looked at Penny for a long moment, and then drew the slender dagger I keep in a sheath on my left forearm, hidden up my sleeve.

"I thought you said you don't like weapons?" said Penny.

"I don't," I said. "But they can be useful, sometimes."

I knelt down and made a long incision in Roger's left wrist, where it rested on the arm of the chair. The razor-sharp edge sliced easily through the charred flesh, severing the main veins, but not a drop of blood fell out.

"This body has been drained of blood," I said to Penny. "So was Diana. And the Colonel was beheaded not to kill him or hamper identification, but to preoccupy people. So they wouldn't realize the whole point of beheading was to damage the neck so much that teeth marks wouldn't show. The killer was still expecting to get away, then. He had time to mess with the body and move it outside into the grounds, and then hide it in the snowman; he didn't expect the body to be found until the thaw, by which time he'd be long gone. He didn't know a storm was coming to trap him here. He's having to improvise now to hide his feeding."

I stood up, still holding the dagger, and looked steadily at Penny. "I'm sorry. There's no easy way to break this to you. Our killer isn't human. We're dealing with a vampire."

Penny looked at me for a long moment, torn between shock and nervous laughter. "*What?* Are you serious? You really expect me to believe that, Ishmael? *That's* your great deduction? We're being picked off by Count Dracula? No. No! I've gone this far with you, but now you've jumped right over the edge. I want an explanation. Right now. About you, Ishmael. Who are you, really? Just what kind of work did you do, for your Colonel?"

"I hunt monsters," I said. "Because I don't want to be one."

I explained, as best I could. About the star that fell from the heavens, in 1963. About the transformation machines, and being made human. About working for the Organization. Penny's eyes grew wide, but she never said a word.

"I am human," I said finally. "In every way that matters. It's just that I was made, not born. I'm stronger, faster, than most people. My senses are sharper. I see and hear things that most people miss."

"You honestly expect me to believe this . . . bullshit?" said Penny. "How can I believe something like this?"

"Because it's true," I said. "And you know you can trust me."

"That was when I thought you were a sane person!"

"They say seeing is believing," I said.

"You're crazy," said Penny. "I'm sorry, Ishmael, but you're crazy! You have to be."

"I did consider that option quite seriously, for some time," I said. "Until I had an accident."

"Ishmael?" Penny said carefully. "Why are you still holding that knife?"

I set the dagger against my left wrist and made a deep incision. Blood ran down my wrist, and it was golden. Penny made a sound, deep in her throat, and backed away, putting half the room between us. The golden blood stopped dripping as the wound healed. I stropped the blade clean on my sleeve and slipped the dagger back into the sheath under my sleeve.

"Seeing," I said, "is believing."

"All right," Penny said hoarsely. "You have . . . golden blood. How about that. If I hadn't seen it for myself I wouldn't . . . There's no way you could have faked that. So . . . I'm still not sure I can accept . . . everything you just told me, but I'll go along, for now. And have some seriously noisy hysterics later, when I've got time. A Close Encounter, in the middle of a country house murder mystery . . . Not what I expected, this weekend. Is everyone who works for the Organization an alien?"

"No," I said. "I'd have noticed."

"Well, that's something, at least. So! An alien passing for human is here to track down a vampire passing for human. Did the Colonel know about this . . . ?"

"Perhaps," I said. "Remember what he wrote in his letter: *A horror has come to Belcourt . . .*"

"Well, why didn't he just say it was a vampire!"

"Perhaps he wasn't sure," I said. "Such things are rare. I've never encountered one before. Don't know anyone who has. But the Colonel must have been given reason to . . . suspect something. That's why he wanted me here so urgently. He needed one monster to take down another."

"So he knew . . . what you are?"

"I never asked," I said. "I have gone to great pains to keep my true nature secret."

"Why?"

"Because I don't want to end up in a cage," I said. "Or on a vivisection table. This planet is not very welcoming to illegal aliens."

"Do we tell the others?" said Penny.

"Probably not a good idea," I said. "They've got enough on their minds as it is. And, I have to wonder, how is it that two of the people in this small gathering know me from earlier times in my life? Diana in the sixties, and Alexander Khan in the eighties."

"Wait a minute!" said Penny. "You mean: when Alex recognized you . . . it was you and not your father? That was you? And Diana really did know you from Paris? You really are that old? Holy shit . . ."

"I worked beside Alex, in a Government department

known as Black Heir," I said. "And Diana and I were lovers, long ago."

"Lovers?" said Penny. "Oh, ick..."

"She was as beautiful as you, once," I said.

"You seem to have got over her death pretty quick," said Penny.

"I have learned to keep my emotions inside," I said. "Because they aren't always entirely human. I will avenge her. And the Colonel."

"And Roger?" said Penny, pointedly.

"Of course," I said. "But I still want to know why two people from my past are here, for the same Christmas weekend. Coincidence? Or something the Colonel arranged? He always did think he knew how to run my life better than I did. I'll never know, now he's gone. He hid me from the world for fifteen years. Who's going to protect me, now he's gone?"

I was genuinely lost for a moment, not knowing what to say or think.

Penny moved slowly forward across the room, to stand before me. "This isn't the time to get lost in the past, Ishmael. Concentrate on the present, on what's happening right now. We're in danger here. You and I, and everyone downstairs, is in danger from a vampire. There. I said the v-word. We're all depending on you, Ishmael."

"Yes," I said. "It's all right, Penny. I'm back. You're quite right, of course. I won't let you down." I stopped and looked at her for a long moment. "Penny...I'm still me. I haven't changed. I'm still the person you believed you could trust."

"Yes," said Penny. "I do trust you. Whatever you are."

We shared a smile. And then we left Roger's room and went back out into the corridor, together.

We stood side by side at the top of the stairs, looking

down. I could hear faint voices, from the drawing room. Just enough to know they were all there.

"What do we know about vampires?" I said. "I mean, really know? As opposed to what we think we know, from all those movies and television shows and weirdly romantic paperback novels. That always struck me as . . . odd. I mean, there's nothing romantic about a leech."

"I know *Dracula* didn't start out as an historical novel," said Penny. "I studied the book at college. We're used to seeing it presented as a period piece. But when Bram Stoker's novel first appeared, Count Dracula moved through the world of the reader, the world outside their windows. And the vampire is surrounded by all the latest technology of his time. Railways, motor cars, telegrams and blood transfusions. Dracula was a supernatural creature, invading a civilization based on science."

"I have encountered many strange things," I said. "Hell, I am a strange thing. And I'm still having trouble coming to terms with this. We need to sort out what parts of vampire lore are likely to be real, and what's just superstitious folk lore and legend."

"Well," said Penny, "I know for a fact that everyone here has been outside in the daylight, at one time or another. And they certainly didn't bring a coffin with them to sleep in. Jeeves would have noticed. We all ate and drank the same things; hell, we all had chicken kiev last night, with bags of garlic . . . No one's reflection has been missing from a mirror . . ."

"Crucifixes?" I said.

"I haven't seen one hanging up anywhere," said Penny, frowning. "Daddy's never been very religious. But no one's been bothered by any of the religious elements in the Christmas celebration. What are vampires, really?"

"A corpse that has risen from the grave," I said. "Broken out of its coffin and dug its way up out of the earth. To walk the world undead and feed on the living. A predator, hiding its true nature behind a glamour. A pleasing appearance. A telepathically broadcast illusion. To make us see it as just another human being, instead of an undead walking corpse. Which is why I can't see or smell anything different about them. Actually, I probably can; it's just that I'm being prevented from noticing. Mentally compelled not to notice. That's actually quite spooky. Like when we didn't notice Diana was missing from the crowd outside Roger's room."

"Until everyone else went downstairs!" Penny said excitedly, bouncing up and down on the spot. "Does that mean the vampire's range is limited?"

"Could be," I said. "It must know it's in danger now. In danger of being recognized and revealed for what it really is. It must know it's going to have to kill all of us, to be safe. Pick us off, one at a time. Not for the blood; it must be sated by now. For the security. It can't afford to leave any witnesses . . . Anyone who might spread wild stories about a vampire . . . People are actually more superstitious these days than they ever were. They'll believe anything. No, it will kill us all, just to make itself feel safe, wait here for the storm to die down, and then head for the nearest village. And disappear. Nothing left behind but a house full of bodies. Or perhaps it'll burn the Manor down. So no one will ever know what happened here. Just another unsolved mystery."

"Why hasn't the vampire already left?" said Penny. "Just, made a run for it? The cold wouldn't affect the undead, would it?"

"I don't know!" I said. "Really, I don't know, Penny! Vampires aren't my field. I never expected to run into one."

"What is your field, then?"

"I'll tell you later," I said.

"You'd better," said Penny.

"We have to identify which of the remaining people here is the vampire," I said. "And deal with it."

"But Ishmael, what if we're wrong? We can't just drive a stake through someone!"

"Don't worry," I said. "We won't do anything until we're sure. Beyond all reasonable doubt."

I always was good at lying with a straight face.

"Why is it picking us off one at a time?" said Penny. "Why not just . . . wipe us all out?"

"Probably because it isn't nearly as powerful as it would like us to think," I said.

"That's the first reassuring thing you've said so far," said Penny.

✣ NINE ✣
MORE DEATHS, AND SOMETHING THAT ISN'T DEAD ENOUGH

I GLANCED THOUGHTFULLY AT PENNY as we made our way down the long curving stairs to join the others in the drawing room. I thought she was taking things rather well, all things considered. In all my time on planet Earth, I'd only revealed my true nature to five people. And four of those hadn't gone at all well. So when we got to the foot of the stairs I stopped Penny and looked at her steadily.

"We can't tell the others about me," I said.

"Oh good," said Penny. "Because I wouldn't know where to start."

"But," I said. "We do have to tell them about the vampire."

"Let's think about that for a moment," said Penny. "It's all right to tell them our killer is a supernatural creature of the night, but not that you're a little green man from outer space? Why?"

"Because I don't want them getting distracted," I said.

"They're going to have a hard enough time believing there's a vampire in their midst, without adding me to the mix."

"I do get that," said Penny. "I'm still having problems accepting what you are, and I saw the evidence."

"The others have a right to know what's really threatening them," I said. "If only so we can work out how best to defend ourselves."

"I'm not arguing," said Penny. "It's just ... how are we going to explain the whole *vampire* thing to them?"

"With our mouths," I said.

"Ho ho ho," said Penny. "Alien humour."

"One of them already knows," I said. "So the one who objects most ..."

"Is almost certainly the vampire!" said Penny.

"See how easy this is?" I said.

Penny smiled widely. "I can hit you from here."

I looked at the closed door to the drawing room, halfway down the long hallway. Inside, people were arguing loudly and angrily and borderline hysterically. None of them seemed sure what to do for the best, but that didn't stop them arguing about it. So I stayed where I was and listened in.

"We should just get the hell out of here!" Sylvia said tearfully. "Leave the house and make a run for it. I don't like it here, and I want to go!"

"Then go," Melanie said coldly. "No one's stopping you."

"I don't want to go on my own," said Sylvia. "I'm scared of the storm. Of getting lost. Won't anybody come with me?"

"It's not safe, Sylvia," said Khan, clearly struggling to sound sympathetic. "We all understand how scary this situation is, but the storm is far more dangerous. Leaving the house now would be suicide."

"Melanie?" said Sylvia.

"Don't be silly," Melanie said immediately. "I can't leave Walter. And he wouldn't last ten minutes, out in the cold."

"Nobody would," said Jeeves. "I took a look out the front door a few minutes ago, and the storm's cold enough to kill any of us, long before we could reach safety or shelter."

"I still say we should all barricade ourselves in our rooms!" said Melanie. She was trying hard for self-control, but only hanging on by her fingernails. "Why won't anyone listen to me? It's the only way to stay safe until help arrives!"

"Help is on its way," said Jeeves. "My people are coming, but there's no way they can get here before morning. At the earliest."

"Locking himself in his room didn't work out too well for Roger," said Leilah. "Did it?"

"We should all stay together," said Khan. "Stay in one place, watch each other's backs. Safety in numbers. Ishmael was right. He may be irritating, and overbearing, but he was right. If we'd listened to him, Roger might still be alive."

"Ishmael, darling," said Penny. "Please tell me what you're doing, because you haven't moved a muscle in quite a while, your face is entirely empty, and I am starting to freak out big time."

"Sorry," I said. "I was listening to the others talking in the drawing room." I gave her the gist of what I'd just overheard.

Penny looked down the hall to the drawing room. "You can hear everything they're saying? All the way down there? Through a closed door?"

"Yes," I said. "It's a gift."

I threw open the door to the drawing room, and everyone immediately froze where they were and fell silent. They relaxed, just a little, when they saw it was only me, and Penny, but they only had to look at our faces to know something had happened. And that whatever it was, they really weren't going to like it.

I looked at Jeeves. "You should have locked the door."

"I did," he said. "But then I had to unlock it, because people insisted on coming and going, so . . ."

"Not a good idea," I said.

"I will not be held prisoner in my own house!" Melanie said loudly.

"Would you rather be dead?" I said.

"Well, really . . ." said Melanie.

"What's happened?" said Leilah, looking at me narrowly.

"Diana is dead," I said, as kindly as I could. "Murdered, in her room."

"No!" said Sylvia. She had both hands at her mouth again. "She was sleeping, so I locked the door behind me when I left. And then, after Roger, I came down here . . . How could I have left her up there, on her own? What was I thinking?"

Penny shot me a meaningful glance. I'd already had the same thought. Could Sylvia's mind have been affected by the vampire? To make her abandon her friend, and then forget about her? Like we all had, outside Roger's room?

Sylvia turned to Khan, looking for him to comfort her, as he had before. Only to find he wasn't ready to do that, this time. He just stood there and looked at her. Not actually suspicious, but not ready to trust her, either. Sylvia turned away, crushed by his rejection, and hugged herself tightly, as though to stop herself falling apart.

"You're the only one here we don't know, Sylvia," Khan said slowly. "Diana brought you here. We knew nothing about you before this weekend."

"You bastard!" said Sylvia, rounding on him. "You're the one with motives for murder! James is dead, and Roger is dead, and you had arguments with both of them! We all saw you! We all heard you! What did you have against Diana? Did she get in the way, when you were trying to pressure Walter?"

Melanie glared coldly at Sylvia. "I never wanted you here. Never wanted Diana here. Conniving little bitch. If you'd both stayed away... I only let Diana come because Walter insisted. He thought we could all be good friends together... He's always been too sentimental for his own good."

"Where is Walter?" I said.

Everyone stopped and looked around the room, only now waking up to the fact that Walter wasn't there with them.

"No..." said Penny. "Please, Ishmael, no, not Daddy..."

"He popped out, just a minute ago," said Khan. "Didn't he?"

"He went back to our room," said Melanie. "To take his pills. He hasn't been gone long..."

"Hasn't he?" said Khan.

"How long?" Penny said fiercely. "How long has Daddy been gone?"

They all just looked at each other, not knowing what to say, surprised they hadn't noticed Walter was gone and confused they hadn't noticed before.

"It's been some time now," said Khan. "Hasn't it?"

"He promised me he'd only be a minute," said Melanie, looking around her for reassurance and not finding any. "He didn't even take his walking stick."

She gestured at it, still leaning against the wall. There was something very significant, and very sad, about the abandoned wooden stick.

"The client," said Jeeves. "We have to check on the client, Leilah."

But I was already out the door.

Only to come crashing to a halt, as I realized I wasn't sure which room belonged to Walter and Melanie. I sniffed at the air, ready to follow my nose.

Penny was quickly at my side, staring at me anxiously. "Are you smelling blood again, Ishmael?"

"Yes," I said. "And a lot more than before."

"Does this mean Daddy's dead?" Penny said steadily.

I was ready to say yes, but I held it back. As long as there was a chance... "Let's find out," I said. "Which is your parents' room?"

By now Jeeves and Leilah had caught up with us. They both had guns in their hands again.

"Everyone please stay put in the drawing room, while Leilah and I investigate," he said firmly.

"Yeah, right," said Penny.

"Where are they?" I said.

She gestured at her parents' door, and immediately we were both off and moving again. Jeeves and Leilah hurried after us, Leilah growling and swearing under her breath. I could hear the others bringing up the rear. They wanted to know what was happening, and none of them wanted to be left behind. And then Melanie went right past me. Running to the room she shared with her husband.

She called out loudly: "Walter! Walter! Are you all right? Answer me, Walter!"

"Please, Mrs. Belcourt!" said Jeeves immediately. "We don't want to alert anyone we're coming!"

She ignored him, calling out her husband's name again and again, until she came to the door to her room and stopped abruptly, because it was open. Just like Roger's. Melanie stood very still, staring into the darkness before her. She started shaking and whimpering. Jeeves and Leilah quickly took her by the arms and moved her gently but firmly to one side. Melanie was stiff as a board, staring into the dark with the wide eyes of a frightened child. I'd let Jeeves and Leilah get ahead of me, just so they could do that. Partly because I'm not good at comforting hysterical people, and partly because I wanted them all out of the way, so I could be first through the door.

But in the end I hesitated, because Penny was with me. I could have asked her to stay back, but I didn't see the point. I knew what she would have said. Jeeves glared at me as I stood before the open door, staring into the darkness beyond.

"I should go in first!" said Jeeves.

And I nodded, in agreement. This close, I didn't need to enter the room to know what had happened. The thick coppery smell of spilled blood was heavy on the air. Jeeves and Leilah handed an unresisting Melanie on to Khan and moved forward, holding their guns out before them. They each took one side of the open door, peered into the gloom, and scowled at each other when they couldn't make anything out. Inside, there was only an ominous quiet. I stepped forward, reached round the door and turned the light on.

And there was Walter Belcourt, pinned to the far wall of his bedroom with one of his own family weapons. A bear-hunting spear had been rammed right through his chest, leaving him hanging high up on the wall. Like some ancient butterfly on display. He hung limply, like a rag doll. His face was entirely colourless, drained of blood. No effort had been made to hide the true cause of death, this time. The savage teeth marks stood out clearly, against the torn and ragged flesh. Blood had spilled all down the front of him and was still dripping slowly from his dangling feet. The vampire had made a real mess of him. A feeding frenzy? Or just a sign that the killer didn't care any more? That it wanted us to know what it was...?

I stood very still, looking around the empty room. There was a gap on one wall, an empty plaque that had once held the boar spear. The killer had come here, done its work, and left, and no one noticed.

Jeeves and Leilah moved quickly round the room, looking at everything...and finally lowered their guns as they realized they weren't going to find anything useful. Jeeves leaned in close to study the bite mark on Walter's neck. He looked simply...disbelieving. Leilah looked sullenly angry, as though their client had let them down by going off and getting himself killed.

And then Melanie came forward, to stand before her dead husband. We were all so taken up with what had happened, no one had given a thought to her. She took in what had been done to her husband and cried out, once. A loud, horrified, almost animal sound of grief and loss. She sank to her knees before the impaled figure on the wall, put out a shaking hand to the dangling feet, and then pulled it back again as blood dripped past her fingertips. She shook her head in silent denial, her shoulders rising and falling as she sobbed.

And part of me wondered: *Is she overdoing this?*

Penny moved slowly forward, to stand beside her mother, staring up at what had been done to her father. Her face was pale, but controlled. "Oh, Daddy..." she said.

She looked back at me, as though she didn't know what to say. I put out a hand to her, and she grabbed it with both of hers, squeezing it tightly. Like someone drowning, hanging on to the only lifeline.

Penny shook her head, looking at her father. "Daddy and I never did get on, but...he had been trying harder, just recently. I should have tried harder too, but...I wasn't pleased at the thought of James coming home again. I was jealous of him, you see. For getting Daddy's attention so easily. Even though James was the one who left and I was the one who stayed. Or, at least, I came home at regular intervals. Now, I'll never know whether Daddy and I might have worked it out. Oh, do keep the noise down, Mummy! All that weeping and wailing isn't helping anyone! I'm sure you'll find another meal ticket, soon enough."

Melanie broke off from her weeping. She lurched to her feet and glared viciously at Penny. "You don't care. You never cared about him! Unnatural child!"

"Maybe if I'd had more natural parents," said Penny.

Melanie wasn't listening to her any more. She'd already gone back to staring pitifully at the body pinned to the wall.

Jeeves and Leilah exchanged a look, took Melanie by the arms again, and led her kindly but firmly out of the room. She didn't want to go, and tried to fight them, but Jeeves and Leilah were professionals. They had a job to do and weren't about to let anyone get in the way. Even the client's widow. Jeeves spoke sharply to Khan and Sylvia, put Melanie in their care, chased them out of the room, and shut the door firmly on their faces.

As the door closed, I could hear Sylvia saying, very shrilly, "I've got to get out of here! I've got to get out of this house!"

I looked at Penny. "We have to work the room. Gather what evidence we can. The vampire must know you and I know. It's not bothering to hide its tracks any longer."

"Give me a moment, Ishmael, please," said Penny. "I can't do the detective thing. Not just now."

I gave her hands one last reassuring squeeze and moved away to join Jeeves and Leilah.

"Thought it best to close off the crime scene," said Jeeves. His gaze was steady enough, but his voice was just a bit shaky. "There's got to be hard evidence here, somewhere."

"We're beyond clues, now," I said. "I know why Walter was killed. And how."

Leilah looked at me sharply. "You do? You know why somebody stuck a bloody big spear through him?"

"That wasn't what killed him," I said.

They both looked at the bite mark in Walter's neck, even though it was something they clearly didn't want to do.

"Of course it wasn't the spear," said Jeeves. "The blood only came from the neck wound. Nothing from where the spear went in. And there's blood splatter on the wall, right there, at neck height, from where he was standing when he was attacked. The killer pinned him to the wall after he was dead. How much strength would it take, to lift a man that high and then drive the spear home?"

"What the hell happened in here?" said Leilah.

"We need to get everyone back into the drawing room," I said. "I don't think it's safe for any of us to be out of sight of the others for long."

"Hear that," said Jeeves.

Back in the drawing room, Melanie sat slumped in an armchair, staring blankly ahead of her, lost in her own grief. At least she'd stopped crying. Penny started to go stand with her, and then changed her mind. She stood alone, Khan stood alone, Sylvia stood alone. No one wanted to be too close to anyone else. Jeeves and Leilah closed and locked the drawing room door and put their backs against it. And then, everyone looked at me. Because it was clear to everyone that I knew something.

I took my time looking round the drawing room, making sure everyone was there. I even counted them up twice, just in case the vampire was messing with my thoughts. "All right," I said. "Who left this room, after Walter did?"

There was a lot of people clearing their throats, and then

not saying anything. It was obvious none of them were sure. They all looked confused and didn't know why.

"I suppose," Khan said slowly, "we were all arguing so much that no one noticed. I think most of us stepped out, at least for a moment, at one time or another. For various reasons..."

"I left the room, for a while," said Jeeves. "I went down the hall to open the front door and check on the weather. See if it had let up any. But I told Leilah I was going to do that. And I was only gone a minute or two."

"That's right," Leilah said immediately. "I can confirm that."

"The storm was just as bad," said Jeeves. "So I came straight back. Leilah was in charge here, all the time I was gone." I looked at Leilah, who shrugged, uncomfortably.

"I let Sylvia leave, to use the toilet."

"I wasn't long!" said Sylvia. "I had to go!"

I looked at Melanie, but she was still too upset to respond. I looked at Khan, and he shrugged helplessly.

"I don't know, Ishmael. I didn't go anywhere, and I don't remember anyone else going anywhere. I know people came and went, but I wasn't paying any attention. Which is odd. You would think, under the current circumstances, that I would be watching everyone like a hawk. Why didn't I notice Walter was missing for so long?"

"There is a reason for that," I said. Everyone looked at me then. Even Melanie. "The killer has been messing with our heads," I said. "Interfering with our thoughts. There is no easy way to say this, so I'll give it to you straight. The killer is a vampire."

I braced myself for loud arguments and angry disagreements, even a blunt refusal to believe, but in the end they all just looked at me. As though I'd made a stupid and very inappropriate joke. They'd all been through too many shocks and losses and emotional upheavals. And then Jeeves nodded, slowly.

"I saw the bite marks on Walter's throat. Human-sized."

"You mean . . . our killer is one of those head-cases who gets a kick out of drinking blood?" said Leilah, scowling hard as she considered the idea.

"No," I said. "Unfortunately, this is the real thing. A vampire. Blood-drinker. Undead."

"Oh, come on!" said Leilah. "There's no such thing as the real thing! There is no such thing as a vampire! It's just a fairy tale, a horror movie . . . What are you trying to pull here?"

"All right, that's it!" said Jeeves. "No more theories, and no more discussion. Leilah and I are the professionals here, so we are taking charge of the situation."

"Damn right!" said Leilah. "No more deaths on our watch. And no more superstitious bullshit!"

"I don't know," said Khan. And just like that, everyone was looking at him. Because there was something in his voice. He realized all eyes were on him, and he shrugged uncomfortably. "Weird shit does happen. Strange things do exist. I know that because I have encountered them before. I used to work for Black Heir."

Jeeves and Leilah reacted to that name immediately and looked at Khan with something very like respect.

"We worked a case with two Black Heir field agents, once," said Jeeves. "A Muti black magic case, in the East End of London. They were . . . scary types."

"Very professional," said Leilah.

"What's Black Heir?" said Penny.

"You know all those secret departments that don't officially exist?" said Khan. "Well, even they don't have high enough security clearances to know about Black Heir. It is an organization specially tasked to deal with . . . weird shit."

"Are we talking X-files?" said Penny.

"Very definitely not," Khan said firmly.

"So . . . you've had experience with vampires?" said Sylvia.

"Of course not!" said Khan. "Never met one in my life. Don't know anyone who has. And I haven't worked for Black Heir since the eighties. With Ishmael's father."

Melanie had been sitting slumped in her chair, only vaguely following what was happening, but suddenly she was sitting bolt upright, to stab an accusing finger at me.

"You! It's you! You're the vampire! Has to be you . . . Because you're an outsider! No one here knows you. What kind of a name is Ishmael Jones, anyway? Has to be fake . . . And besides, you're different. I can tell. Everyone can tell!" She glared around the room. "You must have noticed! The things he says, the way he acts . . ."

"This is no time to be vindictive, Mummy," said Penny.

"You like him, don't you?" said Melanie, smiling unpleasantly. "Unnatural child . . ."

"Mrs. Belcourt does have a point," said Jeeves, looking at me steadily. "Too many unusual things have happened around you, Ishmael. I don't think we can trust you any more."

"Do you trust anyone here?" I said.

"No," said Jeeves. "But you stand out more than most. I'm not taking any more chances. I think the safest thing to do is to lock you up somewhere. Until my people arrive in the morning. Somewhere safe, and secure."

"No," I said. "That's not going to happen."

Jeeves and Leilah both turned their guns on me. Leilah was nodding quickly. "Has to be done, Ishmael. You're the one trying to distract us, with all this nonsense about vampires. And saying you could smell blood . . . That's not suspicious, at all."

"I'm the only one here who can save you from the vampire," I said.

"Yes, well, you would say that, wouldn't you?" said Jeeves. "I think Leilah and I are perfectly capable of dealing with this. We are, after all, professionals. Now, be a good boy and do as you're told, Ishmael. Or I'll have Leilah shoot you somewhere painful."

"Love to," said Leilah. "Never did trust you, Ishmael."

"You've got a bloody nerve!" Penny said loudly. "Where were both of you, when four people died? Including the one who hired you to protect him? My father trusted you . . . and what have you done to find his killer? At least Ishmael's been doing something! I trust him more than I trust either of you!"

"No surprise there," said Leilah, not taking her eyes or her gun off me. "You've been sniffing round Ishmael ever since he turned up. And with your stepbrother and your father dead, you're the only one left to inherit all this . . . If something was to happen to your mother . . ."

"Unnatural child . . ." said Melanie, slumped back in her chair again.

"I swear, if you say that one more time, Mummy, I will slap you a good one," Penny said coldly. "And it will hurt."

"I think we'd better lock you up with Ishmael, Miss Belcourt," said Jeeves. "Just as a security measure. If we're all still alive come the morning, there will be plenty of time for apologies then."

"Lock me up and you won't live to see the morning," I said.

"Shoot him," said Melanie. "Shoot him! He murdered my Walter . . ."

I stepped forward, to say something reasonable, and Jeeves shot me twice. Except I wasn't there. By the time the bullets slammed into the wall I was already somewhere else, heading rapidly for Jeeves and Leilah, ducking and dodging bullets as I closed in. They both fired with professional speed and accuracy, but I was faster. My eyes work better than most people. I can see bullets travelling through the air. It's all a matter of concentration.

I grabbed the guns out of Jeeves and Leilah's hands, careful not to break their fingers in the process, and then stepped back and covered both of them with their own guns. James and Leilah looked at each other incredulously, then at me, and decided to stand very still.

I glanced quickly round the room. Khan and Sylvia were staring at me open-mouthed. Penny was grinning broadly. Melanie wasn't looking at anything. I smiled at Jeeves and Leilah, and then stepped forward and gave them their guns back, again.

"Really," I said reproachfully. "How many times do we have to do this dance? If I wanted you dead, you'd be dead."

"I never saw anyone move that fast in my life," said Leilah.

"What are you, Ishmael?" said Jeeves.

"Busy," I said.

"All right . . ." said Leilah. She hefted the gun in her hand uncertainly, as though I might have somehow substituted a fake, and then looked at me squarely. "Maybe you aren't the killer. But we still have to work the evidence logically. The killer made a real mess of Mister Belcourt, so they should have blood all over them. No one here has had time to change their clothes. But I don't see blood on anyone . . ."

Everyone in the room looked at everyone else, took in the complete lack of blood and actually started to relax a little.

"The killer can't be one of us!" said Sylvia. "The lack of bloodstains proves it!"

"Unfortunately not," I said. "Things are a little more complicated than that. I'm pretty sure the vampire has the ability to mess with our minds, make us see what it wants us to see. To hide its true look behind a glamour, a pleasing illusion. The killer could be standing right here, in this room, soaked in the blood of its victims, and we still wouldn't know it. Because the vampire wouldn't let us know it."

"Oh, that's just marvellous!" said Sylvia. "First you tell us the killer is a creature of the night, and now we can't trust our eyes, either?"

"I'm not buying any of this," growled Leilah.

"I'm not sure I do either," said Jeeves, frowning deeply. "But something weird is going on here. Hiding behind a pleasant illusion . . . You mean, like hypnosis?"

"Something like that," I said. "I think that's how the vampire takes down its victims so easily. It hypnotizes them, overpowers their mind temporarily, holds then in place unresisting, and then attacks them. That's how it was able to take down a seasoned old fighter like the Colonel. He literally never saw it coming. That's why the vampire only attacks one victim at a time, so there's no distraction to break the trance."

"So there are some limits to this thing's power," said Jeeves. "That's something . . ."

Leilah looked at him. "You're buying this . . . ?"

"I'm . . . going along, for now," said Jeeves.

I looked around the room, studying everyone, taking my time. Jeeves and Leilah were standing close together, still guarding the locked door. Still holding their guns, though they didn't seem too sure where to point them. Penny was right there at my side, looking hopefully at me for an answer. Or at least some idea of what to do next. Melanie was leaning forward in her chair, staring sullenly at me, and Penny. Sylvia stood alone, hugging herself tightly, lost and scared and confused by what was happening. Khan stood off to one side, studying one face after another, trying to spy out the real face beneath the mask, through sheer concentration.

"Someone in this room has to be the killer," I said. "Can't be Penny, because she was upstairs with me while Walter was being killed down here. Can't be Jeeves or Leilah because they've been working as a team, and what evidence there is suggests a single killer."

"What evidence?" said Leilah.

"The single set of bite marks on each neck," I said.

"They could be killing separately," Penny said eagerly. "Providing alibis for each other!"

"That would mean two vampires operating under one roof," I said. "How likely is that?"

"How likely is one vampire?" said Penny.

"True," I said.

"Wait just a minute," said Leilah. "Following your logic... you say Penny was upstairs with you all the time, but how can you be sure? How can you be sure she didn't just hypnotize you into believing she was there, while she nipped down the stairs and killed her father? And then hurried back, before you came out of your trance?"

"You are a deeply cynical and suspicious woman," said Penny.

"Just doing my job," said Leilah.

"I don't think it works like that," I said. "It's clear the vampire can overpower human minds, but only when we don't notice. Most of its strength must go into maintaining its cover illusion, keeping us from seeing it for what it really is. Any further mind control must be a real effort, or I'd never have been allowed to work out this much. It kept you all from noticing Walter's absence, but only until I pointed it out. And once the spell was broken it couldn't keep you from noticing any longer. It can't stop us from discussing its existence, not now I've got you all thinking about it. It's probably reaching its limits just hiding from us, now we're looking for it."

"You keep using the word *probably*!" said Jeeves. "I need a hell of a lot more than *probably*, if I'm going to try and take down a vampire!"

"What's it going to take, to bring down a vampire?" said Leilah. "I'm guessing bullets won't do it."

"Silver bullets?" said Sylvia.

"That's werewolves," said Khan. "With vampires, you must drive a wooden stake through their heart." He smiled briefly. "I used to love Christopher Lee, in all those old Hammer horror movies."

"I don't think we can trust what they say in the movies," I said.

"Wooden stakes feature in all the old stories and legends," Khan said firmly.

"What else would work?" said Leilah. "Fire?"

"I'm not an expert in this field," I said. "If you've got Van Helsing's home number, feel free to call him. I'm working this out as I go along."

"Maybe we should start sharpening some wooden stakes?" said Khan.

"You go right ahead," said Leilah. "I wouldn't know where to start. How do you sharpen a wooden stake?"

"No one here has an alibi for the Colonel's murder," I said loudly, to draw everyone's attention back to me. "Or for Roger's, because we can't be sure of when they were killed. And Diana could have been killed before or after Roger. And we can't be sure who was and wasn't in this room when Walter was killed. So, we have to face the fact that we can't rule people out through alibis. That just leaves deductive logic. I wish the Colonel was here; he was always so much better at this than me. But he did do his best to teach me the basics. And I do notice things, even if it takes me a while to realize." I turned slowly, to face Sylvia. "Why did you scream, when you looked through the open door into Roger's room?"

"Because I saw what had been done to him!" said Sylvia. "You saw the state he was in!"

"But how could you see that?" I said. "The room was in complete darkness. I couldn't see anything; none of us could, until I turned on the light. It was an obvious question that didn't occur to me till later. Perhaps you were interfering with my thoughts, or perhaps I was just being slow. After all: a pretty woman, screaming at a gruesome sight? We're conditioned to accept such a scene, from seeing it in so many movies."

"Look," said Sylvia, very reasonably, "if I did kill Roger, why would I leave the door open, and scream, and draw everyone's attention to the murder?"

"To distract us," I said. "While we were all concentrating on the awful thing that had been done to Roger's body, we weren't thinking about how else he might have been killed. And, we weren't thinking about Diana not being there with us. Almost certainly already dead. And finding the body did help to clear suspicion away from you. Poor shocked little thing that you were."

Everyone was looking at Sylvia now, with growing suspicion and horror. Khan backed away from her. From the look on his face, he was remembering holding Sylvia in his arms and comforting her . . . Melanie rose shaking from her chair and moved unsteadily back to hide behind Khan. Penny glared at Sylvia, her hands clenched into white-knuckled fists. Jeeves and Leilah turned their guns on Sylvia, who stood very still.

She gave them her best appealing look. "You don't believe any of this nonsense, do you? You're professionals! I mean, vampires? Really? In this day and age?"

"I let you leave this room to go to the toilet, unaccompanied," said Leilah. "Why can't I remember how long you were gone?"

I walked slowly forward, to stand before Sylvia. And then I sniffed, hard. "My, what strong perfume you're wearing," I said. "Strong enough to hide your true scent from most people. But I'm not most people. Now I know what you're doing, you can't get inside my head any longer. My thoughts are my own, and I can smell blood and decay. Go on, Sylvia, show us. Show us all what you really are."

She smiled at me, and her grin seemed to grow wider and wider and wider.

She dropped her glamour, and just like that we could all see what she really looked like. The others all cried out, in shock and horror and disgust, at the sight of what had been moving unknown among them for so long. Sylvia was just a rotting corpse, with bright shining eyes and huge teeth, dressed in the old-fashioned formal clothes she'd been buried in: spotted with grave mould, and soaked in old and new blood. I fell back despite myself, and Jeeves and Leilah immediately opened fire on Sylvia.

She just stood there, smiling her horrible smile, as her undead flesh soaked up the bullets. She didn't even shudder under the impact. Jeeves and Leilah only stopped shooting when they ran out of bullets. It had been an instinctual thing, like stamping on a spider. Leilah was making shocked, almost feral noises. Jeeves' face was twisted with disgust. And when their guns fell silent, they just stood where they were, unable to deal with something so far outside their experience. Sylvia's smile widened even further, the rotting flesh of her cheeks split apart to reveal even more teeth. She laughed, softly, and there was nothing human in the sound.

"Why are you here?" I said loudly, and her attention immediately switched to me. Looking into her brightly burning eyes was like being hit by a malign spotlight. I met her gaze unflinchingly.

When she finally spoke, in her true form, with her true voice, what issued from the torn and decaying lips was just a liquid, gargling rasp. Something I heard with my mind, or my soul, as much as my ears.

"It's what I do, Ishmael. I go from place to place, striking up friendships with powerful and influential people, using my glamour and charm to get invited to isolated gatherings just like this. So I can feed and move on. Usually just a nip here and there, from everyone present, and they never even notice. Though afterwards they are just that little bit more... susceptible. So if I ever need a favour, or a get out of jail free card..."

"Why don't they become vampires?" said Penny. "Why don't all your victims rise again, to become like you?"

She was trying to sound reasonable and inquiring, but couldn't quite bring it off. The tremor in her voice showed how scared she was. We were all scared. It was the only sane reaction to the horrific thing in front of us.

"Because that's not how it works," said Sylvia. "It takes a lot of effort on our part, to make another of our kind. And I've never really seen the point. Who needs more competition?"

"What are you doing here?" I said. "Why here, and now?"

"Your Colonel thought he recognized me for what I am, at some dreary Ambassadorial reception," said Sylvia. "Don't ask me how he knew. He was only human, after all. Not like you, Ishmael. So I struck up a friendship with his mother, poor lonely old Diana, just so she would invite me here. To the Colonel's family home. I let him know, through certain channels. I thought I could ensure his silence by threatening his family. But he wouldn't play. Came all the way down here to stop me and protect his loved ones. So I killed him. No one defies me and gets away with it."

"And then you were trapped here, by the storm," I said. "And you had no choice but to stay and play along, pretending to be human. You didn't know the Colonel had sent for help."

"But if James was the only one who knew about you, if he was the only real danger to you," said Penny, "why did you kill all the others?"

"You know how it is," said Sylvia. "You get a taste for something, and you just can't stop. You have no idea what it's like, to be undead. There's more to blood than just the feeding. Blood . . . is better than drugs. Better than sex. And there's no conscience to trouble you any more, nothing to hold you back from doing absolutely anything you want. From being a red-mouthed wolf in a world of sheep. I love it . . ."

"That's not why you started killing again, after the Colonel," I said.

"I never leave witnesses," said Sylvia. "The world likes to believe things like me don't exist any longer. Except in safe, romantic fantasies. It makes things so much easier for me."

"Oh my God," said Jeeves. "That thing's going to kill us all. It has to, to prevent anyone from telling what happened here."

"Hold it together!" Leilah said harshly. "There's just one of it! We can still stop it!"

"How?" said Jeeves.

"You hold it down; I'll hammer the stake through its heart!" said Leilah.

Jeeves almost smiled. "Sounds like a plan. Where's your stake?"

"I'm working on it," said Leilah.

Sylvia ignored them, her bright hellish gaze fixed on me. Her hands opened and closed slowly at her sides, pale as death, caked in dried blood, ending in long filthy claws.

"I didn't know the Colonel had sent for another monster. I can tell you're not really human, Ishmael. I can see things most people never even dream of... and I've never seen anything like you, Ishmael. What are you really?"

"Not from around here," I said.

"Why do you side with them?" said Sylvia. She sounded honestly curious. "You're no more like them than I am. They'd kill you in a moment, if they only knew..."

"You prey on them," I said. "I protect them. It's what I do. I still have my... humanity."

"Ishmael?" said Jeeves. "What is she talking about?" Sylvia and I ignored him.

"It doesn't matter what you are," said Sylvia. "You'll die just as easily as the others."

I could feel her reaching out to me with her mind, trying to trap my thoughts inside my head. Hold me in place, as she had with her other victims. But they were human, while I was just a little bit more than that. I could feel her influence, drifting across my mind like cobwebs. I blew them away with no effort at all.

Sylvia snarled, and threw herself at me, moving impossibly quickly. Just a blur on the air, all bared teeth and reaching hands. I went to meet her, moving just as fast. We slammed together in the middle of the room, with an impact that would have killed anything human. We grabbed on to each other, and lurched back and forth, smashing any furniture that got in our way. Everyone else scattered, crying out. I dodged the claws that would have opened me up like scalpels and the fanged mouth that snapped shut near my neck like a steel mantrap.

She was stronger, but I was faster.

Sylvia suddenly broke away from me and sprang up on to the wall, clinging there like some impossibly large insect. She scuttled up the wall and on to the ceiling, hanging upside down. And then she dropped back on to the floor, in front of Jeeves and Leilah. They'd had time to reload their guns, and both of them opened up again. The sound was deafening in the enclosed space. Sylvia surged forward, into the blaze of bullets, and took no harm at all. It was like shooting into water. Her clawed hands reached out for them.

I grabbed her from behind and hauled her away. She spun round in my arms, grabbed my head with both hands, and jerked it round hard, to break my neck. But my head turned all the way round, and my neck didn't break. I'm built better than that. I'm flexible. I grabbed her wrists with both hands and almost cried out with revulsion. It felt like plunging my hands into a mess of maggots. Her undead flesh seemed to squirm inside my clasp. She broke my grip easily and backed away, hissing angrily.

Khan advanced on Sylvia, holding out two silver candlesticks, crossed to form a crucifix. Sylvia laughed at them, entirely unaffected. I hit her in the side of the head with my fist, putting all my strength into it. I felt her rotten flesh spatter under the impact, heard the bone in her skull crack and break, but her head didn't move an inch, soaking up the impact. If I'd hit her any harder I'd have broken my hand.

While Sylvia was distracted by all this, Leilah grabbed up Walter's discarded walking stick, from where he'd left it leaning against the wall. She broke it in two with a single savage blow, to give herself an improvised sharp stake, and then she lunged forward, aiming her stake at Sylvia's chest. And Sylvia grabbed Melanie by the arm and hauled the poor shrieking woman in front of her. Leilah's stake slammed into Melanie's chest and punched right through, protruding from Melanie's back.

She died without making a sound. Sylvia let her go, and Melanie dropped bonelessly to the floor. Leilah cried out in shock and horror.

And while everyone was distracted by that, Sylvia ran across the room impossibly quickly, hauled the locked door open, and ran out into the corridor, laughing happily. By the time I got to the door and looked out after her, Sylvia had already reached the far end. She pulled open the front door and ran out into the cold and the night. Still laughing.

Back in the drawing room, Jeeves was comforting Leilah, who looked like she wanted to cry but didn't know how. Penny was kneeling beside her dead mother looking much the same.

Khan stared at me, his eyes wide with shock and disbelief. "It's you!" he said loudly. "You're him! Not your father. You're the man I worked beside, all those years ago . . . except, you haven't aged a day. I still remember watching you fight that Baba Yaga clone in Moscow, back in eighty-eight. I never saw anyone who could fight like you . . ."

"Save the reunion for later," I said.

"But aren't you going to explain?"

"No," I said. "Not now. Sylvia's gone outside. We have to find and destroy her."

"She won't leave the grounds," said Penny. She rose unsteadily to her feet. I went to offer her my hand, and then pulled it back as she looked at me. She was trying hard to hang on to her self-control. To concentrate on what mattered. She took a deep breath. "If Sylvia could have left, in this storm, she would have right after she killed James. So she can't. The storm traps her here. She'll try to hide in one of the outbuildings. The tithe barn, or the cottages."

"If we go outside, she'll kill us," said Khan. "She'll have all the advantages out there."

"We have to go after her," I said. "Or she'll just sneak back in and pick us off one at a time. Or hide out in one of the buildings, till the storm drops off enough for her to escape."

"She kept saying she wanted to leave," said Jeeves, just a bit shakily, "if only someone would go with her . . ."

"Someone had a lucky escape there," I said. "If anyone had volunteered, she would have fed on them to keep her going. Used their strength to get her to the nearest village. We can't let her get away. We have to find her."

Leilah went over to stand before Penny. "I'm so sorry. I killed your mother."

"That's all right," said Penny. "We weren't close."

✦ TEN ✦
FIRE AND ICE

AND THEN THERE WERE FIVE.

Penny and Leilah stood over the dead body of Melanie Belcourt. The wooden stick still protruded from her chest, because no one felt like touching it yet. Melanie's face wore an expression of sullen regret, as though this was what she'd been expecting all along. Leilah looked shocked. Penny looked like she didn't know what she should be feeling. Alexander Khan stood well back from everyone, staring at me with awful fascination. Jeeves was still doing his best to seem professional. I walked over to him, and he looked at me sharply, the gun jerking briefly in his hand. As though he felt he should be pointing it at someone.

"Well," I said. "That could have gone better."

"You think?" said Jeeves.

"She's out there," I said. "Sylvia. Waiting for us to go and search for her."

"And you think that's a good idea?" said Jeeves.

"Better than waiting for her to come back and pick us off one at a time," I said. "She wants us to barricade ourselves in here and feel safe. She can survive the cold long enough for that. And then she'll break in, supernaturally quietly, and move unheard through the house . . . Unless we take the fight to her."

Jeeves nodded slowly. "We have to take back the advantage. Get the element of surprise on our side. But can we really kill a thing like that?"

"Guns won't do it," I said. "But there are other things we can try."

"We can't all go," said Jeeves. "Too many people stumbling around out there would just make it easy for her. She could pick us off one by one, ambushing us from out of the fog and the snow. And besides, not all of us are up to it."

"Right," I said. "I think you and I should go take a look outside, while Leilah stands guard over the others."

"I heard that!" Leilah said immediately. "You don't give me orders!"

"No, he doesn't," said Jeeves. "I do. Ishmael's going outside because he knows the most about that . . . creature. And I'm going, because that's my job."

"It's my job too!" said Leilah. "How come you get to go out and play the hero, while I have to stay behind and look after the children? I have a right to go after Sylvia! She tricked me into killing Melanie!"

"I know," said Jeeves, not unkindly. "And that's why you can't go, Leilah. Look at you, girl. Still shaking, still upset. Sylvia would take advantage of that. Tracking her down is going to take a cool head and cold professionalism. Revenge would only get in the way. Ishmael and I will kill this vampire in extremely cold blood."

Leilah came forward, to stand before her husband. "You've never had to do that before."

"Neither have you," said Jeeves. "I will spare you that, if I can. So, guard the guests while we're gone. Don't take any nonsense from them. And avenge me if I don't come back."

"Come back," said Leilah.

While they were talking, Penny gave me a hard look, so I went over to stand with her. She'd turned away from her mother's body, so she wouldn't have to look at it. She met my gaze steadily. "Why can't I go with you? I thought we made a pretty good team."

"We do," I said. "As detectives. But this is killing business, now. You have no experience in that area, and trust me, you're better off without it."

"So what am I supposed to do? Just…stand around, wringing my hands, till you come back? Or until it's clear you won't be coming back? I need to do something, Ishmael!"

"Leilah can't guard this room on her own," I said quietly. "If Jeeves and I can't find Sylvia, if she slips past us, she will come back here. She wants everyone dead. For revenge, for defying her…and to ensure there are no witnesses. So, you work with Leilah and Khan to make this room safe, so Jeeves and I don't have to worry about you while we're gone. Can you do that?"

"Of course I can," said Penny. "If you don't come back… I will avenge you, Ishmael. I will hammer a stake through that bitch's rotten heart and spit in her eyes as she dies."

"Of course you will," I said. "Wouldn't expect anything less."

"And afterwards?" said Penny. "If there is an afterwards? What about you and me? Could you use a new partner?"

"I usually work alone," I said. "It's safer that way. For me and for everyone else. I walk the dark side of the road, Penny. I live alone because I hurt fewer people that way."

"That's no way to live," said Penny.

She took me in her arms, and we held each other for a long moment.

In the end I let go of her and pushed her gently away. "There will be time to talk of many things afterwards," I said. "But right now I have a job to do."

"Kill the bitch," said Penny. "And afterwards, I'll show you what living is all about."

"Well," I said. "It's always good to have something to look forward to."

I turned away, to talk with Jeeves, but Khan intercepted me. He stood in my way and looked me over carefully, as though searching for signs he should have spotted before. And then he smiled briefly, uncertainly.

"Look at you," he said. "When we first met we were both the same age. Now I've grown older, and you haven't aged a day. All those years working together, for Black Heir, and I never even suspected that you're . . . What are you, Ishmael? Really? Your name was Daniel when I knew you, thirty years ago, but I don't feel right calling you that now. Daniel wasn't real, but then, I suppose Ishmael isn't either. What are you?"

"In a hurry, Alex," I said. "I have work to do."

"I could come with you," said Khan. "I had the same training you did, at Black Heir."

"You were a paper-shuffler," I said, as kindly as I could. "The one time you worked with me in the field, in Moscow, you hated it. Couldn't wait to get home. I need you here, helping barricade this room and make it safe. Sylvia may be a supernatural creature, but she still has physical limitations. You can keep her out, if you work at it."

"And afterwards?" said Khan. "What's to stop me telling everyone about you?"

"Who would you tell?" I said. "Daniel disappeared from Black Heir, and Ishmael will disappear from Belcourt Manor. And if you start talking wildly about vampires and aliens . . . They'll put you away."

Khan nodded reluctantly. "Who do you work for now, Ishmael? Who did James work for?"

"The Organization," I said. "And now you know as much as I do."

I went back to join Jeeves, who was standing in the open doorway, looking out into the hall. It all seemed quiet enough. Behind me I could hear Penny and Leilah and Khan quietly planning their defence of the drawing room. I looked at Jeeves. "Are you ready?"

"Not really. You?"

"Ready as I'll ever be."

"Then let's get started," said Jeeves. "Before we both have a rush of common sense to the head and think better of it. Leilah!"

She looked round immediately. "Yes? What do you want?"

"Give us an hour, tops," he said, calmly enough. "If we're not back by then, we won't be coming back. Then it will be up to you to decide what to do next. But remember, Leilah: our job is to protect people. Not take revenge."

"The client is dead," said Leilah.

"His daughter isn't," said Jeeves.

"Understood," said Leilah. She looked round at the rest of us. "He's my man. Isn't he wonderful?"

She hugged Jeeves goodbye, kissed him hard, and then pushed him away and went back to the others.

Jeeves looked at me. "She's very warm-hearted."

"I could tell," I said.

And then, together, we went out the door and into the still, quiet hallway.

There was already a distinct chill in the hall as the storm blew snow and wisps of fog through the open front door. I could hear the wind rise and fall, and beyond the open door I could see night had fallen. Blue-white moonlight reflected in from the fallen snow. I looked carefully up and down the hall. All the doors were shut, and nothing moved in the shadows. It was cold inside the house now. Cold as death, cold as the tomb. Cold as a vampire's heart. I couldn't hear anything moving, and I couldn't smell blood or decay anywhere.

"She could have just hauled the front door open, to make us think she'd gone outside," Jeeves said slowly. "And then... sneaked back down the hall, to hide in the house again. In the hope some of us would go outside and split up the group. She'd probably think it a fine joke, to have the two of us stumbling around in the cold and the snow, while she attacked the others."

"She's not in the house," I said. "I can see her footprints in the snow outside. She couldn't have come back in without tracking some of that snow with her. She may be a supernatural thing, but she still leaves traces of her passing in this world, just like us."

Jeeves looked at me. "I thought for a moment you were about to say you couldn't smell her anywhere in the house."

"I'm not that good," I said.

"But you can see footprints in the snow, outside the door at the far end of the hall," said Jeeves. "I couldn't make that out if I had a telescope." He studied me thoughtfully. "Sylvia... the vampire... said you were no more human than she was."

"She's wrong," I said. "I'm a lot more human than she is. Just in case you need me to say it: I am not a vampire."

"Never thought you were," said Jeeves, just a bit too quickly. "But you are quite definitely weird. Did you really work with Alexander Khan back in the eighties?"

"When this is all over," I said, "I'll explain."

"I'm so glad you said *when* and not *if*," said Jeeves. "I'll take all the encouragement I can get."

We both moved cautiously down the long empty hallway and stopped before the open front door. Back in the drawing room, I could hear the others moving heavy furniture about, building a barricade. Jeeves and I looked out into the world beyond. Snow was falling hard, but the wind had dropped away to just the odd gust, here and there. A pearly fog curled slowly on the air, swallowing up the distant view. It was all deathly still and deadly quiet. Just standing there in the open door, exposed to the night and the storm, made Jeeves shiver violently.

I didn't.

"Given that Sylvia is undead," I said, "I think we have to assume the cold won't affect her as much as it does us. So she can survive out here without the need for protective clothing."

"Seems likely," said Jeeves. "The way she looked . . . I swear to God I never saw anything like that in my life . . . Her flesh had rotted right down to the bone, in places! And those eyes, and the teeth . . . Things like that just shouldn't be possible, in any sane and rational world!"

"Mostly, they aren't," I said. "But it's a bigger world than most people ever have to realize. There's room in it for lots of extreme things, good and bad."

"She could be hiding anywhere," Jeeves said unhappily. "In the fog, in the snow. Lying in wait, to attack us as we pass."

"Seems likely," I said.

We stared out into the night. Stark vivid moonlight blazed back at us from the snow-covered grounds. Smooth white dunes everywhere, rising and falling, unmarked and undisturbed. Large snowy objects before us that used to be our parked cars. I couldn't even tell which was mine any more. They sort of reminded me of igloos, which made me wonder whether Sylvia might be hiding inside one of the cars. Safe and unsuspected, and insulated from the cold. But no, there was no way she could have smoothed the snow back again, once she was inside. She was a vampire, not a magician.

I did meet a magician, once. He sawed his wife in half. The police never did find him.

I looked around, taking my time. The tithe barn loomed out of the mists on one side of the manor house, and the terraced row of cottages showed dimly through the fog on the other side. Beyond them, I could just make out the snow-covered gardens, with their trees and hedges and topiary structures. So many dim dark shapes, in the glowing grey mists.

"She could be anywhere, out here!" said Jeeves. "Where do we even start?"

"She's a predator," I said. "They do like to lie in wait. But the longer we put this off, the more chances she has to set her plans against us."

There was a long pause.

"Are you as reluctant to go out there as I am?" said Jeeves. "I mean, once we leave the house, we're committed. No turning back. We hunt the vampire till we find it, and then either we kill it, or it kills us."

"I am extremely reluctant," I said. "But experience has taught me it's nearly always best to hold your nose and jump right in. Because the water isn't going to get any warmer."

"You know what really scares me?" said Jeeves, meeting my gaze with almost brutal honesty. "If she decided not to kill me. If she decided to bite me and make me into a creature like her. A thing of . . . endless appetites and no emotions. Not caring about anyone or anything, ever again. I wouldn't want to go on living if I couldn't care any more. If I didn't care about my Leilah."

"Don't worry," I said. "I'll make sure you're properly dead."

"I was going to say: don't let Sylvia get anywhere near me!" said Jeeves. "Dear God, you have a morbid state of mind, Ishmael!"

"Comes with the job," I said. "And the territory."

We shared a brief smile.

"I'll do the same for you, if I have to," said Jeeves.

"Good to know," I said. "Remember, the way to a vampire's heart is straight under the sternum, and then lean in hard." I looked out at the snow and the fog. "We're going to have to check all the outbuildings, and then make sure she can't conceal herself in any of them."

"How are we going to do that?"

"Set fire to them," I said. "Burn them all, right down to the ground. Preferably with Sylvia inside. But at the very least, we have to drive her out into the open, where we can get at her."

I realized Jeeves was looking at me, apparently genuinely shocked. It took him a moment to get the words out.

"*Are you crazy?* These are all listed buildings! Historical treasures, part of our country's architectural heritage! Each and every one of them is worth a small fortune in their own right!"

"*Antiques Roadshow* can bill me," I said.

"You really aren't human," said Jeeves.

"We both need to bundle up warm before we go out," I said. "There's suitable clothing in the cupboard to your left. I plan to wrap a thick scarf around my neck several times."

"You really think that'll stop a bite?" said Jeeves.

"No. But it should keep the cold out."

"Do we have a plan?"

"Of course. You start the fires, and I'll keep watch."

"So I can take the blame for all the arson," said Jeeves.

"Because you're not planning on being here when my people finally turn up, are you?"

"Like the Organization I work for," I said, "I don't officially exist."

Jeeves sighed, loudly. "This job started out so well. Really good money, just to play bodyguard at a country house weekend. A chance for Leilah to show off her culinary skills. Easy money . . . We should have known better."

I closed the front door to keep out the cold. And so I could be sure the vampire wouldn't sneak back in and ambush us while we were getting changed. I showed Jeeves the walk-in cupboard, and we piled on as many layers of heavy clothing as we could manage, while still being able to move freely. I remembered doing this before with Penny. Remembered walking with her through the snow-covered grounds, with no idea of what kind of day lay ahead of us. I remembered finding the Colonel's body inside a snowman and knowing my world would never be the same again.

When Jeeves and I finished dressing, we both stood back to look each other over. With a scarf pulled up over his mouth and nose, and a woolly hat pulled down hard over his shaven head to just above his eyebrows, all I could see of Jeeves was his eyes. But I was pretty sure he wasn't smiling.

We went back to the front door, and I hauled it open. Both of us were braced and ready, just in case Sylvia was lying in wait on the other side. It's what I would have done. Instead there was just the fog and the snow, and the shimmering moonlight. The air was barely moving, hardly disturbing the heavy mists.

"Easy to hide in," said Jeeves.

"For us, as well as her," I said.

"Unless her undead senses work better than ours."

"I doubt they're better than mine," I said. "I should be able to tell if she's anywhere near us . . . Any sound will travel well on this quiet, and with her glamour gone, she stinks of the grave."

"You sure you'll be able to sense her?"

"I'm going out there, aren't I?"

Jeeves sighed, heavily. "You know the real problem, here? I never once suspected Sylvia might be the killer. I liked Sylvia."

"Everyone did," I said. "I think that's the point of having a glamour."

Jeeves nodded and called back down the hall to Leilah.

She immediately stuck her head out of the doorway. "Yes?" she said loudly. "What do you want? I'm busy! Heavy defensive barricades don't build themselves, you know!"

"I'm going to lock the front door behind us, Leilah," said Jeeves. "So when we come back, we'll need you to let us in. I'll knock like this, so you can be sure it's me." He knocked three times quickly on the door, followed by two slow and hard. "Don't leave me out in the cold, girl."

"I'll be listening," said Leilah. "Dear God, look at the state of you. Are you sure you've got enough clothes on? Don't forget your knock, or I swear I'll leave you out there."

"She would, too," Jeeves said proudly.

"And you say I'm weird," I said.

"You are!" Leilah said loudly.

Once outside, with the front door locked firmly behind us, Jeeves and I stood close together, peering about us. The moonlight reflected back from the snow almost as bright as day, but it was hard to see far in any direction. The fog was getting thicker. I could just make out the tithe barn beside the main house, a great dark looming presence. Any footsteps Sylvia might have left in the snow had already disappeared, covered over by new snow.

Jeeves was already shivering and shuddering from the extreme cold, for all his heavy coats. He glared at me when he realized I wasn't shivering at all.

"It's so desolate out here," he said. "Like being on the surface of the moon. A dead world, harbouring an undead creature. I can't believe I'm really doing this . . ."

"Believe it," I said. "Doubts will get you killed."

"In the old stories, faith was a genuine defence against vampires," Jeeves said slowly. "I never got around to making my mind up about that sort of thing."

"You saw Khan try and stop Sylvia with silver candlesticks for a crucifix," I said. "She just laughed. Have faith in your experience and your abilities, Jeeves. They're far more likely to keep you alive."

"But doesn't all this make you think?" said Jeeves. "She's a vampire; this is Christmas Eve . . . It has to mean something! Doesn't it?"

"I don't know," I said. "I told you, I'm not from around here. I don't know what to believe."

"But if a vampire really does exist," said Jeeves, "you have to ask yourself: what else could be real?"

"I wouldn't," I said. "You'll sleep better at night. Can we please discuss the philosophical implications later, when this is all over and we're back in the warm? I do feel the cold, you know."

"Can you smell anything?" said Jeeves.

"Nothing useful," I said. "Let's start with the nearest building."

"That would be the tithe barn."

"So it would."

We trudged forward through the heavy snow. The great grey shape of the barn loomed out of the mists before us, seeming somehow more solid and more real, the closer we got. The whole world was still and quiet, as though holding its breath to see what would happen next. The only sound was the crunch of our boots as they sank deep into the piled-up snow. The air was cold enough to sear my lungs as I breathed it in. It must have been even worse for Jeeves, because he was making quiet sounds of distress with every breath he took, without even realizing it.

"I don't see any footsteps," he said as we approached the great opening in the barn's front wall.

"Wouldn't expect to," I said. "The snow's had more than enough time to cover them over. If you want something else to worry about... Maybe Sylvia can fly, for short distances. You remember how she clung to the drawing room ceiling..."

"You're right," said Jeeves. "That is something new to worry about, and I would just like to point out that I was a lot happier before you brought it up."

"It does seem unlikely," I said. "But it's best to consider all the possibilities."

"You are not helping my confidence at all," said Jeeves.

"I'm not doing much for my own," I admitted.

We stopped before the tithe barn, to look it over. Heavy stone walls with slit windows, under a slanting slate roof. Little had changed since I was last here with Penny. A lifetime ago. More snow had been blown in through the open doorway, forming a high ledge. No footprints, no gaps, nothing to show Sylvia had entered the barn. Unless she went skittering up the wall... I kicked my way through the snow drift and strode inside, trying to look everywhere at once while still appearing calm and purposeful. Jeeves was quickly there at my side, his gun steady in his gloved hand.

"You do know," I said quietly, "that bullets won't stop her."

"Might slow her down some," said Jeeves. "If I take out her kneecaps. Or her eyes. And it makes me feel better."

"That, right there," I said, "is why I prefer not to use guns. They give you an entirely false sense of security."

"Really not helping . . ." said Jeeves.

"Would you rather I lied to you?"

"Yes!"

"And people say I'm weird."

I spotted an old storm lantern, sitting on the ridged stone floor next to the wall. I picked it up and shook it carefully. Oil splashed heavily in the bottom. I was fumbling in my pocket for something to light it with, when Jeeves hit the wall switch, and bright electric light flooded the barn from end to end.

He looked at me pityingly. "We are in the twenty-first century, you know."

The barn was empty, apart from the hulking shapes of old farm machinery under their heavy tarpaulins. I looked carefully around and behind each of them, even lifting up each tarpaulin in turn for a peek underneath. There was no sign of Sylvia anywhere. Jeeves walked from one end of the barn to the other and back again, just in case. We both took our time, making sure we missed nothing. I could see beads of sweat forming on Jeeves' dark face, despite the cold. The gun in his hand was still entirely steady.

When we'd convinced ourselves the barn was empty, we went back to the open doorway. I looked at Jeeves steadily, and he nodded, reluctantly. I smashed the oil lamp against the wall, spilled oil in a wide circle across the floor, and finally dumped what was left over the nearest tarpaulin. Jeeves produced a Zippo lighter, knelt down, and set light to the floor. Both of us hurried out the doorway as bright yellow flames shot up.

Jeeves and I moved hastily out into the thick falling snow. A great blast of superheated air shot out of the opening, only just falling short of us. Black smoke was already forcing its way out through the slit windows. The electric light inside the barn snapped off, and all that was left was dancing yellow flames.

"Stone walls," said Jeeves. "But wooden rafters in the roof, and old wooden farm machinery . . . The barn will go up fast enough and burn for some time. No place for Sylvia there." He looked at me. "Is it right: fire destroys vampires?"

"I don't see why not," I said. "She's just a walking corpse, and crematoriums deal with dead bodies perfectly well every day. Except . . ."

"I hate it when you pause like that," said Jeeves. "Except what?"

"Sylvia set Roger's body on fire," I said. "Which would suggest she isn't frightened by fire. It is possible that not being scared of something might actually be a weakness. Sylvia's too used to seeing herself as untouchable and unkillable. She might not have the same survival instincts as us."

"It's amazing," said Jeeves. "You keep talking and you keep coming up with things, and yet not one of them is ever remotely comforting."

"It's a gift," I said.

I led the way, past the manor house, past the cottages, and on into the gardens. I didn't think Sylvia would actually be there, but I wanted to look them over anyway, just in case. Sylvia struck me as the type who would do exactly what you wouldn't think she would do, just to catch you off guard. Jeeves didn't make any objections. He thought I knew everything about vampires, which just went to show how little he knew. Our feet sank deep into the snow with every step, making loud crunching noises, as though to warn Sylvia we were coming.

Across the snow-covered gardens we went, through rows

of trees and past the topiary figures, which I found even more disturbing than before, with even more snow to obscure their original shapes. There were no details left to show what they had been. I checked each one carefully, even batting at the branches with the back of my hand to make some snow fall away and reveal the interior.

"Do you honestly think Sylvia would hide inside one of those things?" said Jeeves.

"She hid the Colonel inside a snowman," I said.

I checked between and behind every topiary shape, taking my time, refusing to be hurried. I really didn't want Sylvia jumping out at me. I could sense a growing tension in Jeeves' increasingly abrupt movements. I wondered if he thought I was putting off checking the cottages for Sylvia, and I wondered that too. I finally stopped, at one particular place, and looked at the ground.

Jeeves moved in beside me. "Is that where you found the snowman?" he said quietly.

"Yes," I said. "That's where I found the Colonel. When I first smelled blood and didn't know what it meant."

"I suppose the world still made sense to you, back then," said Jeeves.

"No," I said. "I can't say this world has ever made sense to me."

"Do you ever wonder . . . If you hadn't found James' body, would Sylvia have just bided her time here till the storm was over and then left?" said Jeeves. "And then maybe no one else would have died?"

"No," I said. "I never think things like that. Hindsight never helped anyone. You can only ever deal with what's in front of you. Sylvia killed before she came here, and she would have killed again, afterwards. She's a predator. That's what she does. Stopping her is all that matters." I looked around me. The pale world looked back, pristine and gleaming, cold as death.

Jeeves was shivering hard now. "I think we've seen all there is to see here," he said. "Let's go check the cottages."

"Yes," I said. "Let's do that. Maybe we can set a fire to warm ourselves up."

We made our way back to the row of Victorian cottages, driving ourselves on through the hard-packed snow. I think we both felt more vulnerable, more at risk, out in the open. Where Sylvia could be anywhere. And we both wanted to find the vampire and get this over and done with. Find and stake the rotten thing, and put it behind us, so we could have our lives back again. We stopped before the old head gardener's house, GravelStone Cottage, and looked it over carefully. No lights showed at any of the windows, and the front door was firmly closed. A pleasant scene, in a winter view.

But would an undead creature need light, or heat? Or anything other than a dark place to hide?

Jeeves strode up to the front door and tried the handle. The door didn't budge. "Locked," said Jeeves. "Knew I should have brought my skeleton keys."

I gestured for him to stand aside, and then charged the heavy wooden door. I hit it square with my shoulder and blasted the door right off its hinges without even slowing. The door slammed down on to the floor, and I strode right over it, slowing to a halt in the dark and gloomy hall. Jeeves hurried in after me, waving his gun around in a more or less professional way.

"All right," he said, once he was sure we were alone. "That was . . . really something. I am officially impressed. Doesn't doing that hurt your shoulder?"

"Yes," I said.

We pressed slowly forward, into the gloom of the hallway. Jeeves found the light switch eventually, and the sudden glare was almost blinding. The narrow hall was disconcertingly cheerful and cosy, with pleasant old-fashioned wallpaper, charming furnishings, and a bare wooden floor. A perfect getaway home from home, to soothe the spirits of the troubled guest. Not the kind of place you'd expect to find a monster. But then, that was the point.

We searched all the downstairs rooms and found nothing. No sign anyone had been inside GravelStone Cottage in months. We went upstairs. Jeeves wanted to go first, because he had the gun, but I took the lead anyway, because I knew for a fact I was a lot harder to kill. I kept sniffing the air, but I couldn't smell blood or decay. Just dust and damp.

We searched all the upper rooms, kicking in doors and checking every nook and cranny with malice aforethought. I even opened all the cupboards and overturned the beds, just in case there might be a monster hiding under them. By the time we'd checked all the rooms and gone back out on to the landing again, we were both so tense from unrelieved anticipation that we were exhausted. All my muscles ached, from not being allowed to relax.

"There's no one home," Jeeves said heavily. "Let's get out of here."

"After you," I said.

I let him lead the way back down the noisy wooden stairs, mostly so he wouldn't see me scowling as I struggled to think things through. I couldn't help feeling I was missing something.

Learn to think like the prey, the Colonel always said, *so you can out-think them.* But the prey I went after was usually alive, in some form or another. My cases usually tended more to the super-scientific than the supernatural. I knew such stuff existed; you couldn't operate in my world and not know. But the Colonel had other agents for that. So why had he called for me, specifically, to come and help him? If he suspected Sylvia was a vampire, why not call on a more suitable agent? Could it be that he didn't trust them like he trusted me? I would have liked to think so.

I felt a little easier once we were back in the entrance hall with the open door in front of us. All the way down the stairs, I'd had the horrible suspicion that when we got to the bottom we'd find Sylvia there, waiting for us. Smiling her awful smile. But she wasn't. Jeeves and I hauled furniture out of the living rooms and into the hall, and piled it up. Then we took turns dousing it with bottles of wine we'd found, until the whole hall stank of alcohol. Jeeves and I slipped out the front door, while I left a careful trail of booze behind us, and then Jeeves got to do the business with his Zippo again. The furniture went up in a moment, and a great blast of heat shot out the open doorway. If we hadn't been so thoroughly wrapped up, the intense heat might well have taken our eyebrows off. The entire frontage of GravelStone Cottage was soon wildly ablaze. Jeeves took his gloves off and happily warmed his bare hands against the fierce heat. He pulled down his scarf, so he could grin at me.

"First time I've felt warm since we left the Manor! Look at the place go . . . And you're not even sweating!"

"I don't," I said. "Mostly."

We turned our attention to the long row of terraced cottages. Stretching away for as far as we could see, with the furthest end disappearing into the fog. Everywhere we looked, the doors all stood properly shut, with not a light showing anywhere. Sylvia could have been hiding behind any of the darkened windows, watching and waiting, and we would never have known.

"It's going to take far too long to search each cottage individually," I said. "And it'll give Sylvia far too many chances to launch an ambush. I say . . . we don't go inside at all. Just light them up. You set fire at the far end, I'll take this one; we'll let the fires spread from cottage to cottage till they meet in the middle."

"And then?" said Jeeves.

"And then we wait for the fires to drive Sylvia out, knock her down, stake her . . . and then cut her head off, just to be sure."

"You really think it's going to be that easy?" said Jeeves.

"Well, no," I said. "I was just trying to sound positive."

"You haven't even got a wooden stake!"

"I will acquire one, before the need arises," I said.

"You really don't inspire confidence, you know that?" said Jeeves. He looked down the long row of cottages. "You think it's a good idea for us to split up and go off on our own?"

"I don't see that we have a choice," I said. "If we both start at the same end, she could just make a run for it. So . . . stay in sight as much as you can, and don't let yourself get distracted. Set the fire, and get the hell back here. Call me if you even think you see anything."

"Same to you," said Jeeves.

We nodded briefly to each other. There wasn't anything else to say. Jeeves went stomping off into the snow, while I looked over my end of the cottages. I did look after him once, but Jeeves had already disappeared into the grey walls of fog and falling snow.

It didn't take me long to set fire to my end of the terrace. Kick in the first door, pile up the furniture, soak them with anything incendiary that came to hand, and then light it up. I stopped to sniff the air, now and again, but there was never any trace of blood or decay. Never a sound of anything moving, or even a feeling I wasn't alone. That bothered me. Sylvia had to be here, somewhere. There was nowhere else she could be hiding. I used my own lighter to set the fires. I don't smoke, never have, but a lighter is still a useful thing to have about you. Never know when a sudden inferno will come in useful.

My end cottage went up quickly, and the flames jumped swiftly on to the next. The whole terrace was really just one big fire trap. The first two cottages burned quickly, filling the cold night air with blasting heat and thick black smoke. But when I looked down to the far end of the cottages, there was no sign of Jeeves and no trace of any fire. Something had gone wrong.

I ran past the middle cottages, slamming through the snow, and the far houses slowly appeared out of the mists. No fire, no broken-in doors, not even a shattered window. And no sign of Jeeves, anywhere. I considered calling out to him, and then thought better of it. I sniffed hard at the air, but all I could smell was smoke.

I heard a sound and looked up. And there they were, Jeeves chasing Sylvia across the slanting snow-covered roofs. She still looked like a rotting corpse, dressed in filthy old clothes as she danced lightly along the cottages, laughing easily. Jeeves had to struggle to keep up with her. He had his gun in his hand, but he hadn't fired it yet. I could hear his footsteps, slamming and sliding across treacherous snowy slates, but I couldn't hear Sylvia's. No wonder I couldn't smell her, all the way up there. I could hear her laughing, hear Jeeves cursing breathlessly. He stopped where he was, took careful aim, and opened fire, but if his bullets did hit Sylvia, they didn't even slow her down.

I don't know how they got up there. Whether Sylvia lured Jeeves from one floor to another, then up through an attic opening up on to the roof . . . Something like that, no doubt. And then one last chase, with her beckoning him on, just for the fun of it.

Jeeves went after her again. I called up to him, yelling for him to stop and come down so we could take her the way we'd planned. But either he couldn't hear me, or he didn't want to, caught up in the heat of the chase. He slipped and slid on the treacherous snowy roofs, but somehow still drove himself on, with sheer strength and stubbornness. He almost fell several times, but somehow saved himself at the last moment. Sylvia seemed to float along, supernaturally sure-footed, never losing her balance for a moment. And then she stopped abruptly and spun around, to face Jeeves. He couldn't stop so quickly, stumbling forward, and while he was distracted she launched herself at him. She flashed forward across the snowy roof, so fast she was just a blur, crossing the intervening distance in just a few seconds.

And there was nothing I could do to help him.

She slammed into Jeeves, driving him back several steps. She grabbed his shoulders with both hands, and Jeeves cried out at the horrid strength in her undead grasp. I heard his shoulder-bones break, one after the other. Jeeves struggled anyway, fighting back with everything he had, but he couldn't break free. He tried to bring up his gun, but there was no strength left in his arms.

Sylvia looked down at me, and I knew this had all been arranged for my benefit. A show, staged up on the roofs so I couldn't interfere. Jeeves had been right, after all; she'd just been waiting for us to separate, so she could catch one of us on our own. And have fun with them.

Her head snapped forward, and Jeeves cried out. A horrid despairing sound as her teeth sank deep into his neck. Blood spouted, steaming thickly on the cold air. More blood ran down his chest, soaking into his coat. Sylvia worried at his throat, like a dog with a fresh piece of meat, her sharp teeth tearing at the flesh. The noises she made as she fed weren't even animal; they were somehow more basic, more primordial, than that.

There was nothing I could do. No way I could get up there, before it would all be over.

Sylvia supported Jeeves' entire weight with her undead strength. His legs had gone limp, just dangling. She buried her face in the great wound she'd made in his throat, gulping down his blood. I could hear the awful sounds quite clearly. Jeeves slowly turned his face away, to look down at me. And then he opened his hand and let go of his gun. It clattered down the side of the roof, hit the guttering, and spun out into space, falling down and down through the air. I moved quickly forward and caught it.

Sylvia pulled her face away from Jeeves' neck. She glared down at me, her eyes unnaturally bright in her rotting face. Her mouth and teeth dripped gore. When she spoke, I could hear her as clearly as though she were standing right in front of me.

"See what I'm doing, Ishmael? I'm going to do this to all of them! One by one, until you're the only one left. You get to watch them suffer, and you get to suffer too, for the sin of inconveniencing me. So really this is all your fault, isn't it? And when I finally come for you . . . oh, the things I'll do to you! But for now, just watch . . ."

Jeeves' body was entirely limp, no strength left in it. He was only held up by the vampire's strength. But he was still looking down at me, and I knew why he'd dropped his gun: for me to catch. I raised the gun and took careful aim. Sylvia saw and laughed at me. And I shot Jeeves in the head, twice. I might not like weapons, but I knew how to use them.

It was all I could do for him. To stop his suffering, and to make sure Sylvia couldn't bring him back as one of her kind.

Sylvia screamed with rage as half of Jeeves' head was blown apart, right in front of her. She threw his body away from her, as though it was suddenly contaminated. Jeeves fell through the air, turning and tumbling, until he finally slammed into the snow-covered ground before me, with such force I heard his bones break. I knew he had to be dead, but I knelt down beside him and checked anyway. Because I had to be sure. He would have done the same for me.

When I looked up again, Sylvia was gone from the roofs. Nothing up there but the swirling snow. I'd cheated her out of one small revenge, at least.

The cottages were burning nicely. The fires would reach the far end soon enough. There was nowhere left for Sylvia to hide, now. Only one place left she could go. Back to Belcourt Manor.

Back to the bait I'd left there, waiting for her.

✦ ELEVEN ✦
BLOOD SACRIFICE

THE WIND WAS GATHERING its strength, blowing out of the coldest hell there was. The snow battered against my face as I headed back towards Belcourt Manor, stinging my narrowed eyes. I had to destroy the vampire while it was still trapped here. If I didn't, Sylvia would just kill everyone in the house, wait out the storm, and then walk away. To do it all again, somewhere else. I fought my way through the storm, refusing to let the cold slow me down or hold me back. A normal human probably couldn't have done it.

When I'd left the manor house with Jeeves, I'd known there was a good chance Sylvia might get away. That we wouldn't be able to stop her. That was why I insisted we set fire to the outbuildings. To drive Sylvia back to the one place of shelter left. Belcourt Manor. I could have taken the others with us, to hunt the vampire. Kept the group together. Safety in numbers, and all that. But I needed to be sure where Sylvia would go if she got away. I needed bait, for my trap.

Penny, and Leilah, and Alexander.

I needed to destroy the vampire. For what she did to the

Colonel. For all those she'd killed, and for all those she would go on to kill if she wasn't stopped. But I also needed to save the lives of those I'd left in the house. Because that was what a human being would do.

The Manor slowly appeared out of the swirling mists. As I drew nearer, I could see the front door was still firmly closed. That was something. I paused, a cautious distance away, to look the place over. There were no signs to show Sylvia had got there ahead of me. And then the lights went out.

The glimmers of light shining past the heavy wooden shutters over the drawing room windows just snapped off. And since no one in that room had any reason to do such a thing, it meant Sylvia must have already broken into the house and ripped out the fuses. Good tactic. It was what I would have done. She'd had more than enough time over the weekend to find out where everything was and plan ahead. Predators often prefer to hunt in the dark ...

I hurried forward, slamming through the piled-up snow, sending it flying to either side of me as I headed for the front door. I grabbed the door handle and rattled it hard, and found the door was still securely locked. How had Sylvia got inside? I stepped back and looked up, craning my head right back, and there it was ... a single top floor window open, its shutters pulled away and hanging loose. The same window where I'd thought I'd seen someone watching me when I arrived. Sylvia must have skittered up the outside wall ...

And now she was inside the house with the others.

I hammered on the front door with my fist, making the heavy wood shake and shudder in its frame, and only then remembered Jeeves' special knock. I hit the door three times quickly, two hard and short, and then I stood there breathing hard, planning what I would do when I got inside.

After a worryingly long pause, I heard the door being unlocked from the inside. It swung inwards, and there was Penny. She smiled quickly, her face full of relief on seeing me again, and then her smile fell away as she realized Jeeves wasn't with me.

I hurried forward, into the gloom of the unlit hall, and she fell back. Freezing air and quick bursts of snow followed me in. Penny slammed the door shut in the face of the storm and locked it again. I glared about me into the dark hall. "Have you seen Sylvia?" I said.

"No," said Penny. "I thought she was still outside! Oh bloody hell, the lights! That was her, wasn't it? We all thought it was just the storm."

"No," I said. "She's inside, somewhere."

Penny helped me struggle out of my many layers of coats. I dropped them to the floor and kicked them aside. The outer layers were covered with snow, the inner layers soaked with sweat. I was glad to be rid of them. I scraped layers of frost from my face with my numb fingers, and then headed quickly for the drawing room door. It stood slightly open, spilling warm yellow light into the hall.

"Leilah is lighting candles," said Penny, hurrying along beside me. "There's always lots of candles around. Daddy saw to that. Said it was an important part of the Christmas atmosphere. We used to rely on them a lot, back when I was a little girl and we hadn't quite got the hang of the generator yet . . . Sorry. I'm babbling. Ishmael . . . Where's Jeeves? What happened to Jeeves?"

"He didn't make it," I said.

"Sylvia killed him?"

"Yes," I said.

"Oh God . . . But he was a professional!"

"So am I," I said.

"Yes," said Penny, trying for a smile. "But a professional what?"

"That sounds about right," I said.

More light fell out of the drawing room. I took one last look around the empty hallway, pushed the door open, and went in, with Penny all but treading on my heels.

Just inside the door, half the room's furniture had been piled up to form a barricade. It was pushed to one side now, to let Penny out. I pushed it further back, with one hand, as I entered. It felt solid and heavy enough, but I had no doubt Sylvia could smash right through it without even slowing. I'd always known that. I only encouraged the others to build a barricade because it would give them something to do and help them feel safer.

I closed the door. Firelight and candlelight gave the drawing room an almost cosy atmosphere. Someone had built up the fire, piling the coal and wood high. It blazed fiercely in the massive stone fireplace. I went straight over to the fire and stood before it, letting the heat sink into my body. I hadn't realized just how cold I was, how much my time in the storm had slowed me down. Cold is insidious; it sneaks up on you. I turned around, letting the fire toast my backside, and looked round the room. Candlesticks and candelabras, big and small, stood on every surface. Warm, organic light to push back the shadows.

Leilah looked at me, and one look told her everything. She didn't need me to tell her why Jeeves wasn't with me. She seemed to fall in upon herself, looking suddenly old and tired . . . and then she slowly straightened up again, wearing her strength as armour, taking on her old authority again. Because that was the job, and that was all she had left, now. She met my gaze squarely. "Just . . . tell me he died well," she said.

"He died fighting," I said. "Defiant, to the end."

What else could I say to her? I couldn't tell her the truth. That would have been cruel.

I deliberately looked away. Someone had picked Melanie up off the floor and put her back in her chair. She sat slumped, her head tilted back so that she stared up at the ceiling. Presumably someone had tried to close her eyes, but it's often harder than you think to get them to stay shut. The wooden stick still protruded from her blood-soaked chest.

Khan stood off to one side, looking lost. As though he had no idea what to do. Probably a new experience for a man like Khan, who was used to being in charge and in control. He caught me watching him and saw something in my face. "It wasn't the storm put the lights out, was it?" he said. His eyes were wide and staring, like a deer caught in the headlights. "Is Sylvia back in the house with us?"

"Looks that way," I said.

"Why didn't you kill the bitch?" said Khan, his voice rising even more.

"We did try," I said. "Jeeves died trying."

"It's different for you," said Khan, defiantly. "You're trained for weird shit like this. All I did at Black Heir was push papers around, remember?"

I turned away from him. "Penny, where's the fuse box?"

"I don't know!" said Penny. "How would I know something like that?"

"It's your house!" said Khan. "How can you not know where your fuses are?"

"Because I'm just visiting!" Penny shot back at him. "This hasn't been my home for ages! Anyway, do you know where your fuses are?"

"Of course!" said Khan.

"Poor little rich girl," said Leilah, not looking round from lighting the last few candles, with a Zippo that was a match for her late husband's. "Knows everything except for the things that really matter. Your fuse box is down in the kitchen. Though I don't feel like going back down there at present..."

"Hush!" I said. "Listen..."

We all stood very still, not one of us moving a muscle. Hardly breathing as we listened, concentrating. Outside the drawing room, at the very end of the long hall, we could all hear someone slowly descending the long curving staircase. One step at a time, deliberately drawing it out. Every footstep seemed to last forever, the gap between each new sound tearing at our nerves. And then the footsteps stopped, at the bottom of the stairs. For a long time there was just a slow and steady silence. We all stood tense as statues, straining our ears against the quiet. The footsteps went back up the stairs again, one slow step at a time, all the way to the top. And stopped again.

I hadn't realized how intent I was until I made myself relax.

"She's here," I said. "She wants us to know she's here."

"Why?" said Penny. "It's not like she's scared of us! It doesn't make any sense!"

We stood close together, talking with lowered voices, as though Sylvia might be listening. And perhaps she was.

"Maybe she wants to be with her victims?" said Khan. "They're still upstairs."

Leilah sniffed dismissively. "She wants us to go up after her. Leave the one safe place we have to go upstairs. And be picked off, one by one. Yeah, right, like that's going to happen. I'm not going anywhere."

"She's taunting us," said Khan. "Playing games...because she can. We should push that barricade back into place. Stay here. Safety in numbers."

Leilah sniffed again. "You're just saying that because you're scared to be left on your own."

"Of course," said Khan. "Aren't you?"

"I just want my best shot at killing her!" said Leilah.

"We can't just stand around here, waiting for her to do something!" said Penny. "We have to come up with our own plan!"

"You're right," I said. "We can't let her take the advantage. We have to take the fight to her."

"In theory, yes," said Leilah. "In practice, how?"

"I don't know," I said. "I'm thinking."

Leilah looked hard at Khan. "You worked for Black Heir . . "

"I was an accountant!" said Khan. He glared at me. "You were the field agent, Ishmael! Do something!"

"I'll go after Sylvia," I said. "Barricade the door behind me."

"What?" said Penny. "No! You can't, Ishmael! You already tried once, with Jeeves. And she killed Jeeves!"

"I know," I said. "But someone's got to do it."

"Why does it always have to be you?" said Penny.

"Because I'm here," I said. "And because Jeeves isn't."

I looked at Leilah, and she looked back at me. I could tell she understood. That I felt responsible for not bringing Jeeves back alive. She nodded, quickly. She hadn't forgiven me for coming back alive instead of him. But she understood why I was ready to go out again, and that would do.

I picked up a single lit candle, in a bulky silver candlestick. "I can see better than most people," I said. "Even in reduced light. Sylvia doesn't know that. Should give me an edge."

"You don't have to go on your own," said Penny. "I'll go with you. Watch your back."

Her gaze was steady, her voice less so. But she meant it.

"No," I said.

"Why not?"

"Because I can't protect myself if I have to worry about protecting someone else," I said.

Penny bit her lower lip hard, and then nodded, reluctantly. And then she turned away so she wouldn't have to watch me leave.

I looked at Leilah. "Leave the door open a crack. Stand guard, keep a watch. If you see anyone coming down the hallway that doesn't look like me, shoot it. Jeeves had a good idea, though he never got the chance to try it out: aim for the knees and the eyes. That might be enough to slow her down. I'm going to need a wooden stake . . . Where's the other half of Walter's walking stick?"

Leilah nodded to a side table, where the short length of splintered wood had been laid out, ready for use. I picked it up and hefted it. Such a small and fragile thing, to set against a monster. But it wasn't as if I had anything else. I'd just have to hope this part of the legend was accurate. I went back to the door, holding the stake in one hand and the candlestick in the other. I eased the door open and peered cautiously out into the hall. Nothing moved. I took a deep breath, let it out slowly to settle myself, and went out into the hall.

I heard the barricade scraping back into place on the other side of the door. Light falling out into the hall slowly died away as they pushed the door almost closed. I looked into the crack they'd left open, and Leilah looked back at me. Her face and her gaze were utterly cold. I turned away and set off down the long dark hall, to the great curving staircase at the end. I held my candle out before me, moving cautiously forward in its pool of sane, normal, yellow light. There wasn't a breath of air moving in the hallway to disturb the candle flame.

Not a sound anywhere, apart from my footsteps. They

sounded a lot heavier, realer, than Sylvia's had. But I was worried they also sounded just a bit tentative. I didn't want Sylvia to think of me as weak, as prey. I sniffed the air. I could smell faint traces of blood and decay on the air, ghostly traces from a disturbed grave.

I stopped at the foot of the long sweeping staircase. I held the candle high, and its light showed almost half the stairs clearly enough. No sign of Sylvia anywhere, which left me no choice but to go up and look for her. I started up the stairs, maintaining a steady pace, in the hope that would make me sound confident. Like I had a plan, instead of just a broken walking stick in a sweaty hand. I had faced some scary things in my time, in my various hidden pasts, but never anything like this. As Jeeves said, it wasn't the thought of being killed that was so bad. It was the not staying dead. Of coming back as a walking corpse, with a never-ending need for blood and horror.

There were still faint traces of blood and decay hanging on the air ahead of me, from where Sylvia had walked up and down these steps before, taunting us. I clung to the thought that if I could smell her presence now, when I hadn't been able to before, that had to mean she wasn't influencing my mind.

When I finally got to the top of the stairs, I was breathing hard and my legs were trembling. I still held the candle steadily. I stepped out on to the landing, and Sylvia was immediately right there before me. No warning, no movement, just standing in front of me. Smiling her awful smile, her eyes shining horribly brightly in her rotting face. I almost jumped out of my skin. It had been a long time since anyone had been able to catch me by surprise. Sylvia hovered at the very edge of the candlelight. One step back and she would have been hidden in the dark. She wanted me to see her. So I just looked her over, quite calmly.

She smiled, her mouth stretching impossibly wide, her discoloured skin splitting apart, to show me even more teeth. Her lips still had Jeeves' blood smeared across them. But there were too many old bloodstains sunk into her ragged burial clothes for me to tell what was fresh. What was his. Up close, the vampire stank of slaughter and the grave.

"My, what bright eyes you have, Sylvia," I said. "Why couldn't I see them before, in the dark?"

"Because it is my nature to go unnoticed, until I want to be seen," said Sylvia. Her dead voice still had the power to make me squirm and shudder inside. "Unlike you, dear Ishmael, I am always in control of myself."

"You're nothing like me," I said. "If you were really in control, I wouldn't be able to see you at all."

"What are you, exactly?" said Sylvia. "I can't seem to . . . grasp you. You look human, but you aren't. You're different."

"You have no idea," I said.

"So what are you?"

I shrugged easily. "Not from around here."

"You're scared," said Sylvia. "I can smell the sweat on you. But you don't need to be scared, Ishmael, not yet. I promised you . . . I'll kill all the others first. I'm saving you for last. For dessert."

"Not going to happen," I said. "You have to get past me, to get to them."

"You think I can't?" Sylvia laughed softly, a slow, satisfied sound.

And then she lunged straight at me, just as she had at Jeeves. But I was prepared, and I leapt straight at her. I thrust the candle into her face, catching her by surprise. She paused a moment to slap the candlestick away. It hit the wall and fell to the floor, still somehow miraculously burning, giving me just enough light to see by. I punched Sylvia in the head with all my strength and felt, as much as heard, her skull crack and break and cave in. Sylvia rocked back on her feet, half her face collapsed in on itself. She struck out at me with a clawed hand, and I ducked under it. I could feel the disturbance in the air just above my head. I brought the wooden stick up, to drive it through her chest, but she sprang back immediately, out of my reach, almost disappearing out of the light and into the dark. She stood her ground, hissing at me like a cat. And I could hear the broken bones in her head creaking and rasping as they put themselves back together again.

Her stench was almost overpowering now, up close: the smell of blood and slaughter about to happen.

And then she turned and vaulted over the banisters, jumping all the way down to the hall below. I grabbed up the candle from where it had fallen out of its holder, sheltering the flame with my hand, and hurried over to the banister to look down. Sylvia was still falling, gentle as a leaf. She landed easily in the hallway, graceful as a cat. She didn't make a sound. Just looked up at me, and smiled, and moved silently down the hall. I shouldn't have been able to see her in the deep dark gloom, but she wanted me to.

I ran back to the top of the stairs. Sylvia was still drifting down the hall, silent as any ghost. She stopped before the drawing room door. It was almost closed, just a thin slice of light falling out into the hall. For whatever reason, Leilah wasn't there, watching. Sylvia considered the door carefully, and then knocked: three quick, and two hard and slow. She had been listening.

There was the sound of furniture being dragged back, and then the door swung inwards and Leilah looked out, expecting to see me. Sylvia lunged forward and slammed the door open with one hand, and I heard the barricade beyond the door collapse and fall backwards. Leilah stepped forward and shot Sylvia repeatedly in the face. It didn't even slow the vampire down. Sylvia grabbed Leilah's head with both hands and ripped it off. I cried out, but Sylvia didn't even look back. Leilah's body slumped slowly, to sit on the floor, blood pumping and jetting from the ragged neck stump. Sylvia held the head right up before her rotting face and smiled happily into Leilah's still rolling eyes. The mouth tried to say something, until Sylvia stopped it with a kiss.

The vampire threw the head aside, and it bounced and rolled away down the dark hall and out of sight. Sylvia leant over the headless body, thrust her face into the still-spurting stump, and drank greedily. And then she stood up, wiped at her dripping mouth with the back of one hand, and strode forward into the drawing room.

In the time it took for all this to happen, I jumped over the banisters and dropped heavily through the air. I braced myself as best I could. I seemed to hang on the air for ages, and then I slammed into the floor, hard enough to crack the wooden boards. The impact knocked the breath out of me for a moment, and I dropped my candle. The light had gone out anyway. But I still held on to my wooden stick. I ran down the hall and back into the drawing room.

And all the way, I could hear Sylvia laughing.

When I burst through the open door, Khan and Penny had retreated all the way across the room, to stand with their backs pressed against the far wall, facing Sylvia. Khan had smashed up a chair, with some last desperate strength, to make a wooden stake from one of the chair legs. Penny had one of the other legs, and she threw it at Sylvia with all her strength. The vampire slapped it easily aside.

"You killed my daddy, and my mummy, you bitch!" yelled Penny. "I'll find a way to kill you!"

"I never get tired of hearing that," said Sylvia. "Warms my

old heart . . . But better than you have tried, Penny my sweet, and I'm still here, and they aren't. Now, hush and hold still. It's feeding time. You don't want to leave an ugly corpse for whoever finds you, do you?"

"Get behind me, Penny," Khan said roughly.

"Oh, how lovely!" said Sylvia, clapping her dead hands together. "A last-minute hero! I love those . . ."

Penny tore her gaze away from the bloody-faced vampire to look at Khan. He was looking steadily at Sylvia, the wooden chair leg shaking just a bit in his hand. Penny fell back a step, to stand behind Khan. The trust she placed in Khan seemed to encourage him, and the chair leg was suddenly steady. Sylvia moved slowly forward, taking her time, savouring the moment. I stayed where I was, in the doorway, trying desperately to come up with some plan that wouldn't get the other two killed. I didn't dare move. If I did anything to let Sylvia know I was there, she might kill the other two immediately, just to spite me.

"Never thought to see you play the hero, Alex," said Sylvia. "Bit out of character for you, isn't it? The man who only ever cared for himself?"

"You make it easy," said Khan. It was clear he wanted to back away, but he wouldn't let himself show weakness in front of the vampire. "You're so corrupt, you make me look good. I have to be the hero, Sylvia, because I couldn't bear to be like you."

"Now that's not a very nice thing to say," said Sylvia. "Bad things happen to people who say bad things."

Khan's face was grey with fear, but he stood his ground and glared at her defiantly, still holding his wooden stake out before him.

"We talked," he said hoarsely. "You and me. We shared confidences. I thought I knew you . . ."

"You don't," said Sylvia. "No one does."

"So what's it like?" said Khan. "Being dead?"

Sylvia surprised me then, by stopping her advance to consider the question carefully. "Undead, dear," she said finally. "It's very . . . freeing. I love it! And any moment now, I'll love you. For as long as you last."

"Do you remember anything, of what your life was like before this?" Khan said desperately. "Don't you miss it?"

"It's always so sweet," said Sylvia, "when the prey wants to talk. To beg or bargain with me . . . To try and understand the horrible thing that's happening to them . . . To hold off the dreadful moment, with one last attempt at communication . . . To bridge the gap between us. Well, Alex dear, life was a nightmare from which I have woken up. Free, at last! No conscience, no mortality, no civilized chains to hold me down or hold me back. I can do whatever I want, now, and I do!"

"You kill people!" said Penny, from behind Khan. "That's all you do! You destroy lives!"

"That's what they're for," said Sylvia. "I feed and I kill, I butcher and I slaughter . . . and it's all such fun! I'll tell you what, Alex dear, give me the girl. Give me Penny . . . and I'll let you go."

Penny glanced anxiously at Khan, but give the man his due, he didn't flinch and he didn't hesitate.

"Never," he said.

"Ah, well," said Sylvia. "Worth a try. I do so love it when they turn on each other to please me."

She darted forward impossibly quickly and slapped the wooden chair leg out of Khan's hand with such force that it flew across the room and buried itself half its length in the wall. Sylvia jumped on Khan and sank her teeth into his neck, biting deep, worrying at the bloody flesh. Khan swayed on his feet, but didn't fall. Sylvia wouldn't let him. He made a sick, horrified sound, and tried to push her away from him, but already there was no strength left in his arms. He was dying, and he knew it. Blood coursed down the front of him as Sylvia worried at his neck with her sharp teeth. Penny beat at Sylvia's head and shoulders with her fists, trying to drive the vampire away, but Sylvia didn't even notice her.

Khan slowly raised one hand and dipped it into the blood running down his front. He put a fingertip to Sylvia's forehead and drew a cross there. Her head snapped back, and she glared at him with foully shining eyes. And then she broke his neck, with a sudden spiteful move. The sound of bones breaking was very loud on the quiet. Sylvia threw the dead body aside and grabbed Penny by the arm. Penny fought the vampire fiercely, but couldn't break free. Sylvia pulled her forward, so they were face to face, and Penny spat in Sylvia's eye.

The vampire spun Penny around, still holding on to her arm, and glared at me. I was still standing in the doorway; she'd known I was there all along. Everything had happened so quickly that I still hadn't worked out what I was going to do. Sylvia was so much faster than me, stronger than me . . .

The vampire hauled Penny forward, to stand her between the two of us. Penny cried out as dead fingers sank deep into her arm, and then she stopped abruptly as Sylvia put her face right beside hers, resting her rotting chin on Penny's shoulder. Fresh blood dripped off Sylvia's face, running down to stain the top of Penny's dress. She stood very still and looked at me imploringly. I gave her my best reassuring smile.

"Now, Ishmael," said Sylvia. "Throw away that nasty wooden stake."

I looked at the walking stick in my hand and let it drop to the floor. I kicked it away. It made a small, sad sound as it rolled across the floor.

"Now," said Sylvia, "come forward, dear Ishmael, and surrender yourself to me."

"Why would I do a thing like that?" I said.

"Because if you do, I'll let little Penny go."

"No, Ishmael!" Penny said immediately. "She'll kill you! And still kill me anyway! You know that... Get out of here, Ishmael. Just... leave."

"Hush, hush," I said. "There's nowhere to go, Penny. And anyway, I wouldn't leave you, even if I could."

"Oh dear," said Sylvia. "I hate it when they go all maudlin and sentimental."

"You really think I'd trust you?" I said. "To keep your word?"

The vampire laughed breathily. "You don't have a choice. Because, dear Ishmael, if you don't do exactly as I say... I will bite dear little Penny here, in a very special way. And make her like me. Forever and ever and ever. I could use a companion..."

She opened her mouth wide, blood still dripping from her teeth, and set the points daintily against Penny's neck. Penny shuddered violently despite herself and squeezed her eyes shut; she couldn't stop the tears rolling down her cheeks.

"All right!" I said. "All right... That's enough. Please, don't hurt her. Look. I'm coming forward."

I moved slowly towards them, across the drawing room, one step at a time, while Sylvia watched with bright, hungry eyes.

"Please, Ishmael, don't," Penny whispered. "She'll kill you. And I wouldn't want to live anyway, without you."

"Quiet, child," said Sylvia. "You won't care about any of that, soon."

"It's all right, Penny," I said. "I know what I'm doing."

Sylvia waited till the very last moment, and then threw

Penny to the floor. Hard enough to drive all the breath out of her, and keep her from interfering. Sylvia grabbed me by one arm and pulled me to her, those unnaturally bright eyes fixed on mine. And then her head snapped forward, and she sank her teeth into my neck. It hurt like hell, but I wouldn't let myself cry out. I made myself stand my ground, and not struggle, even as a horrid soul-deep revulsion ran through me. I clenched my hands into fists at my sides as she bit deeply into my throat, nuzzling the side of my face with her own. I could feel the strength draining out of me . . . Until Sylvia suddenly jerked her head back and threw me away from her. She staggered backwards, looking at me incredulously. She was shaking and shuddering as my blood dripped from her mouth.

My golden blood.

"You should have listened, Sylvia," I said. "I told you I wasn't from around here."

Sylvia screamed. Smoke issued from her mouth. My blood was no good for her. It poisoned her; ate her up, from the inside out. Her decaying flesh darkened and fell apart. Her hands dropped off her wrists, and great wounds opened up all over her body. She fell to the floor, screaming and screaming as she fell apart, until finally there was nothing left of her but a bloody sludge on the floor, already dissipating and disappearing.

I hurried over to Penny and helped her back up on to her feet again. We clung together for a long, long moment. I could feel my strength coming back, but for the moment I let her hold me up. She needed to do that, and I needed her. Eventually, we let go and looked each other over.

Penny put a hand to my neck. "The wound, it's almost gone! You still look a mess, though." She produced a handkerchief from somewhere and pressed it to the side of my neck.

"It's all right," she said. "It's a clean one."

We shared a smile.

"It's over," I said. "It's finally over . . ."

"So that was your plan," said Penny. "I never saw that one coming, and neither did she. Were you really sure it would work?"

"Of course," I lied.

"You did that for me. Risked your life, for me."

"Yes," I said. "I couldn't let her kill you."

"You wanted to kill her, for what she did to your Colonel," said Penny.

"But I killed her for you," I said. "It's all right. The Colonel would have understood."

Penny smiled. "I think . . . this could be the start of a wonderful romance."

"Yes," I said.

✤ TWELVE ✤
After the Party is Over Comes the Mopping Up

THE STORM BLEW itself out by morning.

By the times Jeeves' people arrived, well after breakfast, the wind had stopped blowing and the snow had stopped falling, and there wasn't a trace of fog anywhere on the crisp clear morning air. I heard the security people coming long before they arrived, stomping and trudging and cursing their way up the snow-packed drive because they couldn't get their transportation any further. So Penny and I were already there, sensibly dressed for the cold, waiting for them at the front door. A dozen men and women, in matching anonymous quasi-military outfits. A competent enough bunch. They didn't seem all that happy to see me and Penny, or to learn the emergency was over and everyone but us was dead, including the killer, and that Jeeves and Leilah were among the fallen.

The team leader didn't even want to tell us who they worked for. I was used to that. You meet a lot of people who don't officially exist, in my line of work. The team leader was all set to launch into serious interrogation mode, and I was getting ready to tell him where to stick it and provide a physical demonstration if necessary, when another figure came striding confidently up the drive to join us. The team leader took one look at him and immediately hurried off to be busy somewhere else.

The new arrival was a sharp-faced sort, in his mid-thirties, with a military moustache, wearing a smart tweed suit and rugged hiking boots, and I knew who he was immediately. Who he had to be. He took charge with calm efficiency, sending the security people into the house to start the cleanup. They brushed past Penny and me as though we weren't there, loudly conferring with each other as to how many body bags they'd need and whose job it would be to go back to the van for them.

The newcomer looked steadily at me and Penny. "Hello, Ishmael. And Miss Belcourt. I am the Colonel."

"Funny," I said. "You don't look like the Colonel."

"I am the new Colonel. The King is dead, long live the King, and all that. There is always a Colonel to represent the Organization."

"I suppose you'll do," I said.

The Colonel raised an eyebrow, briefly. "My predecessor wrote in his files that you were frequently insubordinate. Apparently, he admired that in you. I do not."

"Tough," I said.

I met his gaze, and the Colonel went into the house to take charge of the clean up. I let him. I didn't see any reason to get involved. By the end of the day, every disturbing piece of evidence would have been sanitized or destroyed, all the bodies would have disappeared, and a cover story would be set firmly in place. No one in the everyday world would ever have to know what really happened here.

"How will they explain all the deaths?" said Penny, after I'd run through the procedure for her.

"Food poisoning, probably," I said. "That's always a good one. The bodies will be cremated, all the proper doctor's certificates will be placed on file, and the local media will be encouraged to bury the story. Is that acceptable to you?"

"I suppose so," said Penny. "Though no matter how well they clean up, I'll never feel the same about this house again. For me, this will always be the place where too many people died. And there really was a monster hiding in the dark, just like I believed when I was a little girl."

"Let's go for a walk," I said. "Leave them to it."

It was still bruisingly cold, but nowhere near as bad as before. Just another winter's day, with a bright shining sun in a clear pale-blue sky. Snow-covered grounds stretched away before us, rising and falling like a frozen white sea. Penny and I strode along together, arm in arm.

"People can always surprise you," said Penny, after a while. "All these years, I only ever thought of Alex as Daddy's faintly creepy business partner. I don't think we ever said a pleasant word to each other. But when the time came, he stood up to Sylvia, to protect me. I think it genuinely never even occurred to him not to."

"We are what we do when it matters," I said. "And when it mattered, Alex was a good man. Brave and true."

"That makes it worse, somehow," said Penny. "I'll never be able to tell him how much that meant to me. Same with Daddy and Mummy. All the things I meant to say to them and never did, because I always thought there'd be more time. Until suddenly, there wasn't. And poor Roger, and poor old Diana..." She stopped and looked around her. "I suppose... this is all mine, now. The house, the grounds, everything. Except you seem to have burned down most of the everything."

She had a point. The terraced row of Victorian cottages were now just burnt-out ruins, parts of them still steaming and smouldering. Last night's raging winds had also picked up the flames and carried them out into the trees and hedges and topiary shapes, leaving them just black twisted shapes.

"How typical," said Penny, "that Belcourt Manor should end up in the hands of the one member of the family who really didn't want it."

"No one says you have to keep it," I said. "Sell it all, and be free of it at last."

"I'd like that," said Penny. "But then: where do I go? I can't go back to my old job, my old life. Not knowing what I know now, about how much bigger the world really is."

"I have been thinking about that," I said. "And it has occurred to me that just possibly I have been on my own for too long. I could use a partner."

"I was hoping you'd say that!" said Penny, smiling brightly. "I thought we worked well, together. But I have to ask, Ishmael, if aliens are real, and vampires are real . . . what else is real? What else is out there? Just how big is the world, really?"

"Come with me," I said. "And find out."

"Love to," said Penny.

We walked on, together.

"You really don't remember what you used to be, before you were human?" said Penny.

"I have . . . dreams, sometimes," I said carefully. "Flashes, images; none of it ever seems to make much sense."

"So . . . Have you ever wondered what you would do, if your people ever come back for you?" said Penny, looking earnestly into my face. "I mean, would you want to go back with them? Be . . . something else? You've been here for so long . . ."

"Penny," I said. "This is my world, now. I may not have been born human, but I have learned to be human. Everything I need is right here on this planet."

"Everything?" said Penny, snuggling in close.

"Yes," I said.

"Did you ever work out why James called you down here?" said Penny, after a while. "I mean, why he wanted you here in particular?"

"I think so," I said. "Ironically, you supplied the final piece of the puzzle, when you told me Diana was already pregnant when she married Walter. Who almost certainly wasn't the father. Am I right in believing Diana and Walter were married in 1970?"

"Yes," said Penny. "Why?"

"One year after my affair with Diana, in Paris," I said. Penny stopped dead and looked at me, eyes wide. "But . . . Dear God! I never made the connection! You mean . . ."

"Yes," I said. "I think the old Colonel, James, was my son. It would explain why he wanted me here, to protect his family."

"You think he knew?" said Penny.

"It would explain why he went out of his way to track me down and offer me the protection of the Organization," I said. "I doubt I'll ever know for sure. It's not the kind of thing he would have put in his official files. I always thought of him as a father figure, and all along he probably thought of me in much the same way. I wish . . . we could have talked about it."

"Hold it," said Penny. "Does this mean . . . we're related?"

"Not in any way that matters," I said.

"Good!" said Penny. "The last thing our relationship needs is more complications."

"So, we're in a relationship, now?" I said.

"You'd better believe it," said Penny.

"What is this thing called love, earth woman?" I said solemnly.

"Don't you know?" said Penny.

"Yes," I said. "I know."

"Hey!" said Penny. "I just realized! It's Christmas Day! Merry Christmas, Ishmael!"

"And a merry Christmas to you, Penny. Peace and good will to all men, including those who aren't actually all men."

"One last question," said Penny. "I have to ask, why Ishmael?"

"Why not?" I said.